MW00423925

Praise for *The Other Side of Night*

"Mind-bending! This intriguing and thought-provoking thriller is a profound exploration of how far some are willing to go in the name of love. A fantastic twist you'll never see coming."

—Liv Constantine

"A strange, compelling, and ultimately moving head-spinner of a novel."

—John Connolly

"Inventive, clever, and completely original, Hamdy's latest effort is simply terrific. Don't miss it."

—J. T. Ellison

"What can I say about *The Other Side of Night* that won't be a spoiler? Ingenious, constantly surprising, and deeply moving. Put yourself in the hands of a master storyteller, and strap in for a mind-bending ride."

—Joseph Finder

"*The Other Side of Night* is a mind-bending mystery that, by the time it reaches its extraordinary end, leaves no twist unexplained, no thread untied. An utterly satisfying read."

—Ryan Gattis

"Hold onto your sanity. This psychological thriller will keep you wondering which strange details are real and which emerge from the minds of the characters. The lonely boy, the disgraced police officer, the bizarre scientist—each has a dark secret, and a dark problem to solve. *The Other Side of Night* is imaginative and thought-provoking, fiction at its best."

—Michael and Kathleen Gear

"Remarkable. Adam Hamdy may have created a completely new crime genre."

—Anthony Horowitz

"In this inventive and intriguing novel, Hamdy mixes in just the right amount of mystery, uncertainty, and relational tension and brings them all simmering to delicious effect. Stunningly good writing. Don't let this one slip you by."

—Steven James

"A fantastic read. Mind-bending, gut-wrenchingly tense, and one of the most original stories I've read in years. An absolute treat."

—John Marrs

"A gorgeous, legacy-defining, genius work of art that Adam Hamdy will long be remembered and revered for creating and gifting to readers. *The Other Side of Night* is astoundingly breathtaking and one of the most memorable, thought-provoking novels I have ever read. Destined to be included in any conversation about the best books of 2022."

—Steve Netter, Best Thriller Books

"*The Other Side of Night* is like no crime novel I've ever read. The pages almost turn themselves and when I was finished, I couldn't stop thinking about the story's incredible twists, turns, and surprises."

—James Patterson

"Stellar . . . Intelligently plotted and powerfully told, Hamdy's deviously twisty tale of fate and coincidence, love and courage, and profoundly tough choices will shock, stir, and haunt readers long after the final page."

—*Publishers Weekly* (starred review)

"*The Other Side of Night* is a surprising and cleverly constructed roller-coaster read."

—Karin Slaughter

"A genre-bending page-turner—existential, emotional, and packing a twisty, gut-punch of an ending."

—Matthew Sullivan

"*The Other Side of Night* is a thrilling novel with multiple tricks up its sleeve. Part detective story and part philosophy, Adam Hamdy has written a clever and moving concoction."

—Peter Swanson

"A big-hearted, big-brain novel that you'll finish in three days and think about for the rest of the year. Wonderful."

—Stuart Turton

"*The Other Side of Night* is gut wrenching, explosive, and absolutely original, with a twist that made me gasp. A master class in crime fiction."

—T. A. Willberg

DEADBEAT

A NOVEL

ADAM HAMDY

ATRIA BOOKS

NEW YORK   TORONTO   LONDON   SYDNEY   NEW DELHI

An Imprint of Simon & Schuster, LLC
1230 Avenue of the Americas
New York, NY 10020

First Atria Books hardcover edition December 2024

ATRIA B O O K S and colophon are trademarks of Simon & Schuster, LLC

Simon & Schuster: Celebrating 100 Years of Publishing in 2024

For information about special discounts for bulk purchases, please contact Simon & Schuster Special Sales at 1-866-506-1949 or business@simonandschuster.com.

The Simon & Schuster Speakers Bureau can bring authors to your live event. For more information or to book an event, contact the Simon & Schuster Speakers Bureau at 1-866-248-3049 or visit our website at www.simonspeakers.com.

Interior design by Erika R. Genova

Manufactured in the United States of America

1 3 5 7 9 10 8 6 4 2

Library of Congress Cataloging-in-Publication Data has been applied for.

ISBN 978-1-6680-3152-0
ISBN 978-1-6680-3154-4 (ebook)

For everyone out there struggling to do the right thing.

I was offered a fortune to kill a stranger
I was told he was evil, but the truth was far more complicated
And his death was only the beginning . . .

CONFESSION

My name is Peyton Collard and I am a killer.

I was a stand-up guy. Once, long ago, but I've since lost count of the number of people I've harmed. People whose lives I've ruined.

If you don't know what I did, congratulations, you're one of the 80 percent of people who don't read the blurb on the back of a book and you must have missed my story on the news, but the rest of you who already know my name and the headline-grabbing aspects of my story already know what I was accused of doing.

But what I was accused of and what I actually did are two different things. The pages that follow are my story, and you can decide whether they are the truth. Doesn't matter whether you believe them. Real or fiction, the effect is the same. A cautionary tale for all you wholesome folk, and an atonement for me.

My confession.

I sent people down to the worms before their time, and each death was worse than the one before it, but I didn't feel it at the time for reasons that will soon become clear.

I'd like to say the proceeds of this book will be going to a good cause, but to me there's no better cause than my daughter, Skye. I want her to be everything I'm not.

I was a fool. So damn foolish. I trusted a stranger with my innocence and killed for money. I turned detective, investigating the very murders I'd committed to find out the truth of them. Can you imagine? A serial killer chasing down his own work, bringing his victims justice. Sounds outlandish, but that's what happens when you mix desperation and idiocy.

I don't expect you to like me, and I'd be surprised if by the end of my story you do, but my tale is one you won't have heard, so if there's a chance my daughter might profit from this story, then it's one that needs telling. Some of you might find my story entertaining, and folk with minds so inclined might even laugh, but I hope those on a crooked path will take the lessons and divert to a better life.

We're presenting this as a work of fiction for reasons that will become clear, but my publisher tells me true crime sells, so you, the reader, should take as much or as little truth as you find useful.

Other folk can beat you physically, mentally even—trust me, I know—but you're the only person who can harm your soul, down at the very core of you, deep where you're bound to a world beyond the physical. To God or karma, or the universe, or whatever you believe in, a place where the pain is so intense each self-inflicted wound is like star-fire, burning away who you are. Hurt yourself there enough times, and you'll die. Maybe not on the outside, where your breathing body can still pass for something close to human, but on the inside you can scorch yourself dead.

That's what a deadbeat is. Someone who's lost their connection to the greatness that binds us all. We cast the word around as a joke, much like when we call someone a witch or a devil. But these are curses in the old tongues, and a deadbeat is someone who's burned their soul until the light within has gone out.

That's me.

And this is my story.

CHAPTER 1

An angry god had snapped his fingers in my skull, killing half my brain cells and traumatizing the leftovers. I opened my eyes and got lightning flashes across my vision. White fireworks that were regular features of my worst hangovers.

But who was I kidding?

I wasn't hungover.

I was still wasted.

Last night's session with Jim had run up my tab at Rick's Bar like the counter on a gas crisis fuel pump. Jim and I had rounded off the night by doing a couple of lines of K in the fetid cesspit Rick calls a men's room, and my world had taken on a muffled, comatose, "fill in the blanks" quality. I have no idea how I got back to the tiny rathole I leased by the Long Beach Freeway. It was a dump, but it was my dump, and most of the stains on the threadbare faux-Persian rug were mine, so I didn't mind coming round face down on the raggedy red floor.

There was thunder to go with the lightning flashes, and it took me a moment to realize the cracking noises weren't imagined. Someone was banging on the front door, no more than ten feet from my head.

"Open up, sir. Mr. Collard, we know you're in there."

I glanced around to see shapes at my window. My eyes wouldn't focus properly, but the blocks of dark color suggested man-shaped lumps in uniform.

"Open up," someone else said, rapping on the window.

"Yeah. Okay," I replied, voice hoarse, throat raw.

Had I thrown up? I belched some bile, which burned when I swallowed. Tequila, rum, vodka, and bourbon had all featured in past me's smorgasbord of drinks. Booze always convinced me I was invincible, and the more I drank the more invincible I became. I didn't feel invincible now, though.

Left hand on the 1970s teak coffee table I'd found in a thrift shop, and I pushed myself onto my side. Right hand on the arm of the green corduroy couch someone over in Compton left in front of their house, and I forced myself up from the floor. The room whirled like a spinning top. Thankfully I wouldn't have to do anything as complicated as get dressed. I was still clothed in my light jeans and a blue checked shirt worn unbuttoned over a black T-shirt, all crumpled and stained. I looked down at my bare feet and wondered where my shoes and socks were.

A mystery for another time, I thought as I staggered to the door.

The heat hit me first. For all the flaws of my rathole, at least the AC worked. Then came the blazing sunlight, which set the fireworks flaring behind my eyes, until they'd had a moment to settle to the new, brighter reality. The sky was blue, so blue that if you'd lain in the gutter and looked up at the cloudless, you'd have thought yourself in paradise. But from where I was standing, the place was purgatory.

Edgebrook Avenue lies in the shadow of the Long Beach Freeway. My home, a single-story, two-bed bungalow, had a tiny backyard that ended in a high wall that ran directly beneath the freeway's edge. High above, a few yards to the east, thousands of vehicles raced past every hour. Apart from in the morning and evening when tens of thousands rolled by in ten-lane, nose-to-tail, slow-moving rush-hour frustration, the noise from the freeway never stopped, and it was a constant reminder of failure to everyone who lived on Edgebrook. Maybe I'm being hard on my old neighbors, but none of them liked me, so who gives a hot damn? About half kept their homes and yards in order and did their best to fight the pollution and malaise that clouded every waking day. The rest of us didn't mind much about appearances, and our overgrown yards and derelict homes spoke to our busy-doing-nothing schedules. If pride was a sin, we had some devoutly holy folk living on Edgebrook.

My car, a twenty-year-old lime green Chrysler Sebring convertible with a soft top that didn't work, was parked in my short driveway. I must have driven home from Rick's. Not good.

Past me's crimes weren't my most pressing worry, though. Instead, I was struggling to figure out why two bored-looking mechanics in gray overalls had started hitching my car to a tow truck.

A sweaty red face filled my vision. The man who'd been knocking on my door. The lawman who was so eager to see me. He wore an LA County sheriff's uniform and a bulletproof vest and looked sad and tired as he held a piece of paper in front of me.

"Repossession" was the only word I caught as he spoke.

I felt sorry for the guy. Imagine this being your job. Robbing from people too poor to pay, to enrich people too wealthy to care. And dressing it up as law enforcement. He knew what he was, and even in my semi-wasted state, I could see the self-loathing in his eyes. It was like looking in a mirror.

My pity was short-lived, and when my slo-mo mind finally caught up, my thought process became real simple.

Car. Mine. Stop.

I pushed past the sheriff and ran across my bone-dry, weed-infested lawn, fumbling in my pocket for my key.

"Hey, man, don't," one of the mechanics said.

He had the same weary look in his eyes as the lawman and turned with outstretched arms like a linebacker trying to block an oncoming rush.

To this day, I don't know whether it was intentional or the luck of inebriation, but I stumbled and fell forward so my shoulder hit his gut, knocking him on his ass. I almost went with him, but my experience as a seasoned drunk meant I recovered my footing with a hop and skip that took me to the driver's door.

"Stop!" the sheriff yelled, but freedom called, so I ignored him and yanked it open.

The other mechanic, a junior with a shaved head and a frame that hadn't been turned soft by hot dogs and beer, tried to stand in front of the car.

"Don't do it, man," he said.

I jabbed the key in the ignition, turned, and the engine stuttered and died. The sheriff was almost at the car, so I locked the doors. I was drunk, possibly high, not thinking. Where was I going to go?

The young mechanic banged on the hood, and the sheriff slapped the window.

"Get out!" he yelled.

Spurning reason, addled by booze, with an instinct only to run, I tried the ignition again, and this time the engine coughed into life.

I threw the old Sebring into gear and stomped on the gas. As the car lurched forward, I spun the wheel and the front right tire bounced on the curb, and I raced across my lawn and met the road. My deranged plan had been to speed away, head south along Edgebrook, and lie low at Rick's until who knew what? I hadn't thought that far ahead. But my fantasy silver screen escape was to live only in my mind. In the real world, my slow reactions, intoxication, and general lack of competence saw me rip the bumper off my neighbor's car, which sent me veering out of control across the street toward the sheriff's liveried vehicle.

I tried to step on the brake but hit the gas by mistake, and the Sebring gave a final roar before it rammed straight into the sheriff-and-star logo on the driver's door. The airbags failed to deploy, so I cracked my head against the wheel, and the world became even more hazy and distant. I fumbled with the door, but my hands weren't working. In fact, my whole body felt as though someone else was in charge, so I gave up and just sat there for a few moments before I blacked out.

CHAPTER 2

I came around in the VA Medical Center on Wilshire. The cops who took me into custody were thorough and ran my background. Fifteen years in the Engineering Corps had gotten me decent veteran's coverage, and the doc checked me for signs of trauma before clearing me for jail.

Afterward, the cops delivered me to the regional headquarters of the LAPD on 77th Street. The sandstone building looked like something Pharaoh might have built to honor Ra, and it stood out in a run-down neighborhood of low-rent condos, motels, and bail bond offices.

I'd been in jail once before, but they treated me like I was a seasoned ex-con who knew the drill. I was processed and relieved of my few personal possessions: a near-empty wallet, prepaid cell phone, and car and house keys. After a couple of hours in the holding cell, I was finally taken to see my court-appointed attorney.

There are few things more depressing than meeting the lawyer charged with getting you out of a jam and realizing they're the George Constanza of the legal world. All neuroses, tics, and hang-ups, along with a rapid-fire array of nervous smiles to try to mask the darkness within. My public defender, Mitch Hoffman, looked a little like Costanza, but thinner, as though he couldn't even find comfort in a good meal. He sat across from me stinking of chewing gum and stale cigarettes, and his yellowing, stub-nailed fingers suggested a nervous fifty- or sixty-a-day smoker. Heavy breathing and an intermittent hacking cough confirmed my diagnosis.

Yellow concentric semicircles spread out from his armpits, old sweat stains on a crumpled short-sleeve shirt. I couldn't see his trousers because he was seated at a table when I was brought in and cuffed to the anchor point between us, but I just knew they'd be polyester.

I didn't bother to hide my disappointment as I looked at Mitch, and if it hadn't been for the anchor, I'd have slouched back in my chair with what my grandma used to call haughty disdain. This guy wasn't going to get me off. He hadn't even spoken yet, and I already had a ripe dislike. If he had that effect on the judge, not only would I be back inside serving out the remainder of my six years, but I'd also probably get another six on top for wrecking the sheriff's car.

If Mitch took offense, he didn't show it. He barely looked at me and focused on the file on the table. What was a guy like him doing in the public defender's office? Had he graduated bottom of his class? Angered a higher-up? Career criminals would have chewed him out, and I could just imagine him being steamrollered by a prosecutor and yelled at by a breathless, red-faced angry old judge.

"So, erm, Mr. Collard, we're looking at a year for resisting arrest, six months for assault, vandalism carries a maximum of three years, and another three years for DUI," Mitch said.

"DUI?" I interjected. "I went less than twenty yards. It could hardly be called driving, let alone under the influence."

"Nevertheless," Mitch replied. "You could be looking at another seven and a half years on top of the three you have unserved on your"—he looked away awkwardly and cleared his throat—"your prior conviction for the accident."

I was grateful he used the word *accident*. It went easier on my conscience. A stronger man would have used the correct term: *vehicular manslaughter*.

"Ten years?" I couldn't believe it. "You're telling me I could be facing another ten years?"

"Ten and a half years, actually," he replied. "You're in a bit of a pickle."

Pickle? Was this guy for real?

"Does a pickle extort you with threats of sexual violence?" I asked, and he blushed. "Because that's what happens in federal prison."

"Well, no," he said. "I'm sorry. *Pickle* is the wrong word. *Squeeze* or *jam* would probably be better."

I glared at him, and he wilted.

We listened to the muffled sounds of the precinct until he finally plucked up the courage to speak. "I, well, I hate to bring bad news, but they're going to hold you in county until we get a trial date."

"How long?"

"Well, er, it depends on case assignments and court availability and—"

"How long?"

He looked up and held my gaze. "Three months."

"Three months?"

"Any time you serve will count toward your sentence." His tone was similar to the slicked-back salesman who'd sold me the Sebring. Trying to convince me the poison I was being fed was just bitter-tasting medicine.

"What about bail?" I asked.

"Well, you've been put in the high rollers' club. Judge set it at a hundred thousand dollars because of your prior. You're on probation, Mr. Collard. Probation."

"A hundred thousand. I don't even have a hundred bucks."

"Do you have any assets?" Mitch asked. "You'd need ten thousand for a bondsman."

"Assets? I'm in here for driving a junker into a cop car while under the influence of liquor and ketamine," I said.

"Ketamine? I didn't know about ketamine." He flicked through the paperwork quickly.

"Do you really think I've got more than a gutter-soaked twenty to my name?"

"You shouldn't see me as an enemy, Mr. Collard. I'm here to defend you to the best of my abilities." His eyes met mine, and I thought he might cry. "We'll go for a deal."

If you're a square who's never crossed the line and felt the hand of the law on your throat, you probably imagine a con like me fronting up for his day in court, watching his lawyer deliver an Oscar-worthy speech, cheering when the jury foreperson announces the inevitable innocent verdict, and jumping into his convertible Porsche to race off to a pool party celebration.

In truth, most criminals don't have the money or the stomach for justice. Run the risk of twenty years in jail, or cop a plea and serve two. Was I going to gamble ten years of my life on the legal skills of the skinny Costanza sitting opposite me? He'd probably screw up the plea deal and get me sent to the electric chair.

"Don't take this the wrong way, Mr. Hoffman, but is there anyone else who could represent me?" I tried to keep my voice neutral. "No offense intended."

He seemed to melt into his seat, but then tried to reassert himself by sitting up straight. "This is an open-and-shut case. A deputy sheriff and two officers of the court witnessed what they describe as a drunken rampage. Deputy Buckman said it was the guiding hand of the Lord that kept anyone from being killed."

I shook my head with the lazy disbelief of all sinners.

"That's right, he's a godly man, and that plays well in court." Mitch sat forward. "And to answer your question, no. No, there is no one else who can represent you."

I sighed.

"I might be able to make something of your military service, but frankly, with you still being on probation, we're going to have to throw ourselves on the mercy of the DA's office and the court."

I prayed he wasn't going to say it, but he did, and as the words left his lips, I wanted to punch him in the face. But my hands were bound, so I had to take the clichéd hack wisdom that would have been rejected from a fortune-cookie factory.

"Beggars can't be choosers."

CHAPTER 3

If you've ever taken ketamine, you'll be familiar with the K-hole, a dark cavern that follows the dreamy high. On a normal day, it can turn folks in on themselves, force them to cast a critical eye over their lives, but stuck in jail with the prospect of a long prison stretch ahead of me, my K-hole ran deep.

I followed it down, feeling every inch the failure I was. I was in the holding cell with four hard-luck, tough-life, broken souls, and we kept our distance from each other. This wasn't a losers' social mixer. It was a human trash can, where society's waste was held until it could be processed, hidden from view, recycled into model citizens, and released—or consigned to the heap forever. I couldn't believe I'd ended up here again. And for something so stupid: defending my hunk of junk car.

I'd been given a second chance at life when I'd made parole, but here I was right back in the slammer for doing something that stupid.

Getting high with Jim had seemed a good idea at the time, but now the happy K-dream had well and truly worn off, and as I looked at the grubby, sweaty men in the cell with me, the full weight of my mistake hit me. Would I have fought for that junker sober? No way. They could have towed the car and the house too. Four years ago, I'd never have been seen dead in either.

And here I was, facing a hard ten, at risk of losing the only good thing I had. I was a terrible father, but my thirteen-year-old girl, Skye, was a great daughter, and she brightened every moment I spent with her. She was more than I deserved, and she deserved better than this. Deep in my K-hole, the thought of being separated from her again brought a tear to my eye. But I wasn't going to cry. Not here, in this place with these men.

Mitch's math made me sick. I knew from bitter experience how bad ten years in federal prison would be. If I had money, I could have hired one of those Monopoly lawyers who can magic up a get-out-of-jail card. One of those slick, sharp-suited, forked-tongued attorneys who were always lunching with the mayor, had the DA on speed dial, and could get a billionaire standing over a body with a smoking gun compensation from the city for the inconvenience of an arrest.

Money would have gotten me out of this place, too, with its grimy walls covered in carved graffiti, smelling of bleach and piss and misery. Money would solve all my problems, but I didn't have a bean and didn't know anyone who did either. Least not anyone I could ask for a loan. So, my life was mapped out. A transfer to county jail, some fights, threats of sexual violence, until I settled somewhere in the pecking order, a long wait for the formality of a trial that would deprive me of freedom for too many years. Rare visits from Skye, under the disapproving eye of her mother, Toni, until teenage life would prove too much of a draw and even my daughter would forget about me.

When I first came to Los Angeles seven years ago, I was handsome, successful, married. Someone told me LA is known as the City of Angels because every inhabitant gets their own heavenly guardian who watches out for them. Mine must have taken a wicked strong dislike to me or something, because true enough, I had a little over two decent years before I lost everything.

I was stirred from self-pity by one of the cops banging on the cage.

"Collard," he said. "Get up. You made bail."

I didn't move, thinking this was some twisted joke.

"Come on." He didn't bother hiding his impatience. "Unless you want to stay here."

I sat up and looked around in disbelief. Who the heck had sprung me? Was my guardian angel back after so many years away?

I got off the hard bench and went to the cage door, which buzzed open. This couldn't really be happening, could it? I put my hand against the wall. It felt real enough. No dreamlike qualities whatsoever.

"Who sprung me?" I asked as the cop stood aside and let me pass.

He shrugged. "No clue."

He took me to the custody desk, a surprisingly mundane place considering how many people tasted free air here for the very last time.

High with the euphoria of good luck, I said as much to the desk sergeant who handled my release paperwork. He sat on a stool behind a high counter. Jaded, he pursed his wrinkled lips and gave me a perfunctory nod.

"You know who posted my bail?" I asked.

"You got that many friends?" he cracked.

"I didn't think I had any. Least none who could front this kind of dough."

He sighed and checked the computer next to him.

"Syd Ryder," he said after a moment. "He's a bondsman. Works out of an office couple of blocks down Broadway. Someone must have given him security."

I signed for my stuff and went outside in a hurry, just in case there had been a mistake. I stood in front of the Pharaoh's monument, baking in the June sun, and looked up and down Broadway. I could see plenty of signs for bail bonds to the south, past 77th Street, but couldn't pick out anything that identified Syd Ryder. My luck really must have been turning, because my phone still had a little juice. I found him on Google and pinpointed his office two blocks south of my location. It was too hot to walk, so I made a call.

The voice that answered was as rough as an armadillo's hide. "Ryder Bail Bonds."

"Syd Ryder?" I asked.

"Who is this?"

"Peyton Collard."

"Oh. Mr. Lucky."

"Yeah. I want to know who posted my bail."

"No can do, Mr. Lucky," Ryder said. "Client demanded they remain anonymous."

"Was it my ex-wife?"

"I doubt it. You ain't that lucky, Mr. Lucky."

I guessed from his response my savior was a woman. A real-life beautiful guardian angel.

"Don't I have a right to know?"

"You have a right to jack shit, Mr. Lucky." I heard him take a draw of a cigarette, and there was a pause as he held in the smoke and then exhaled. "Go live your life. Someone gave you a second chance. At least until trial."

He took another drag of smoke.

"Make sure you show. I hate leaving the office to hunt the stupid. Always puts me in a head-crackingly bad mood."

He hung up and left me standing on the sidewalk outside the regional police headquarters, wondering why anyone would have paid to spring a deadbeat from jail.

CHAPTER 4

When I was in the engineering corps, driving my Honda CR-V around the city, I was always in a hurry to get from A to B. I never paid the in-between places any mind. I missed people and places that would have broadened my understanding and made me a real local. And if you're a tourist, forget about it. The so-called authentic local experiences your hotel concierge recommends always show a place at its best. They're designed to conceal the blemishes, which, like the scars on an old warrior's face, are part of their story.

You want to know a place—the truth, good and bad? Ride the bus.

Why am I hitting you with a bus commercial when you're here for murder and mayhem? Well, it goes, as any good attorney will tell you, to character. I used to be an optimist. Mr. Glass-half-full, and my attitude to having to schlep across the city on a bus from time to time is one of the last vestiges of that. I look for the positive, rather than think about how far I've fallen and the decline that's evidenced every time I plant my ass on one of the hard plastic seats.

Of course, riding the 115 bus from the corner of Manchester Avenue along Firestone Boulevard I wasn't just optimistic, I was elated. Years in prison had been lifted from my shoulders. My unknown benefactor might well have saved my life. I took in the sights and sounds of the city, and the low-rise mini-malls, auto shops, and fast-food joints looked like the finest museums, art galleries, and palaces to my eyes. Ask any ex-con; freedom has a tint all its own.

Even the bad houses on Edgebrook didn't look too shabby as I hit the street that had been my home for five months. I'd leased the place from a big bear of a Greek man, who didn't mind leasing the house to an ex-con, but charged me 20 percent over market rate and insisted I paid two months' rent and two months' security deposit. He called it a poverty premium.

But the place suited me. It had a spare bedroom for Skye when she stayed over, which wasn't often because Toni didn't approve of me or the neighborhood. They might have been poor, but my neighbors kept to themselves and just wanted a bed to crash on while they slept off whatever misery tainted their lives.

My socializing happened at Rick's, a bar a couple of blocks away that had once been a Blockbuster video store. Socializing was probably too strong a word. I would normally talk only to my buddy Jim Steadman, but every so often I drank enough booze to make others tolerable and had instantly forgotten conversations with complete strangers about life's most profound secrets.

I haven't always been a cantankerous antisocial jerk, but life grinds hard on some people, turning their warm welcomes to dusty suspicion.

I neared my home and saw the crumpled front end of my car being hooked up to the same tow truck by the same two mechanics from this morning. I'd taken a painful and long trip to jail, only to return to the start. But this was no board game of monopolists and losers. It was my life, and these two were robbing me.

I ran over with a "Hey!"

"Stay away from me, man!"

The guy I'd tackled squared up to me and raised his arms to make himself big.

"You're still supposed to be in jail," his younger colleague said.

"I'm not normally a violent man." I stopped just out of the big guy's reach. "I'm sorry I hurt you. I wasn't thinking straight."

"You didn't hurt me. You caught me off guard is all." He puffed out his chest and looked at his colleague, daring him to challenge what was clearly bullshit overcompensation.

"I don't want trouble. I just want my car," I replied. "I'll make good. Look at it. It's not worth anything now."

"Ain't our job to decide what gets taken. We just do the taking."

It was the way of the world. Like Caesar, the Man decided with his thumb who won and who lost, and his minions made his wishes real. No one was responsible because the Man wasn't sufficiently dumb enough to let himself be identified. People like me, angry and carrying pitchforks, might come looking for him. So, he hides in the swamps of shareholding, crouches in the weeds of contracts and liens and legal doublespeak, and says, "It's just the way things are, buddy. Better luck next time."

And the victims of the grandest of all grand swindles think themselves unlucky and start again, while their competitors in the game of life are busy accruing more and more, hardly skipping a beat, passing it on to the next generation so their children gain all the advantages while the victims' offspring have none.

I'd become a victim yet again, and with the theft of my car, my slate was almost clean. Do over. Start from scratch, poor man.

"You can't leave me without a car. This is LA," I protested.

"I know where we are, man," the older mechanic said.

His young associate smiled and the two of them shrugged at each other, and, realizing I really didn't pose a threat, returned to their work for the Man.

I shook my head in disbelief and took a seat on my front step. I watched in the fading light as they hooked the car to the truck and winched it onto the flatbed.

The mechanic I'd tackled gave me a mocking salute as he climbed in the cab, and they drove away, taking my bashed up old Sebring with them.

Deadbeat to carless deadbeat in the space of minutes. I didn't have much further to fall, and feeling every inch the heel, I turned for my front door. But I stopped when I saw something in the corner of my eye. The tiny, crooked flag on the mailbox at the edge of my front yard was raised, like the arm of a hesitant child about to ask an awkward question in class.

DEADBEAT

I walked the small yard and opened my old-fashioned aluminum mailbox. Inside was a single small, padded package. It was addressed to me, but there was no stamp, so it had been hand-delivered. Above the typed label was a sticker marked Urgent. Bills and court summonses were the only urgent things I ever received, but I could feel something thick inside. Too thick to be simple paperwork.

I tore the flap as I walked toward my front door, and almost gasped when I saw a flash of green, the familiar but rarely sighted color of money.

I shook as I unlocked my door and glanced over both shoulders nervously. This much cash didn't belong in my neighborhood. I hurried inside, slammed the door, and leaned against it as I put my hand into the package and pulled out a stack of fifties. The Bank of America paper collar told me I was holding a thousand bucks.

CHAPTER 5

I moved an old pizza box and sat on my couch to try to figure out who'd send me a thousand bucks. The same person who bailed me out, maybe? I want to be real clear; this kind of thing did not happen to me. Getting my car towed, being arrested, facing hard time behind bars were the normal flavors of my life in recent years. Bail? Cash in the mail? There was a different chef in the kitchen. Maybe I'd had a lifetime of bad luck these past few years, and everything from here on would be gravy.

I reached into the package and found a folded piece of paper. Instead of the expected explanation, when I opened it, I saw a web address.

www.96423789.com

I pulled my phone from my pocket and typed it in. After a short pause, the screen went black. It looked like a dead site, but I scrolled down to find a single audio file and clicked play.

"Mr. Collard," a machine voice said. It was female and reminded me of Siri or Alexa. "I put up the security for your bail. You are in my debt, and your ledger stands at the amount of eleven thousand dollars. I'd like to make you an offer. If you do as I ask, you will become a very rich man. If you don't, I will take the money you now owe me in other ways."

Looking back, I should have been more wary. The implied threat should have told me I was dealing with a foe not friend, but hindsight is the fool's curse, opening our eyes long after the time for action has passed.

"I would like you to kill a man for an additional one hundred thousand dollars. He is a stranger to you. A drug dealer suspected of multiple homicides. His name is Walter Glaze. He owns the Ultima nightclub in Venice. I have sent you one thousand dollars as a gesture of good faith, to enable you to buy a gun. Two shots to the head. He is not to die any other way. Kill this evil man, and the next time you open your mailbox, you will find one hundred thousand dollars in cash."

CHAPTER 6

The message ended, leaving me with the continuous rumble of the freeway. I looked at the bundle of fifties in my hand and the audio file on my phone, and wondered what was happening.

Was this for real?

Was it a joke?

Or worse, entrapment?

Someone had fronted ten grand for my bail and another grand in cash and offered me another hundred to kill a stranger. A drug dealer. Maybe a murderer. You ever have one of those fork-in-the-road days? A moment you replay when you wish you could go back and pick a different path? There, right there in that dirty, messy living room, in that raggedy house in the shadow of the freeway, seriously considering an invitation to murder, that was one of those moments for me. I should have deleted my search history, pocketed the cash, and waited to see how the mechanical voice came to extract my supposed debt.

Instead, I found myself seriously considering the offer.

I was desperate. A shadow of the man I'd once been. Old me would have refused the offer.

I couldn't.

Had I been roped in to settle an organized crime beef? Had this guy, Walter Glaze, rankled the wrong person? But why hire me? Gangsters would have their own people. Sure, I had military experience, but I'd been an army engineer, not some James Reece, Jack Reacher medaled super soldier. I couldn't believe any villain would have singled me out because of my service record. I was solid. Above-average shooter, decent engineer, careful, methodical, but never going to win any combat medals.

Whoever my wannabe patron was, they were smart. I'd read stories of people hiring assassins through Facebook or supposedly super-secure message boards only to get busted by the FBI or ratted out by would-be killers who choked at the last minute. Maybe it was just random chance that had brought us together? A connection that couldn't be traced by any conventional detective. That would be very clever.

And keeping me in the dark meant if I didn't do it, the client could move on to another candidate without fear of exposure.

Listen to me talking about clients and killers like some body-bag-filling assassin. At that point I was green and bewildered. It might have been a prank, and there I was taking it seriously. I mean, a total stranger offering me a hundred grand to kill a man. Me? A deadbeat?

What would you have done?

Would you do it?

Would you kill someone who deserved to die?

That's what kept running through my mind. If the offer was genuine, and this Walter Glaze guy was a villain, could I do it? Did he deserve to die? And if he did, why shouldn't something good come of his death?

The bounty on his head was a future for me and my kid.

That's what desperation does to a person. It gets you testing the limits of what you're prepared to do, because life isn't about living anymore. It's about survival.

I was startled by a knock at the door.

"Peyton?"

It was Toni, my ex-wife.

"Peyton, are you in there?"

"Yeah. Just a minute." I shoved the bundle of fifties behind a couch cushion and went to the door.

"Where were you?" Toni asked before I'd had a chance to take in her sour expression.

I'd let Toni down. Like boiled candy with a sour center, all the sweetness of our life together had been sucked away to leave only the mouth-puckering kernel. I remembered how happy and carefree she'd been as a teen, her hair so long it used to blow around her face in the Chicago winds. Now it was cropped short, giving her a severe appearance that was at odds with the carefree girl I'd known. Resentment shone from her eyes and worry lines marked her face. She'd never lost the figure that had initially attracted me to her and wore tiny shorts that looked as though they'd been sprayed on and a T-shirt that was tied above her belly.

"You were supposed to see Skye this afternoon," she went on.

Skye was right there beside her mother, watching me with the pitying look a farmer might give a least-prized hog about to be taken for slaughter. She had her mother's eyes, hair, mouth, and physique. Heck, she was Toni's mini-me twin, and looking at her always made me remember the lost days of youth when the future had been unwritten and the blank pages full of nothing but promise. Before she'd lost me to prison, she used to be so alive she sparkled with the excitement of each new day. When I was sentenced, part of my little girl died.

I didn't resent their combined judgment. With the repossession and the arrest, I'd forgotten this afternoon was one of my allotted times with Skye.

"I'm sorry—" I tried, but Toni cut me off.

"Skye, honey, can you wait in the car?"

Our daughter glanced at me, and I nodded. "Your mother and I need to talk. I'll see you in a couple of days, kiddo."

"Tomorrow, Dad," Skye corrected with a sense of weary sadness that almost crushed me.

Toni gave an emphatic eye roll and slow shake of her head.

I sighed. I couldn't do anything right.

"Tomorrow. That's right. Sorry, kiddo."

Skye withdrew to Toni's ancient, rusty gray Honda Civic, which was parked in front of my house.

"What happened? Where the fuck is your car?" Toni asked, her anger bubbling over now that our daughter was out of earshot.

"It's a long story," I replied. "Something came up."

"Something booze? Or something lazy?" Toni asked.

Her questions stung just enough to remind me of the man I used to be.

"Something work," I said, and I moved away from the door to the couch, where I peeled four notes off the deck of fifties.

I sensed Toni craning round the doorway to see what I was doing, but I was shielding my stash with my back. I replaced the rest of the money behind the cushion and turned to see her face puckering further as she surveyed the disgusting condition of my home.

"Clean this place, Peyton. Skye isn't coming here until you pick up. You probably got rats and racoons living in this dump."

"I will," I assured her. "Meantime, here's a couple of hundred."

I handed her the cash, and she frowned. I think she'd given up hope.

"You still owe me thirteen grand alimony," she said sharply.

"I know. I'll get it to you. I promise."

I'd spoken empty words before, but this time I might have a way to fulfill them if I was prepared to end a life. It was a slim hope, but it was better than none.

She eyed me suspiciously. "What kind of work you doing?"

"Just helping a guy out with a problem."

"Criminal problem?" Toni's eyes narrowed.

"It's good, paying work," I said.

We eyed each other for a moment.

"Is it dirty?" Toni asked, brandishing the money I'd given her. "Because I need to know if you're giving me dirty money."

"No," I replied truthfully. I hadn't done anything yet. "But let's say it was. Hypothetically. Let's say there was a way to make a lot of money that strayed across the line."

"What line? Sex? Violence? Drugs?"

I didn't answer.

"Are you fucking kidding me? After what you've put us through? What you do is your business, but don't you be giving me any money that comes from across any lines." She gave me a fierce look. "Your kid needs better than she's got, and I'm working every hour I can just to stay above water."

She hesitated.

"And the pool might be about to get deeper."

I knew her well enough to sense the bad news just over the horizon.

"Skye's been losing weight. Fatigued. Funny moods. Irritable. Not sleeping right." Tears came to her eyes but didn't fall. "Always thirsty. The doc is testing for diabetes."

"Oh shit," I said, shaking my head, my heart sinking down low, lower than it had ever been. My kid. You can take pain for yourself, but the suffering of a child hurts in a whole different place. I knew Skye had lost weight, that was kind of hard to miss, and she'd been kind of lackluster, but I thought that was teen growing. I didn't know about the other stuff. I was familiar with only type one because I was at college with a guy who'd been diagnosed as a teen, but what I knew wasn't good.

"Don't go doing anything stupid. And don't say nothing neither. It might be an infection or something, and I don't want you scaring her. But you need to know, because if it is, we're gonna need money, Peyton. We're gonna need a lot of money. Insulin is free, but if she develops complications, it's going to cost a lot of money to keep her safe. We need to come through. For her. For our daughter."

I nodded gravely. This was as real as life gets. My baby. My poor baby girl.

"So, I'm going to ask you again, and I want to know the truth; is this dirty money?"

"No," I replied. "It's clean."

She gave me a skeptical look.

"It's clean," I assured her.

"Then if there's more of this to be had, don't you go crossing any lines. Get earning honest dollars and provide for your daughter, Peyton. Make sure she's okay, whatever happens. It's Saturday tomorrow and you've got Skye until after lunch, so don't be late."

She turned and marched to her car. Skye looked at me sadly from the passenger seat. There are few things less satisfying in life than getting a full-blown blast of pity from a kid, particularly your own, but that's where I was in life. If not at rock bottom, then clinging onto the step just above it.

I'm not going to be a stereotypical ex-husband and portray my ex-wife as a bitter serpent who made every living moment hell. She is a wonderful woman—that's right, Toni, if you're reading this, I still think you're the best. When we were together, she was sweet and kind, beautiful and sexy, smart and tenacious, everything I could ever have hoped for. We'd been sweethearts at Mather High School in Skokie, Illinois, where we spent scorching summers on the beaches of Lake Michigan and frozen winters tracing patterns in the condensation on the windows of Cindy's café as we sat drinking our hot chocolates, watching the world go by.

We'd married shortly after graduation, and she'd come with me to LA when I studied mechanical engineering at Cal State. After growing up with the full force of four seasons, we both fell in love with the predictable sunshine of Los Angeles, and agreed that wherever my deployments took me, we'd always aim to end up back in the City of Angels. I had no idea we'd succeed, but as individuals living separate lives.

Toni had reserves of strength I could only dream of. But this wasn't about me. It was about Skye, and I couldn't bring myself to picture her coping with the diagnosis if things fell that way. I couldn't imagine how any of us would cope. We weren't coping as it was. Toni didn't even look back as she walked away. She got into the car, fired up the rattling engine, and drove west.

CHAPTER 7

I shut the door and returned to my seat on the couch.

I picked up my phone and searched for complications of type one diabetes. My screen filled with search results from the Mayo Clinic, Johns Hopkins, and the American Diabetes Association, and a quick scan revealed cardiac, kidney, neurological autoimmune, and ophthalmic complications were a risk even if the condition was well managed. I had no idea it could be so serious, and it seemed Toni had been right to flag the need for money. These would be choppy waters to navigate in a leaky boat. We needed something more solid beneath our feet.

But could I kill a man?

This wasn't just about my debts anymore. If Skye was sick, there was no question I had to do whatever was needed to take care of her. And if I could put a little money in my pocket, I might even be able to fire Mitch Hoffman and buy justice in the form of an Ivy League, high-flying lawyer. Someone with perfect teeth, easy charm, and a back-of-the-hand loophole map that could clear me of assaulting the mechanic and trashing the sheriff's car, and make sure I'd be around to be a better father. I couldn't go to prison now. I couldn't leave Skye and Toni. Not with this hanging over us.

You're nuts, I told myself. *No one hires a killer like this. Even if you had the balls to kill Walter Glaze, the money would never come. It's a scam.*

I grabbed the rest of the cash from behind the cushion and looked at it closely. Seemed real enough, and my would-be patron claimed to have paid my bail. Why couldn't this be real? Who said a killer had to be hired with a briefcase full of bearer bonds? This is the digital age. People put out contracts on Craigslist. If you wanted someone dead, didn't it make sense to choose an assassin who had no connection to you?

Is that what I was now? An assassin. This morning I'd been a deadbeat drunk.

I picked up my phone and typed "Walter Glaze Ultima" into the search bar. My screen filled with search results. Most related to reviews of his popular nightclub, but as I scrolled down, I saw a couple of links to *The Gray Letter*, a gossip site. I clicked through and found a story that suggested Walter had underworld connections. It seemed my anonymous patron was right about ties to organized crime.

I couldn't take this seriously, could I?

A hundred grand.

The sum rolled around my mind like a cloud swollen with potential. After a long, hard drought I needed green rain.

Could I kill a man? Could I murder someone with malice aforethought? Could I double-tap someone at short range?

Why should someone bad enjoy life if their end could ease my daughter's way through life?

Part of me couldn't believe I was even considering an execution, but make a person sufficiently desperate and their mind will turn to anything. And Toni was right; Skye needed money not just if she was ill, but for her future, for college. She needed a good start in life. Toni and I had our shot, and we were broken and battered beyond repair, but there was still hope for Skye.

The sins of the father shouldn't pass to the child.

Skye was shiny and new, and I prayed with every ounce of my depleted faith that our daughter wouldn't end up like either of us. If the offer of a bounty for the head of an evil man might be real, didn't I have a responsibility to consider it?

Put yourself in my shoes. Sitting in the wreckage of a life gone most bad, facing jail and ruin, and someone throws you a lifeline, not only for you, but for your loved ones; what would you do?

People have killed for greed, revenge, ambition. How would it hurt the world to lose one evil man and gain one healthy successful young woman?

I mean, what would you do if someone offered you a way to transform your life? How much would it take? Does everyone have a price?

Don't be fooled into thinking this is a rare choice. People are faced with this very question every day. We just don't see it clearly because it's obscured by the pollution of life, but allow me to blow that smoke away. The CEO who knows he or she could reduce workplace accidents, deaths even, by implementing higher standards at a mine, the hospital board that could improve clinical outcomes by investing in better diagnostics, the clothing company that could increase health outcomes for sweatshop workers by setting minimum wages for subcontractors; life is taken from people every single day. We really notice only when it's taken quickly, or when a lot of people are robbed. When it happens slowly, far away, it's invisible.

Think back to your most desperate moment, when you felt defeated. Imagine yourself drowning in the sea of life, overwhelmed by wave after wave of bad news, bad luck, bad judgment. Imagine if someone had thrown you a lifeline. No matter how thin and tenuous, you'd have grabbed it even if you knew it would snap, because holding on to something is better than dying with empty hands.

Desperation makes people cross seas in tiny boats, ingest baggies full of smack, sell their minds, bodies, and souls. My anonymous patron had put up my bail, so this person clearly had some money, and I was already in his or her debt. Desperation made me take the offer seriously. A stronger man might have laughed it off.

One life, and I could change everything.

One soul.

This wasn't a decision I could make alone. I needed advice and I was short of friends, so I stuffed the remaining fifties into my pocket, grabbed my keys, and headed for Rick's.

CHAPTER 8

Rick's Bar is a single-story former Blockbuster video store on the corner of Long Beach Boulevard and Pine. The windows that had once been packed with display boards of rifle-toting action heroes or invading aliens had been covered by drapes that now concealed what went on inside. The old glass-and-steel doors had been replaced by solid wooden ones, and when I walked through them, I got a comfortingly familiar lungful of beer and sweat.

Rick had put the bar where the old counter had been, and the racks that had once housed videos and DVDs had been replaced by cheap benches and tables that were bolted to the floor. The place felt bigger than it really was because it was always quiet. Rick focused on cultivating high dependency in his customers rather than trying to appeal to a larger, but more fair-weather, crowd of social drinkers.

"Peyton Collard!"

The slurred words came from a familiar mouth. Jim Steadman, the only friend I'd made since my release, was sitting on his usual stool at the bar. We'd bonded over military service. At forty-seven, Jim was ten years older than me, and he'd seen a ton of frontline action in the Marine Corps. Unlike me, he had added beef since discharge and was probably carrying three hundred pounds on his five-ten frame. Until he got to know a person, he was cold, bordering on hostile, and when I'd first stopped in at Rick's I'd been a little intimidated by the huge guy who would often be found in khaki shorts, camo T-shirt, and combat-green LA Lakers baseball cap.

"Jim," I said, hauling myself onto the stool beside him.

"Fix my young bud whatever he wants," Jim said to Rick, who sauntered over with one eye on the college basketball game showing on the giant wall-hung TV.

"I'll have a draught," I said.

"Put it on his tab," Jim added, and I couldn't help but scoff. "We ain't socialists here, Collard. Man pays his way."

"Tab's getting pretty heavy for both of you."

Rick was a quiet guy who usually minded his business, except when there was money due.

"What do we owe?" I asked.

Rick checked the ledger below the counter. "Ninety-six fifty for Mr. Peyton Collard and an even forty for Mr. James Steadman."

"Let me take care of it," I said, peeling four fifties off my fold.

I have to admit I enjoyed not being a deadbeat for once.

"What were you saying about socialism?" I asked Jim.

"I ain't gonna fight a man who wants to buy me a drink," he slurred.

"There's two hundred." I handed Rick the money. "Put whatever's left on my account."

Jim laughed. "Your account? You the fucking king of England now?"

Rick grinned and pocketed the cash.

"And forget the draught," I said. "Set me and my friend up with a couple of depth charges."

I'd conned myself into thinking I'd come here for advice, but my inner demons and I knew I intended to get hammered.

"I appreciate it." Jim raised his glass before draining the dregs of his beer.

Rick took a few moments to pull a couple of fresh beers and pour two shots of bourbon. He put the drinks on the counter in front of us, and Jim handed him his empty glass.

"You lose family?" Jim nodded at my pocket.

I was suddenly conscious of the $600. Way too much walking-around money for a joint like this.

"There was a pension charge I shouldn't have paid," I replied. No one, not even vets, could figure out the maze of military retirement benefits. "I got a rebate."

"I see." Jim nodded, but his eyes narrowed farther than usual. "Whatever, man."

We dropped our shots into our beer glasses, and the dark bourbon diffused into the amber ale. I took a sip, and suddenly life tasted a lot sweeter. The cold beer came with an oaky bourbon aftertaste.

"You do what you got to do, man," Jim remarked.

"Is that your motto?" I asked before taking another drink.

"How do you mean?" He eyed me with the suspicion he usually kept for strangers. How many drinks had he had?

"I didn't mean anything, Jimbo. I was just shooting the breeze."

A heavy beat passed, and the sound of the basketball game filled the time between words.

"I was just wondering, you know, if 'do what you gotta do' was a general rule. That's all."

"You know I killed people," Jim snarled. He was real drunk. Mean drunk. The death stories usually came only later. "Ain't nothing to it. Counselor wanted to PTS-fucking-D me, man, but I said if my commanding officer points at someone and says this is our enemy, kill them, life gets pretty simple. Ain't no drama in dropping bad guys."

Another heavy beat.

"So, yeah, you do whatever the fuck you've got to do," Jim said, "is a general rule for life."

"And if you had to kill someone now?" I asked. "Someone bad."

"Drop 'em before they can blink." He snapped his fingers. "Why?" He leaned over conspiratorially. "You got someone in mind?"

I laughed, but it was hollow and off-key. "What? No. I was just—we were just talking, man."

He eyed me for a moment before breaking into a broad grin. "Well, that's all right, then." He raised his drink. "Salut."

We tapped glasses and got to business.

CHAPTER 9

I got so drunk, I went on another pilgrimage, the third since my release. My recollection is patched together like a homemade quilt, but after seeing Jim off, I think I hailed a cab and had the driver take me to Bel Air, where I hiked the Santa Monica Mountains, using my phone's flashlight to avoid stumbling and cracking my head on the rocky trail. Finally, I looked down at the home of the man whose life I'd destroyed.

Joseph Persico.

Billionaire, technologist, recluse.

There wasn't much about him in the public domain, but I'd found him and searched out his address. Part of me wanted to knock on his door and beg forgiveness, but I didn't have the courage to look the man in the eye, so instead I'd gone into the hills behind his house, a huge sprawling estate, and looked for signs of the man. But I'd never seen him, just the hard glint of the garden lights shining off metal.

Persico had several Boston Dynamics "Spot" robots patrolling his property. Designed to look like dogs, these devices moved on four legs, and from my distant vantage point, it was easy to believe they were alive. I knew from my engineering days rich folk had been incorporating drones and mechs into their personal security arrangements for a few years. For them the future is now. Machines with infrared sensors, motion-activated cameras, self-charging, always on, always vigilantly defending the space between the haves and have-nots. Watching the canine machines patrolling the grounds gave me a degree of peace. Persico was still alive and believed he had things worth protecting.

I had been drunk each time I'd come up here and had spent an hour or so swigging from a bottle. The first time I'd cried with guilt, the second I'd prayed for forgiveness. Tonight, I watched the huge house and asked the spirit of the man sleeping inside for peace. I needed calm to make the right choices in life.

Eventually, I must have staggered down the mountain and made my way to West Hollywood, even drunker than when I'd arrived—thanks to the six-pack I'd taken from Rick's. I vaguely recall hailing a cab to take me home.

Life came into sharper focus when I reached Edgebrook Avenue a little after three in the morning, but I spent too long on my front step, trying to get my key into the door. After what felt like years, I finally jammed it in, turned it, and stumbled into my living room, where I collapsed on the couch. But I couldn't sleep.

I thought back to my conversation with Jim. Did he know? Had he been trying to tell me I should kill Walter Glaze? Was he my patron? Had he sent the package? He always seemed to have money and was secretive about where it came from. He'd been pretty clear that he'd drop a bad guy. And Walter Glaze was most definitely a bad guy. Why shouldn't I end him?

A hundred and sixty thousand people die every single day. I've looked it up. A couple of stadiums full of people with each spin of the earth. What did it matter if I added one more dirtbag to that number? No one would skip a beat if Walter Glaze got hit by a car or fell out of a window, but if someone killed him, suddenly it isn't bad luck, it's a crime and everyone gets uptight. But is it really a crime to kill a bad man if an innocent child gets a better life?

Was I finding the peace I'd prayed for out on the mountain? Was this Joseph Persico's spirit giving me absolution through the clarity of action?

I squirmed around until I managed to get my phone out of my pocket, and I tapped at the warped, dancing letters until I managed to spell out "Walter Glaze Ultima."

The same set of results I'd seen earlier materialized, but this time it took much more concentration to make sense of them. I scrolled down to another gossip site called *LA Exposé* and clicked the link. This page was styled like a 1930s pulp magazine and had a silhouetted man in a trilby hat as its logo. *LA Exposé* was packed with salacious headlines about city notables. The piece on Walter Glaze was titled "Club Man, Drug Man, Murder Man." I concentrated on the opening line of the first paragraph, and when the letters finally came into focus, I started to read.

Club Man, Drug Man, Murder Man
From *LA Exposé*

In 1885, Charles Rentz was commissioned by Charles Goldstein to design Webster Hall, the world's first nightclub. The building was completed in 1886 and hosted a mix of high-society functions and socialist and union meetings. Revolution and revelry, strands of night culture that still resonate today.

Some dispute Webster Hall's claim to be the first nightclub, and point instead to McGlory's and Haymarket, establishments that predated Rentz's building, but McGlory's and Haymarket were akin to wild theaters with a mix of performance and vaudeville acts. They were also known for the third strand of night culture: crime.

Gambling, prostitution, stabbings, and shootings were regular occurrences at these establishments, along with the ensuing police raids.

Ultima, a modern nightclub near Venice Beach, would seem to have little in common with those ancient redbrick East Coast institutions, but beneath the expensive concrete and black steel, faux-industrial urban design, multimillion-dollar light and sound system, and wealthy clientele, the three strands of night culture are never far away, and some might say they're inexorably intertwined in this venue.

Step inside Ultima and you will be promised a night of wild adventure by the greeter, and the wide-eyed expressions of many of the patrons suggest the club makes good on its promise. The music is loud, perhaps a notch or two below painful, pounding out beats faster than any human heart. The vibe is electric, and the place is always packed, but never overcrowded. The uniformed staff are polite and professional, as one would expect at ten dollars for a beer and twenty-five for the house margarita.

And as you drift through the place, sipping impossibly expensive alcohol, watching the young bohemians' adventures in sound, sight, and imagination, you are so distracted by the pulsing energy of it all, you never stop to think who's behind the eternal party and why.

Then you see Walter Glaze, all six-four of him. Handsome, broad smile, powerful shoulders, glad-handing regulars, smiling at less familiar patrons, making everyone feel welcome. Walter Glaze, high school and college football star, family man, philanthropist, anti-racism campaigner. Walter Glaze, the all-around golden hero.

You'd be forgiven for looking no deeper, such is the shine coming off the man. It dazzles most, but if you scratch at the gold plating, you find something underneath. Something that most definitely isn't precious. Something tarnished.

There's Walter Glaze the juvenile delinquent. Walter Glaze the adulterer. Walter Glaze the nightclub owner questioned after the fatal shootings of two drug dealers who'd been arrested by police outside his club. Had they been killed to stop them revealing who they were really working for?

There are rumors of a connection to the Southside Boys and whispers they use a nightclub to launder money obtained from their various violent criminal activities.

Then there's the story of Roger Balloux, a French artist and philosopher who claims Glaze beat him nearly half to death in a drug-fueled rage. Balloux initially filed charges but dropped them suddenly. Did the Southside Boys pay him a visit? What convinced him to give Walter Glaze a free pass?

Nightclubs have come a long way since their nineteenth-century heyday, but some things never change.

If you ever wind up in Ultima, ask yourself this: Who is Walter Glaze?

Thanks for reading *LA Exposé*, your guide to the city's most pressing, unreported news. If you liked this story, please consider buying us a Ko-fi.

CHAPTER 10

My alarm woke me, and as I opened my heavy eyes, I thanked my past self for remembering Skye, even if he had left me only thirty minutes to get to Toni's. I stood, took a moment to steady myself as the blood settled into new pipes, ran to the bathroom, relieved myself of the night's toxins, necked a couple of Advils, grabbed my keys and wallet, and raced from the house.

I don't know if you've ever run in Los Angeles. The heat makes it feel as though an angry dragon is constantly misting you with hot breath. The heat is tinglingly close, and there's no breeze for even a moment's relief. I definitely wouldn't recommend running outdoors in LA when it's approaching high noon, and I particularly wouldn't suggest doing it hungover.

I covered the two miles to Toni's place in twenty-eight minutes. I used to clock six-minute miles when I was a proper man, but now even fourteen-minute miles involved a near-death experience.

I arrived, dripping sweat, dizzy, panting, lungs burning with exhaustion and pollution, and I'm pretty sure I stank.

Toni lived in an apartment building on North Hickory Avenue. Four white buildings, now streaked with grime, were connected in the shape of a cross that stood in a small garden. Each block was three stories and contained twelve apartments. Toni had one on the ground floor. Her barred windows overlooked an alleyway that ran beside the building and gave her a view of a restaurant parking lot and auto body shop. It was cheap and functional, a place to pass the night before the daily grind.

Every visit kick-started feelings of guilt and shame at having failed my wife and kid. They lived with the constant rumble of traffic from Rosencrans, an ugly view, bums, and weirdo neighbors, a galley kitchen and combined living room that wasn't big enough to pass for a dog kennel in Beverly Hills, two bedrooms little bigger than jail cells, and a wet room with a shower over the toilet.

I slowed to a walk and caught sight of Toni standing by her kitchen door. She had the Look, her familiar expression of disappointment and anger. Like her favorite T-shirt, she wore it often, and I felt every inch the heel each time I saw it.

"Just in time," she said as I pushed the six-foot-high green gate that was meant to guard the main entrance. It was always broken.

"I know, I know. I'm sorry," I replied, sucking in as much air as my sore lungs would take.

She glared, dialing the Look up to a six out of ten. "She's your daughter, Peyton. She deserves better than this."

"I know," I conceded honestly. "But I made it, didn't I?"

"Just."

"Any news from the doctor?" I asked.

"They said it would be a few days before we'll get the results," Toni replied.

We couldn't afford proper health care for Skye, which was another source of shame. Whatever tests the white coats needed to do, our daughter would be bottom of the heap.

"You got no car," Toni said sourly. "So, what are you going to do with her?"

"Take her to the park."

My allotted morning with Skye would be spent in an LA public park because I'd totaled a vehicle I hadn't finished paying for. I couldn't help but feel like a loser.

"She's thirteen, Peyton, not eight. The park." Toni frowned and shook her head in ill-disguised disappointment.

Skye appeared behind her. I wanted to wrap her in my arms and tell her everything would be okay, but even I couldn't be sure of that.

The apartment was too small for her not to have heard Toni doing me down. She sized me up, and while Toni's eyes blazed with anger and frustration, Skye's glistened with sadness. It broke my heart to see her feeling sorry for me.

"Hey, kiddo," I said. I felt so inadequate. I didn't deserve to be her dad. I had to do better. "You ready?"

CHAPTER 11

There's nothing like being humiliated by your own child. Doesn't matter whether they've caught you having sex, woken you up after a night of hard drinking when your breath is 90-proof, or busted your balls about how they said you were driving too fast while the cop who pulled you over is weighing up whether to write you a ticket. Kids are supposed to look up to you and see a hero. Pity coming from a kid has a particularly bitter taste.

Skye offered hers with silence and awkward looks. It had been a long time since I'd felt okay about myself, so there was no question of me suffering the ego shock of being knocked from hero status, but on Alameda Street, sucking in the fumes from the passing cars, my shriveled ego was desiccated even more. She used to be a chatty girl and her eyes had once been like stadium floodlights, shining with love and admiration for me. I was Daddy the soldier man, the clever, handsome engineer who could build and fix stuff. She'd slip her child's hand into mine and shine those floodlights at me so brightly I knew I was the center of her world. Her blond curls would bounce as she chatted enthusiastically about animals and planets, her two favorite interests, and I would listen and share whatever learning I had to offer. Those were the good times, before I ruined all our lives by getting myself locked up.

By the time I got out, her golden locks had turned a sandy brown and the child had been replaced by a teenager. Teen Skye was a young woman whose hair was cut short and accented red in places. She wore grungy T-shirts and baggy jeans, and usually had on a wide baseball cap that concealed most of her face.

I wanted to ask about her symptoms, but Toni had told me to steer clear, so I couldn't talk about the biggest thing in our lives right now.

"How's school?" I asked, deploying a trusty reserve question.

"We're on vacation."

My ego shriveled a little more. I couldn't even ask a good question.

"But there's summer school," she added. "Mom's booked me in when she's working."

Toni did paperwork and helped keep the books at a Goodwill store on Redondo Beach Boulevard not far from her apartment. It didn't pay well, but it was all she could get as a high school graduate who'd worked to help finance her ex-husband's tuition. We'd been able to afford for only one of us to go to college and had made the mistake of choosing me. Toni would never have screwed up the way I had.

"And it's good," Skye said. "A lot of my friends from regular school are there."

"Kelly? Sam?" I asked.

She scrunched up her face and shook her head. "No. My new friends from high school. Brook, Laura, Gloria."

"Oh." I didn't know who any of those girls were.

"What happened to your car?" Skye asked.

More shriveling.

"I, well, I, er . . ."

There was no good answer.

"Mom says you probably totaled it while wasted."

A shriveled husk now. If it shrunk any more, my ego would vanish.

"Your mom can jump to conclusions sometimes." It wasn't a lie.

"What happened to you, Dad?" Skye asked with the earnestness only a child can pull off.

It was a real good question and one I'd asked myself in my darkest moments. I had a grab bag of theories, but none I was prepared to share with my kid, so I just replied with a weak smile and walked a little quicker.

Skye was smart enough not to press for an answer, so we both hurried on, pretending the question had never been asked. Wilson Park was a concession against concrete, an island of green, resisting the encroaching sprawl. The skate park and adventure playground were busy, and the paths were crowded with joggers, dog walkers, and families. There were softball, Frisbee, and touch-football games happening on the lawns.

Fate smiled on me, or so I thought. Turns out it was the mocking grin of a god with a wicked sense of humor.

"There's Laura." Skye pointed at a girl about her age. "She's one of my friends from class."

She ran toward the girl, who had platinum-blond hair and was about the same height and slight build. She was walking with a rugged man I assumed was her father.

"Skye," I said, but she was gone, so I followed her and a few moments later joined the trio, who were standing to the side of a path that led to the adventure playground.

"Hey," the man said. "I'm Bill. Laura's dad."

"Peyton," I replied, shaking the man's hand.

His skin was rough and his fingers tough and ridged with callouses. Maybe I was seeing qualities I was missing, but in my mind, he had the strong grip and honest eyes of a man who wouldn't let you down. He was probably five years my junior but hadn't lived my life and looked as though he worked out, so I felt much older.

"Wanna go watch the soccer?" Laura asked, and Skye nodded.

They ran off before Bill or I could respond. He smiled indulgently, and we fell in beside each other as we headed for the soccer field.

"Some days they're still kids," he remarked. "Others they're too-cool-for-school grumpy teens. Or in this case, hormonal teens watching boys play sports. One of Laura's friends is playing, so she dragged me down here. I haven't had the courage to ask if he's a boyfriend. It's a tough age."

I nodded absently as the girls settled at the sideline of an impromptu soccer match. Boyfriends? How were we here already? I realized with a sinking feeling that I still thought of Skye as a little kid, as though she hadn't aged while I was inside, but time hadn't stood still for her the way it had for me.

"Laura said you were in the army."

"Yeah," I replied, surprised Skye would even talk to her friends about me. "Army engineering. You?"

"I went straight into a job after high school. Never thought about the military and couldn't afford college." He hesitated. Was I supposed to say something? "I got work at an auto shop. Trained as a mechanic and never left. Been there fourteen years."

I wished I could trade the man his steady, dependable life for my mess. I hadn't been able to find a job since my release.

"You still serving?" he asked.

I shook my head. "I'm between jobs. Figuring out what to do next."

He nodded at the girls, who were shouting at one of the players, a handsome boy with hair that fell about his face. "Got to give back better, right? Our parents gave their best for us, now we've got to pay it forward for the next generation. Laura says Skye wants to be a doctor. Med school." He exhaled sharply, and I pictured him presenting a customer with an astronomical quote for a new head gasket and an engine rebuild.

I had no idea Skye wanted to be a doctor. She was too young to be thinking about careers, right? How did this stranger know more about my daughter than me? Why hadn't Toni told me our daughter wanted years of college education?

"Loans or paid up front, either way it's expensive. Even with scholarships," Bill said. "But that's what kids are there for, right? To keep us on our toes. Got to pay forward our good fortune."

I nodded as my ego shriveled to nothing. I couldn't fulfill even the most basic of my daughter's dreams—a new dress, a pair of shoes. Even with the hundred grand for Walter Glaze, how would I have any hope of helping her achieve her life goal?

CHAPTER 12

Because what's the point?" Toni told me when I asked her why she hadn't shared Skye's Big Dream. "You can't even put food on her table, let alone pay for college. And you're weak, so you'd just string her along with lies and false promises. She'll just take loans and try for scholarships when it's time. We can't rely on you, Peyton."

Her words were like stab wounds, and I wanted to defend myself, but what with? I was many things, but delusional wasn't one of them, and she was right, so I backed away from her kitchen door and waved at Skye, who was peering at me from her bedroom window.

She waved back but didn't smile.

She'd spent an hour with Laura watching the match, laughing more than she ever did with me, and chatting to the boys at halftime. Bill had invited us to join him and his daughter for a late lunch, but I didn't have much money left after my night at the bar, so I declined, and, feeling more like a heel than ever, just said goodbye to them. Skye and I did a couple more silent laps of the park. I'd wanted to talk to her about becoming a doctor but didn't have the courage to expose more of my failings as a father.

I left Toni's and walked home, taking it easy in the afternoon sun. I had nothing to hurry for. No one waiting. No job. Not even a dental appointment. I couldn't afford one.

I replayed my conversations with Skye, Bill, and Toni, and as I remembered how small they all made me feel, I had the strangest experience. For a moment, I wasn't me. I was a passerby looking at myself, judging myself with the words of my daughter, her friend's father, and my ex-wife echoing in my head. I saw my dirty clothes, my rough stubble, smelled my body odor, heard my self-pitying sighs, and sensed the fog of failure that swirled around me. I looked at myself in disgust and wondered what the hell had happened to the man I'd once been.

All the excuses, disappointments, and unlucky breaks came to the surface, but I didn't have the strength to face them today. Toni, my ex-wife, the love of my life, didn't even think I was worth bothering with. That I was some kind of dream-eater who would destroy our daughter's future.

There had been a time before my life went to pieces when I'd see a target, take aim at it, and hit it. No questions, no doubts. Engineering taught faith in human ingenuity. With enough time and thought, any problem could be solved. Past me had been unstoppable, but was he dead? I prayed he was only sleeping. What would it take to bring him back?

I took a detour on my way home, heading for Rick's.

It was a little after six when I arrived, and the place was pretty quiet. Rick nodded absently. He was watching the buildup to a football game from his perch behind the bar. Jim was on the other side of the counter, drinking a beer as he kept his eyes on the TV.

"Hey," I said, sliding onto the stool next to him.

He nodded without looking away from the pregame interview, but when he finally turned to me, he scrunched up his face in disgust.

"Jeez, Peyton, you look like shit. Rick, get this man a drink."

"Stow that," I said, and Rick shrugged.

"You're not going to twelve steps me, are you?" Jim asked. "That would be too depressing."

"No. I need to take a drive somewhere, and I don't want a DUI to add to my troubles."

"Now *that* I can understand." Jim raised his glass in salute before knocking back the amber.

I felt awkward as his attention shifted back to the game. I was loitering with intent, and he finally felt me looking at him. He eyed me with suspicion.

"You gonna ask me out?"

"I was wondering . . ." I hesitated.

"Yeah? Fucking favor coming. I can feel it."

I nodded. "I was wondering if I could borrow your car."

I'd seen his black 1981 Lincoln Continental in the parking lot, which is where it spent most of its time. He was usually too drunk to drive home.

Jim scowled. "You wanna borrow my car? My baby? My beautiful child?"

How long had he been drinking?

I nodded uncertainly.

"What's wrong with yours?"

"I . . ." I wilted as Jim glared at me.

"Relax, man. Everyone heard about you trashing the sheriff's car. Some of your neighbors frequent this here establishment." He smiled like a little devil. "You're a total screwup, Peyton, but you've come in here, refused a drink, which shows responsibility, and you've asked a favor, which shows you think we're buddies. I gotta say yes, don't I, Rick?"

The barman was too wise to get involved and didn't react.

"Cynic might say you paid off my tab to put me in your debt, but I know you ain't that cunning."

He delved into his pocket and produced his keys.

"Take her, but make sure you bring her back like you found her," he said. "Exactly how you found her."

"Thanks, Jim," I replied, taking the keys. "I owe you one."

CHAPTER 13

I still don't know why I went there. I wasn't fixed on killing Walter Glaze. Maybe I was curious about the guy? Or needed to clear my head after my afternoon with Skye? One of those high-flying LA prosecutors with half an eye on the mayor's office would have started rapping about malice aforethought and intent and such, but I was a deadbeat with nothing better to do, and the honest truth is the only thing I was planning to kill that night was time. Lord knows I had plenty of it. A night at Ultima might help me understand why someone wanted Walter Glaze dead.

I took Jim's car, which handled like a tennis court on wheels, but gave a smooth easy-chair ride, and went home to shower and changed into a sky-blue T-shirt, black jeans, and dark blue sneakers. I hadn't been to a nightclub in years, but the uniform couldn't have changed that much, and I left the house feeling and looking good.

LA roads are best at night. Like a smoker who spends their days coughing up congestion, the city finally clears its pipes after evening rush hour, and when the salary folk are safe in their homes, watching TV with their family, or gathered around their tables shoveling takeout onto their plates, the roads with their wide lanes, bright lights, and gaudy billboards are their own world of fun.

Jim was such an alpha male. Of course, he was going to have one of the biggest production cars ever made, but it wasn't just a proud display of manhood; the car was practical. If I'd had to spend hours in LA traffic, where better than cruise control, ice-cold AC, grand seat comfort? A car so big you could park a smaller car on the back seat and still have space for the family. I motored through the City of Angels without so much as a ripple, watching the world glide by.

I found Ultima nightclub on Grand Canal, a side street off North Venice Boulevard. The club was located in a huge, whitewashed concrete warehouse on the northwest corner of Grand Canal, and I slowed to case the joint as I drove by. Reconnaissance, we call it in the army. It was an art in which I'd had some training. See without being seen.

Ultima wasn't like any nightclub I'd ever been to. The people lining the street wore outfits that made Lady Gaga look plain. Hats, boots, chain-mail dresses, scaffolded costumes; this place catered for the clubber as an artist, and I was seriously underdressed.

A pair of gorgeous greeters in matching black trouser suits checked names as VIPs arrived, and nodded people through from the line. Four doormen in black shirts and trousers kept an eye on the crowd. A small, discreet blacklight sign advertised Ultima, but that was the only give-away. Passersby would have seen nothing but a line of living artworks waiting to get into a large, windowless building.

I parked on the next road along and walked back to the club. I could smell rotting food and other ripe, offensive odors coming from the alley-way behind Ultima, and saw a row of industrial dumpsters that stretched into the darkness beyond a staff entrance.

Good place to hide out, I caught myself thinking.

I wasn't there to kill a man, I promise, and even back then I felt annoyed at the fact I was considering lying in wait between the huge trash cans and killing Walter Glaze as he left his business.

You could kill a bad man and start a college fund with the money, a little voice told me. *If Skye's sick, you could make sure she's okay. Maybe even buy a decent lawyer to get you off the charges for the car thing so you can be there for her. Take care of her. It's money for good. Good money.*

The thought was like woodworm eating away at what little integrity I had left. I wasn't going to kill anyone. Not tonight anyway.

I pushed death from my mind and felt a tremor of excitement for the first time in years as I turned the corner and joined the line on Grand Canal. Alcohol and drugs usually numbed my senses, but here I was sober, on an ill-defined mission, waiting to get into a high-end nightclub.

"You laying on the irony?" a woman asked, and I turned to see a woman, a work of art made flesh.

She was looking at me as though I was a living joke.

Attica Douglas.

The most beautiful woman I've ever known.

CHAPTER 14

Your outfit," Attica explained. "Either you made no effort at all, or you made every effort to satirize the rest of us. Both are cool."

She was with four friends dressed like Cirque du Soleil backup dancers. I was transfixed by Attica, who wore needlepoint heels, sheer black tights, and a body-hugging black silk minidress embroidered with silver skulls. Her blond hair was shaved on one side and hung down in a shoulder-length cascade on the other. Her arms were covered in sleeve tattoos of flower vines woven between ornate skulls. She exuded confidence, and the impish glint in her eye told me she had a wicked sense of humor.

"Do we have to wait?" one of the guys in her entourage asked. "Walter said we should go right in."

I took note of the use of my target's name. Target? Like I was an assassin.

"I'm just mingling," Attica replied. "Keeping it real."

"Reality sucks," the guy shot back. "Let's live the fantasy."

He and the others left the line and made for the entrance. I felt the chill of disappointment as Attica followed.

"Coming?" she asked, glancing over her shoulder.

I smiled like a lottery winner as I hurried to catch up with her, relieved the difficult years hadn't totally killed my game. I was soft around the edges, but in this dim light I might still pass for handsome.

"I'm Peyton. Peyton Collard," I said, offering her my hand.

She looked confused before she took it awkwardly while we were walking.

"Attica Douglas."

I've spent a long time thinking about life. There isn't much else to do in prison, and even after I got out and spent months swimming around a beer glass of self-pity or praying for forgiveness on the mountain overlooking Joseph Persico's house. I don't say this to brag or to set myself above anyone, because I'm the lowest you can get. I'm a killer. A taker of lives. I mention my hard thinking hours because I want you to know the amount of time I've devoted to such things. I may not have the right answers, but at least you know my wrongthink has been carefully considered.

Take Attica, for example. I lusted after her from the moment I saw her. I was charged with excitement as we walked side by side. You know that feeling? The promise of a thousand new tomorrows, because that's what a fresh relationship represents. It isn't just a connection to a person; it's a fork in the road of life, a chance to reinvent ourselves, to live as different people.

Attica didn't know Peyton Collard the drunk ex-con without a cent to his name. She knew Peyton Collard the Silicon Valley billionaire, music producer, or heart surgeon. I wasn't going to lie to her, but such was the energy I felt, I truly believed I could have become any of those things if it would have put me in bed with her.

Her friends said something to one of the greeters and we were waved inside.

I still think about stepping through the dark entrance, a near innocent with no idea I was about to be given a glimpse of heaven on my way down to hell.

CHAPTER 15

It can be hard to distinguish memory from dream. Ultima was one of those places where the line between reality and fantasy was blurred. The people in their strange costumes came from another world, and the building, with only a single portal to the outside, seemed to protrude into another part of the multiverse.

I followed Attica and her friends through a lobby that was built of screens playing a kaleidoscope of star fields, galaxies, and universes that made me feel even more insignificant. God knows what this place would be like high or tripping.

One of Attica's friends pushed a heavy door open, and a heavy rhythm and light choral vocals hit me.

We stepped onto a crescent balcony above the dance floor. There were three other balconies and a huge bar, where black-clad staff hustled to serve a crowd of customers three rows deep.

A magnificent laser system wove patterns in the air and alternated colors with the bass line. Every so often the rainbow was punctuated by black light, and that was when I saw the true beauty of Attica's dress. The silver embroidery shone brightly in the UV light, and as she moved, the skulls rippled with life. She was a work of art and shone so brightly, all the other ornately clad clubbers faded into the dull background.

She took my hand and led me down a curved staircase to the dance floor. Her friends left us, but I hardly noticed them or any of the bodies pressed around us. She pulled me, and her hair smelled of vanilla. It was the sweetest scent I'd encountered in a very long time. I held her in my arms and lingered in the moment, wishing it could last forever.

Things like this didn't happen to a deadbeat like me. I'd been raised Protestant, but I wasn't a religious man. It was hard to keep faith in God after all that had happened, but was this the universe's way of telling me I was on the right path? Was I destined to kill Walter Glaze?

She produced a pair of pills from a tiny clutch that matched her dress and took one. She pressed the other into my mouth, and I relished every instant her finger was on my lips.

"What is it?" I asked.

"A key," she replied. "A mirror. Perhaps. We call them Sidewinders. Here," she said, producing a baggie from her clutch and slipping it into my pocket. "You'll want more."

I didn't object. I liked the feel of her hand in my pants, and someone this beautiful could never give me something that could hurt me.

I've said Ultima was heaven and hell, and at that very moment, I was in heaven, but whatever she'd given me was my ticket to the other place. When I look back on everything that's happened since, I wonder how different things would have been if I hadn't swallowed that pill.

CHAPTER 16

We danced close. I'm not talking American close. I mean Argentine-tango close, finding our own slow rhythm in contrast to the mass of bodies around us. As the music coddled us, I felt whatever was in the pill hit.

Attica blazed white, her aura so dazzling I could hardly take it in. She smiled, took my hand, and we pushed through the crowd, and the flares of souls burst into vivid color all around me.

I was tripping, of course. Attica said something to the club bouncer standing by the stairs, and he allowed us into the VIP section. I followed her upstairs, and we found her friends sitting at one of twelve tables on the large balcony. They were all mirrored, and I saw myself in the tabletop as we sat on the crescent-shaped couch. My pupils were like saucers, and I was so high I didn't register it was me until my ass was on plush velvet.

I tilted my head back, closed my eyes, and tried to compose myself. I felt Attica against me, her hand rubbing my inner thigh, and wherever her fingers traveled, they electrified my skin. I was supposed to be here on a mission, I reminded myself.

I opened my eyes, but instead of Attica's beautiful face, I was greeted by Walter Glaze, as though he was an evil spirit I'd summoned.

The man I've come to kill.

To investigate, I corrected myself. I was just about sober enough to reason with my dark side, but only barely.

Walter Glaze didn't acknowledge me. He was leaning over me so he could whisper in Attica's ear. I already hated the man, so it was no surprise my drug-tainted eyes saw his aura as a cloud of soot-gray smoke. He had his hand on Attica's knee, and his muscled shoulder kept brushing my body, pushing me back into my seat.

Attica took her hand away from my leg and put it on Walter's shoulder. Her unblemished skin looked right at home on the man's black silk suit. Was Walter's indifference to me a way of showing he was the man she should have been with?

Memories swirled up from the depths. Nights crying in prison, days spent being beaten, humbled by bigger, stronger men. Men like this one.

I punched Walter in the ribs and stood up, pushing him onto the mirrored table, knocking over a round of drinks.

He seemed more surprised than hurt.

"Easy, friend," he said. "You just had to ask me to move."

Had he even felt the punch?

"Sorry, Walter," Attica responded before I could answer. "Peyton is pretty wasted."

"Happens to the best of us." Walter got to his feet and waved at one of the servers who staffed the section. Soon the man came with a tray, tidying the mess I'd made.

"Get them another round. On the house," Walter said. "I should have been more careful."

I hated his casual confidence, his wealth, his crimes, the wool he pulled over other people's eyes, but most of all I hated his hands on Attica as though I wasn't there. I wasn't no one. I was the man who might kill him.

I don't remember whether I said anything to him then, but I didn't feel so good all of a sudden, and I left Attica, her beautiful friends, and Walter Glaze, and staggered in search of a restroom.

CHAPTER 17

I stumbled down the stairs. The dance floor, which had been shining with positive energy only a few minutes earlier, was just a gloomy mass of sweaty bodies, and as I pushed my way through, I saw hostile, angry faces every step of the way. Demons everywhere, teeth long and wolfish, protruding from snarled mouths, hair of fire and thorns.

My trip was turning bad.

When I finally broke through the other side, I ran into the men's room like a velociraptor on the hunt for prey. I was about to hurl, and the sight of an elderly man with large prescription glasses standing beside a tray of colognes and candy packets almost stopped me in my tracks, but I rushed into the nearest cubicle and hunched over the can like a devout worshipper.

I desperately wanted to be sick, to purge myself of my bad history, but nothing came, and as the moments passed and my rapid breathing subsided, I realized I'd suffered a full-blown panic attack. Now that I had the safe haven of a toilet, I didn't need it. My toes straightened, my stomach untangled, and the sweat started to dry against my skin.

I heard the attendant shuffling and breathing outside the cubicle. I turned red with shame at the thought of this man, my elder, and almost certainly my better, bearing witness to this moment of humiliation.

I rose, flushed the empty bowl, took a moment to compose myself, and stepped out. As I left the cubicle, Walter Glaze sauntered into the men's room with a casual confidence that reminded me of Bruce Lee. Only he was at least twice the size of the great martial artist.

"Give us a minute, Ed," he said to the attendant, who nodded and left.

I thought about pushing past Walter and following the old man but couldn't get my limbs to work. Was I scared? Or high?

Walter went to one of the basins and watched me in the full-width mirror.

The sound of water rushing over his hands was captivating. I saw a waterfall in my mind's eye, more real than any of my mundane surroundings.

Focus, I told my swaying reflection. *This is the man you were sent to kill.*

Was I muttering? Had I said that out loud?

"You're pretty fucked up," Walter remarked as he lathered his hands. "If I didn't know better, I'd say you tried to sucker punch me back there."

So, he had felt it.

"Hard to tell, though." He continued watching me throughout. "More of a tap than a punch. You get jealous or something, friend?"

He paused.

"No need. Attica and I go way back, and I'm happily married."

He showed me a thick silver band, slick with soap suds.

A happily married, lying, rich, handsome gangster, who peddles drugs and violence.

How was it right he had so much more than me?

I looked around the marble room and settled on the attendant's tray. Gum, Tic Tacs, cologne, Life Savers, a tip cup, and a metal pen. Jason Bourne had killed a man with a Biro. This solid-steel Parker would be more lethal. I just had to find the courage to pick it up and drive it into a man's throat. Pass "Go," collect a hundred thousand bucks, and join the winner's circle.

He startled me by grabbing a paper towel from the dispenser, and turned to face me as he dried his hands methodically. They were so very big.

"If I wanted her," he said, looking at me square. His features were being distorted by whatever was in that pill, turning him devilish, but I had no doubt his eyes were fixed on mine. "If I wanted anything you have." He stepped forward, closing the gap between us. I felt a force trying to push me back, but I stood my ground. "I would just reach out and take it."

He put his hand on my shoulder and squeezed me a little too hard for me to mistake the gesture as friendly.

"You're just a fuck to her," he said. "I've seen her do this before. Pick up some random from outside our social circle for sex. You're disposable, friend. You mean nothing. You are nothing."

I had to do it. I had to take that pen and drive it home. I imagined him raging, clutching at his throat, choking on his own blood.

I could do it.

This one thing.

This one brave thing would change my life forever.

Just reach out.

Take it.

Do it.

"There you are," Attica said, an instant before the men's room door crashed against the wall.

"I've been looking for you," she said, and I thought she was talking about Walter, but her eyes were on me.

"I think he's had too much of everything," Walter sneered. "Pretty sure he was aiming to hurt me, but I know his kind. Pussy."

This arrogant, corrupt criminal was making judgments about me, humiliating me. He didn't know I'd been a soldier once. He had no idea I'd had to fight my way through hard years in prison.

I swung for him instinctively, but my fist failed to hit its mark. I seemed to be moving in slow motion, but Walter Glaze suffered from no such affliction.

He caught me with a gut punch that buckled me in half, and as my head came down, his anvil fist came up and smashed into my chin, knocking me on my ass.

I don't remember much else. Something set Attica and Walter to laughing, at least that's my recollection of things. But I might not be the most reliable of narrators because I crashed in and out of consciousness, and even when I was awake and aware, the world spiraled violently. Concussion? Or just the effect of the Sidewinders and a head injury?

I'm pretty sure Walter Glaze dragged me from the restroom and handed me off to a pair of bouncers who weren't gentle as they took me out back and tossed me into the alleyway beside the dumpsters, the very spot I'd thought would make a good hiding place to lie in wait for murder.

My ego bruised, my heart hot with anger, I staggered away, picturing the murder of the man who'd just humiliated me. If I'd had any doubt about killing him before, Walter Glaze had just erased it by showing me exactly what kind of man he was. He'd made it easy for me to see this as a battle of good versus evil and to tell myself he was to blame for what came next.

CHAPTER 18

I woke in the doorway of a consignment store, disturbed by the cashier opening up for the day. I mumbled what I hoped was an apology and staggered into blinding sunshine, squinting as I tried to get my bearings. I was somewhere near Santa Monica Boulevard and shuffled toward a bus stop by a busy intersection a few hundred feet away.

I sat at the back of the 260 bus with my head against the window, a Ratso Rizzo figure, feeling sick and sorry for myself. The smell of bleach overlaid on trace vomit and urine added to my nausea. There were a handful of other people on the bus, and we avoided each other the way big city folk do, but even their fleeting glances in the glare of daylight made the previous night's thoughts of murder wilt.

Maybe I'd just stay on the bus to the depot and get lost like so many people who came to California? Here at the western edge of the world, tens of thousands of people wander the coast, hiding from their pasts, homeless, transient, dipping into mainstream society only when necessary.

Only a fool romanticizes a life on the street, I told myself. *You ready to take that final step because some prick knocked you on your ass? You want respect? Stop being a deadbeat.*

It was hard not to hate myself. I hadn't always been so pathetic. In high school I'd been voted most likely to succeed, I'd done well in college, and I'd been tipped for command in the army. I didn't recognize that man now. A different me, who might as well have been a character from a movie. He wouldn't have given in to self-pity and booze.

My phone rang, and I shifted in my seat to get it out of my pocket. The incoming profile showed a photo of a Lincoln Continental.

"Hey, Jim," I said.

"You sound fucked up, man," he scoffed. "You crash my car?"

"I left it in Venice. I'm on my way to get it now."

"Two-day rental is four hundred bucks."

Jim could turn on a dime, so it was sometimes hard to tell whether he was fooling or for real.

"I'm kidding, you dumb fuck. Bring it over to Rick's."

"I will."

I was about to hang up when Walter Glaze's smug face flashed through my mind. I saw all the ways he'd ruined my night, hurt me, humiliated me. I thought about Skye, about her diagnosis, and her hard-luck future. I imagined all the kids getting hooked on whatever Walter Glaze peddled. I looked around the bus and didn't want to be there anymore, stuck at the back and on the bottom. I wanted a better life for my daughter. And for me.

"Hey, Jim, if I wanted to get a piece . . ."

"You gonna kill someone, hotshot?"

"No. Nothing like that. After the thing with my car, I dunno, I just want more home protection."

"Ex-cons aren't allowed firearms in the good state of California."

He was right. My prison sentence, which had been longer than a year, disqualified me from legally owning a gun.

"I know. That's why I'm asking you."

I'd never been able to figure out exactly how Jim earned a living. Something to do with private security. Either he used to work in the field, or he still did. He was incredibly discreet. Or maybe he just didn't trust me. All I knew was that he'd run with some heavy dudes.

"You know Rudy's on Compton Boulevard?"

"No."

"It's the pawn shop by the market, opposite Pollos, the chicken place. Tell him I sent you."

"Thanks."

"And we never had this conversation," Jim said.

"It's not what you think," I protested.

"None of my business, hotshot. Just bring my car back when you're through playing bad guy."

He hung up, and I looked at my fellow passengers to see if any of them had overheard. Like good angels, they kept to their own business.

Was I really going to do this? Was I really going to drive over to Compton and buy a gun?

I settled back into my seat and thought about my life.

Why didn't I deserve good things? What had pricks like Walter done to deserve all the luck? Sold drugs? Exploited people? Killed them? He'd shown me nothing but cruelty, and a price had to be paid, didn't it?

Besides, just because I own a gun, doesn't mean I'm going to use it.

CHAPTER 19

Could I kill a man? That's what I kept asking myself as I walked a block along Compton Boulevard in the roaster that was Los Angeles and found Rudy's, a double-fronted pawn shop with bars across the windows protecting a trove of artifacts plundered from ordinary lives: phones, jewelry, guitars, laptops, tablets, clothes, and even shoes. I wondered if anyone had ever left the store barefoot, clutching a handful of dirty notes. More likely they were a haul from the dead. Relatives taking advantage of the fact neither heaven nor hell has a dress code and footwear is most certainly not required.

The door was locked. An old man in a baseball cap and a Metallica T-shirt looked me up and down with the eyes of a seasoned trouble hunter. He buzzed me in, and I stepped into air-conditioned comfort. A radio played hard rock, which seemed a fitting soundtrack for the purchase of a deadly weapon.

"You Peyton?" the old man asked.

He wouldn't have looked out of place leaning up against the hitching post in front of an old-time western saloon. Narrow lips, weathered skin, and, behind those sharp eyes, a calloused soul that was just waiting for the world to disappoint him.

I nodded. "You Rudy?"

"Jim said you were coming. I got your purchase here."

I moved toward him. He was behind one of three huge glass counters

DEADBEAT

that formed a U around the edges of the store. Beneath the transparent countertops was more plundered treasure. How many tears had been shed over the loss of these precious things? There was a whole section of wedding and engagement rings.

I'd rehearsed a speech about needing a gun for personal protection from someone who'd been threatening me and my kid, explaining why I couldn't go legal, but I needn't have bothered.

He leaned below the counter and picked up something wrapped in a Coors beer towel.

"I've got your piece here," he said, placing the bundle on the thick glass.

He unwrapped it to reveal a nickel-plated revolver.

"It's a Smith & Wesson Model 19," he said. "Takes a 357."

I picked it up and was surprised at how heavy it felt. Not the weight of a man's life, though.

"You'll need these." Rudy put two boxes of cartridges on the counter. "Three hundred for the lot."

No questions. No judgment. Just the tools of death.

I nodded, put the gun back on the beer towel, and reached into my pocket. As I counted out the money, I kept glancing at the shining revolver and wondered whether it had ever been used to take another life. Was it already familiar with the task that lay ahead?

CHAPTER 20

I was shaking by the time I pulled up outside Rick's. Bile kept rising and falling, scorching my throat. I could have played stupid and pretended it was alcohol withdrawal or the comedown from the pill, but I knew it was guilt. Not for what I'd done. Remorse about the past had a different flavor. It was smoky, burning my soul quietly, until it crumbled like a red dead coal. This was the guilt of precognition, unruly and wild, as some part of me fought against the inevitable, tried to cry out that what I was going to do was wrong, but got strangled by the cold logic of selfishness.

I was really going to kill a man.

I'd bought a small used Nike sports bag from Rudy for six bucks, and I grabbed it from the footwell, put it on the seat, unzipped the main compartment, and checked the parking lot. The Lincoln was the only car, apart from Rick's gray Toyota Camry. I opened the glove compartment, and it gaped wide like a tiny hippo's jaw. There at the back of its throat was the Coors towel, bundled in a ball. I grabbed it and the boxes of ammunition and put them into the sports bag.

I checked the parking lot again to make sure no one had seen me, got out of the car, and double-timed it to Rick's.

Jim was in his usual spot at the bar, but the place was otherwise empty.

"Rick's gone for some snacks," Jim said as I approached.

"And he left you in charge?" I tried to crack wise to hide my anxiety.

"Yeah," Jim replied belligerently. "I'm trustworthy. Like I know you have a piece in that bag you're holding."

I burned with sudden shame.

"But I ain't gonna tell nobody, because I'm trustworthy," he assured me. "You want a drink?"

"I can't," I replied, placing the keys to the Lincoln on the bar.

"You gotta be sober to kill a man?" He grinned like a mocking troll.

"Shut up, Jim. Of course not. I'm going to see Toni and Skye. I don't want to be sauced."

"Whatever you gotta tell yourself, man," he said. His eyes were glassy, and his words were curling at the edges. Not quite slurring, but not far off. "And thank you too." He picked up his keys. "I bet you didn't even fill her up."

I was a little ashamed. "Thanks for the car, Jim. I appreciate it. Let me buy you a beer."

"Sure. When you got time to sit and drink with me." His belligerence was unmistakable. "Well, run on then."

He fixed his eyes on his beer.

"Thanks for the connect," I said, holding up the bag.

He grunted, and I left him to his drunken anger. He could be so unpredictable. Best friends one minute, hated enemy the next.

As I pushed the door open and bright sunshine flooded in, Jim spoke.

"Peyton, for the love of everything holy, don't do anything stupid."

"I won't," I assured him, but wondered if that advice had come too late for me.

It seemed stupidity was my best buddy, always with me, guiding my life, and he brought his pals hard luck and misery to the party every single day.

I left the bar and walked to Toni's place. I felt the urge to see her and Skye one last time, just in case things went wrong. A little over thirty minutes later, I was on the rough, dry grass outside her apartment. I heard movement inside, and the kitchen door was opened by a man who was about an inch taller than me. A few years younger, slimmer, wavy blond hair, a deep surfer tan, and a Chiclet white smile, which he flashed at me. He wore a pair of shorts and nothing else, giving me the chance to take in his ripped abs and tight pecs.

"Hey, bruh," the guy said. "You must be Skye's dad."

I was too stunned to respond. This younger, better man wasn't here to install cable or repair the AC. I mean, who'd do that shirtless anyway? He was my replacement.

"I'm Jack," he said, offering his hand. "Jack Harper."

I shook it weakly.

"Toni and Skye just went to Ralphs to get some chow. They won't be long."

He smiled but didn't move.

"Can I come in?"

He scrunched his face like I'd pinched him. "Toni said I'm never to let you in." His smile returned. "Got to respect the rules, right?"

We said nothing for a while.

"Listen, dude, I just want you to know you won't get any weirdness from me. Toni and I are taking things slow, but whatever happens, you're always gonna be Skye's dad."

Nothing I'd ever heard had panicked me more. The idea of this tanned young Brad Pitt replacing me was worse than a hundred gut punches. He would very obviously be better than me at everything. Even at being a father.

"What you got there?" he asked, nodding at the bag.

"Nothing," I replied awkwardly, feeling every inch the deadbeat for bringing a weapon within five hundred miles of my daughter. Stupidity was with me. Always.

"What are you doing here?"

I turned to see Toni and Skye approaching. Our daughter was drinking a bright purple slushy, and Toni was carrying a grocery bag.

"It's not your day," Toni said. She and Jack exchanged an awkward look. "You two have met, then?"

"Yeah," Jack replied. "He's exactly how you described."

What had my ex-wife said about me?

Toni squeezed by to get into the apartment. She smelled great and had done her makeup. She was wearing short shorts and a white vest that showed off her cleavage. It wasn't a subtle look, but Jack's roving eyes suggested he clearly liked it.

"Hey, Dad," Skye said.

She loitered beside me.

"Hey, kiddo. You enjoying that?" I nodded at her slushy.

Should she even be drinking something with so much sugar?

"Yeah." She stuck out her tongue, which was a bright purple.

Toni put the grocery bag on the floor.

"Can you make a start?" she asked Jack. "While I see what this is about."

His smile didn't falter. "Sure thing, hon."

They were at the "hon" stage, and I hadn't even known he'd existed until I'd turned up like an unwanted insurance salesman. Had there been other Jacks?

She smiled back at him as he took the bag, but it drained from her face the moment she turned to look at me.

"How long have you and he . . ." I trailed off.

"This part of my life," she said, drawing a globe with her hands in the air around me, "is the past, a connection that only exists because of our daughter. And then there's that part of my life"—she gestured inside—"which is my future, shared with people I want to share it with. What happens in that part of my life has nothing to do with anyone in this part of my life, and frankly if you two never met, that would be just fine with me. I don't want you knowing my business, Peyton."

"I see," I replied, doing my best to conceal my hurt.

"What do you want, Peyton?" She glanced at my bag. "What's that?"

"I—"

She cut me off. "If you need that money back, it's too late."

"I don't need anything. I just wanted to see you and Skye before . . . Well, I didn't know you'd be entertaining."

"Entertaining? Who the fuck are you? Martha Stewart?" She laughed. "We're dating."

I felt nauseous again.

"I just wanted to let you both know that I love you." I turned to Skye. "And I'll always try to do right by you."

"What the heck has gotten into you?" Toni asked, ruining what I'd hoped would be a touching moment. "Are you drunk?"

"I'm more sober than I've been in years. I'm gonna make things right."

"You better not be planning anything stupid," Toni said.

Did she know? Was I that transparent? She'd always been able to read me, even when we were kids.

"I don't want a Seth Walker," she added.

"Who's Seth Walker?" Skye asked.

Walker had been one of my army buddies. He'd gassed himself in his garage, running the engine of his Hyundai while his family slept in their beds. Toni was worried I was going to take my own life. The thought had crossed my mind more than once, but Skye always kept me here. I had to be there for her. Particularly now. I needed to be a better dad, especially as there was a potential replacement on the scene.

"Jeez, Toni, not in front of Skye. I'm not going to— Come on. I mean, I'm going to make things right for both of you, and I want you to know I love you."

I put my hand behind Skye's head and kissed her temple. It felt like a really awkward gesture because I was very aware of the gun concealed in the bag in my other hand. What had I been thinking bringing it here?

"I love you, kiddo."

"Love you, too, Dad," she replied, looking very puzzled.

I backed away from them.

"I love you both," I said. "And I might not be your now love, Toni, but I will always be your first love, and that will just have to do. I'm going to get you what you need and more. I'm going to be a good father and a good ex-husband."

Skye smiled, but Toni just watched me, as perplexed as she might have been if she'd seen a cat wearing sneakers or a dog riding a bicycle. I was an oddity to her, and the visit almost certainly hadn't been my best idea, but I wanted them to know why I was doing what I was about to do.

It was all for them. I still loved them and I wanted that to be clear. Everything I did was for love.

CHAPTER 21

So, I'd met my ex-wife's new squeeze and got her thinking I was suicidal, been beaten up and thrown out of a club I was casing to explore the possibility of murdering a man after an anonymous patron, who'd sprung me from jail, offered to pay me.

This all felt pretty normal to me, because my life had become a shit show of hard luck and random happenings.

You might be sitting there in your warm bath, toasty bed, on the train to your square job where you get to be a fully paid-up, productive member of society, and you might be wondering why someone might accept the word of a total stranger. An anonymous promise isn't worth the words used to make it, right? Not to me. At this point, the word of a stranger was the only hope I had.

I walked home from Toni's place, planning what I was going to do. Disused, almost forgotten regions of my brain flickered to life as I recalled my old methods of preparing for a military operation. Past me had been an obsessive, it was part and parcel of being an engineer, and whether our challenge was to build a bridge, secure a base, or repair a highway, I liked to rehearse everything over and over in my mind, until I'd pictured every possibility and prepared myself mentally for each outcome.

Failure here would involve being arrested. Success meant another man's death.

I wasn't a frontline soldier, but I'd been deployed in Afghanistan and knew plenty of guys who'd experienced the fire and brimstone of war. They killed men with families, fathers, grandfathers, and sons. And when they'd come back from the slaughter, some polished brass whose glory days were faded black-and-white memories would pin shining medals to their chests.

People die every single day. Tens of thousands of them all over the world. The removal of one nasty gangster should make no difference to the tally. At least that's what I told myself when I felt my queasy misgivings rise.

By the time I arrived home, I'd rehearsed Walter Glaze's death every which way. It wasn't a murder. It was a sanctioned killing, but instead of my authority deriving from the state, it came from my patron, and the application of my own judgment that this here was a bad man who'd served more than his fair share of time on earth.

I showered and changed into black jeans and a black T-shirt. I put on a black hoodie with a large front pocket, into which I shoved the pistol and twelve rounds. As an afterthought I also pocketed the pills Attica had given me. The military history module I'd taken during basic training had taught me even the most hardened soldiers need mind-altering substances to cope with the business of killing and its aftermath.

I pulled my old dress uniform from a suitcase under my bed and laid it on the frayed divan, a reminder of better times. If anything went wrong, I wanted people who came here to know I'd once been an honorable man.

I kept being unsettled by waves of sickness, so I went into the kitchen for a glass of water. After I'd finished it, I found a working pen and sat down at the small table with a piece of paper. It was a warning letter from the power company that it was going to cut me off for arrears, but the back was blank and clear. The uniform wouldn't be enough for Skye, so I started writing.

My dearest Skye,
When you were two, I'd take you swimming every Sunday morning when I wasn't on deployment. You'd stand at the side of the baby pool, your chubby

little arms stuffed inside your water wings, and you'd smile and giggle before jumping in. You were so brave, but every time your head went under the water, my heart stopped. Even though I knew I was there to catch you, to bring you up, I couldn't help but go to those dark places and imagine the pain of something bad happening. I'm sorry I haven't been there for you these past few years, I really am, but I'm here now and I'm doing right by you, because you are the light that brightens my world.

If you are reading this, things have gone wrong, and people will be saying terrible things about me. I want you to know that I was trying to give you a better life. I don't want you to face the struggles that have made my life a mess. You deserve better because you're a beautiful spirit, a wonderful soul. If we never see each other again, I want you to remember me at my best—a good man trying to provide for his daughter in a difficult world. Know that I love you and always will,

Peyton (Dad)

I left the note beside my uniform. Family and honor, testaments to the man I'd once been.

Maybe after today, I could become that man again.

CHAPTER 22

I took my time getting to Venice. There wasn't any rush. I rode six buses to get to Culver City, doubling back on myself, walking blocks in between each route so it would be harder to figure out where I'd come from or where I was going if anyone reviewed the transit cameras.

I was on the 260, my last bus, sitting near the back, trying not to think about what lay ahead, finding distraction in my surroundings. Most cities followed a familiar design. They had a heart, usually a financial district, a soul, theaters and culture, organs of retail, commerce and industry, brains of education, and suburban limbs where people lived. Los Angeles wasn't most cities. It was as though a great creator had tipped all the body parts onto the map and cloned some of them at random. There were a lot of suburban limbs growing through what should have been organs of commerce, the soul had been shrunk, cut up, and scattered throughout the huge sprawl, and the heart was a place few people went. Folk lived in their cars, using the city's veins to travel from one part to another, and that made for a sense of isolation among the millions who lived in the huge Frankenstein. I shared space with the handful of people on the bus, but I didn't know them or their lives, nor they mine. Today, that was a good thing.

High above the streets was the billboard life we aspired to: smiling faces promising happiness from a soda can; artful photos of GM wheat wraps hugging factory-fed, machine-slaughtered fried chicken; movies selling us the lie heroes always win. But down on the ground was life as lived, up close and for real. Jaundice-yellow signs in barred windows promising cash for gold, homeless folk foraging in trash cans, seemingly productive citizens doing their daily rinse and repeat—work, home, sleep—occasionally wondering why no matter how hard they tried, they could never reach the life the billboards promised.

Don't think on it, friend. The billboard life is there to tantalize, not to be realized. There isn't enough happiness to go around. It's as rare as gold. The folk living the billboard life know it. They sell us the dream of their life and we pay dearly for it, climbing over each other in the hope we'll be the ones to join them. Put two cars in your drive, make your mortgage payments, take that vacation, keep your head down and work hard, and . . . what's that?

Financial crash, road crash, medical crash.

Crashes of all kinds, unforeseen and unexpected.

Impacts.

Due to circumstances beyond our control, we're going to have to take the little ladder you were building toward the billboard life and snake you back down to the gutter where you belong.

See, when you've had bad luck, you know it can happen to anyone. You know just how much of it there is to go around. But folk at the top living the billboard life haven't had bad luck. That's why they're on the billboard. They think they made it there through hard work, that the people far below them, seen dimly through their privacy glass, are stuck in the gutters of the real world because they didn't work hard enough, dabbled in drink or drugs, or lack the ambition to climb to the shining world of the billboards. They never think about the good luck, or lack of bad luck, that put them in paradise. Why would they?

Do you ever think about what really put you where you are? It becomes much harder to justify the big house, the fast car, the full bank account and toned Pilates belly, if you realize it hasn't been earned. I work hard, they say. So does the nurse who inserted your father's catheter, the driver who takes your kids to school, the construction workers who laid your swimming pool. The billboarders don't realize success self-selects an entitled outlook on the world. I earned this, they think, without any sense that millions of smarter, harder-working people are stuck in the gutter, far, far below.

Every face I saw on the street was yet more justification for Walter Glaze's death. He was one of the billboarders, living high above the rest of us, but he'd risen on wings of evil. The poor folk on the bus, those drifting in the gutters of life, each and every single one of them had more right to Walter Glaze's wealth. I was going to take a stand for all the little guys and girls, and most importantly for the one I loved most: Skye.

By the time I got off the bus in Culver City, my churning stomach had calmed, the bile wasn't rising quite so much, and I was resolved.

I walked along Venice Boulevard to the corner of Motor Avenue and bought a green ski mask from the surplus store. I slipped it into my hoodie pocket, pressing it against the heavy revolver. I got a pair of blue latex gloves from a late-night pharmacy.

It was 9:45 p.m. when I left the store, and I walked the streets for a while, aimlessly wandering block after block, watching the slow-moving minutes tick by. Habit got the better of me, and the bright lights of a liquor store on Washington Place drew me like a tractor beam. I bought a bottle of Jack Daniel's from an emaciated clerk who didn't even turn her dead eyes toward me as she slipped it into a brown paper bag.

It was mission fuel, I told myself as I started drinking. By the time I reached Grand Canal, I was a third of the way to the thick glass bottom. My belly felt warm and my mind clear and calm, like the stillest Lake Michigan beach day. As I neared the nightclub, I put on the gloves, pulled the ski mask over my head, and jogged a little to reach the alleyway. I ran along the back of the building into the dark shadows near the staff entrance and wedged my way between two of the large dumpsters. It was a dank, grimy place that stank of urine and garbage, but the smells didn't offend me. I sat on the ground with my back against the alley wall, watching the staff entrance through the narrow gap, drinking.

Always drinking.

After a few minutes sitting in the shadows of waste, I realized I hadn't scoped the place out properly, that Walter Glaze might not even be in tonight, but by the time I hit the halfway mark, I was bottle happy and didn't care.

CHAPTER 23

After drinking myself into oblivion, I was visited by the ghost of my better self. He held my clammy hand and took me to the beach, and within the dream I cried with joy at the sight of past me racing a four-year-old Skye across the wet sand on her birthday.

Toni watched us from the picnic mat, all indulgent smiles and happy futures.

I let Skye beat me and chased her down, scooped her in my arms, and swung her around, her hair catching the California sunlight, her smile shining ever brighter. She was my guiding star.

She still is.

I dreamed of teaching her how to swim, of squeals and smiles as she jumped and disappeared beneath the surface only to emerge from the water laughing, me scooping her up in my arms, of saying, "I love you," of hearing her tiny little voice say, "I love you, too, Daddy," of her words swelling my heart to bursting.

That day on the beach, her birthday, best represents past me, or at least what I like to think of as the man I was before prison.

I carried Skye back to the picnic mat and set her down. I leaned over to kiss Toni, who was busy unboxing the food we'd bought. We sat on the beach, watching the ocean roll in, eating cold hot dogs and chips, drinking fresh OJ, and laughing at little Skye's jokes. We had a party planned for her friends the next day, but today was just for us.

Future me longed for this past to be present again. I wanted to call out to the man I'd once been and warn him what lay around the bend, but my dream had rendered me mute.

I've wondered why subconscious me took me back there as I lay in the alley behind Ultima on the night I went to kill Walter Glaze, and I think the dream was actually a wake. If I killed Walter Glaze I'd be murdering the man I'd once been. The good man, the moral man, the family man would die with Walter, and whatever ghost is at the controls of the machine we call self wanted me to see what I'd be losing. I think it was a cruel attempt to stop me, but it had the opposite effect.

In the warm moments with the sun on my face, my wife and child beside me, sharing laughter, I was reminded of my obligations as a father. This man didn't know self-pity. He didn't know failure. His was a life of love, smiles, and contentment, and there was no way he would ever let his little girl down. He would always do what was necessary.

So perhaps my subconscious wasn't replaying a happy scene from my past to taunt me. Perhaps it was reminding me of the man I had once been and hoping the memory would stir the strength of my past self to do the job at hand.

I wanted to stay in the past to inhabit the body of the man on the picnic mat, to do my life over, to avoid the mistake that had ruined everything, but even as the longing swelled within me, I felt the pull of the future. Something was dragging me back to the terrible reality of my life.

CHAPTER 24

"What the fuck?"

The words hit me like a trio of slaps. I was half out of my hidey-hole, on my back, my head and chest sticking into the alleyway from between the dumpsters.

"Who the fuck are you?"

I rolled onto my hands and knees.

Walter Glaze was by the staff entrance. He looked mad as he came toward me. Had I seen him coming out? Or had I slid into the alleyway, and he'd seen me? Judging by the warp and spin of the world, either was possible because I was stomach-pump drunk. Don't judge me harshly. Soldiers in long-gone wars were often intoxicated in order to be efficient ministers of death. Alcohol in the First and Second World Wars, amphetamines and hallucinogens from then on. I won't deny I was feeding my addiction, but some part of me was also numbing my conscience.

My eyes watered and burned, but I still tried to draw my piece as Walter Glaze walked over. One hand and two knees weren't enough to stabilize a man in my condition, and I toppled forward onto my face.

"Jeezus," Walter said, crouching over me.

"Don't," I mumbled as I felt his hand on the top of my head.

I resisted feebly as he pulled off my mask.

"You?" he remarked. "What the fuck are you doing here?" He pulled me by the arm. "Get the fuck up."

Alcohol and anger raised my temperature as he hauled me upright.

"Attica was in here tonight," he went on as I shuffled a little to find my feet. "Laughing at you. If she could see you now, she'd laugh some more."

I remembered the last time he'd humiliated me.

"I've got something for you, Walter," I slurred.

Was I really that drunk?

I managed to register his frown of confusion as I pushed him away and reached for my gun. I stumbled back, collided with one of the dumpsters, managed to free the Smith and Wesson from my pocket—

And promptly dropped it.

The gun clattered onto the concrete, bounced, and skidded between my feet beneath the dumpster that was holding me up.

I looked up to see Walter had also watched it disappear.

"Was that a fucking gun?" he asked. Sober or drunk, there was no mistaking his disbelief. "Did you just pull a fucking gun on me?"

Walter Glaze was a fit, strong man, and if I'd been sober, I might have been terrified, but I was too drunk to care when he came for me. I still don't know the polite response when you've failed to murder someone. Maybe there's a fancy Georgia finishing school that can tell me. Apologize? Laugh it off as a joke?

I didn't get a chance to do anything. He threw a right cross that hit me like a sniper's shot. My legs crumpled and I toppled over with such force, I cracked my head against the concrete.

Everything went disco crazy with flashing lights, and the world danced and whirled around me. I groaned and rolled onto my side as Walter started kicking me in the ribs and gut. I scrabbled around trying to get up, but he stamped on my hands, and despite being numb to the other blows, I felt his heels on my fingers and howled.

I lay in the alley next to the dumpster, surrounded by garbage water, sodden Kleenex, scraps of rotten food, and other unidentifiable matter, crying as I took the beating of a lifetime.

CHAPTER 25

For a while, part of me wished Walter had kept going. At the time, lying balled up, taking my punishment, wasted, the world was just a carnival of pain, humiliation, and confusion. I wasn't the man on the beach. I hadn't been for a long time. I had a dim idea Walter might kill me, and I think I cried out for him to stop, but he kept coming with his shiny six-hundred-buck shoes, and I couldn't do anything except take it. I thought of Skye, how her life might work out without me in it. Probably better.

Then to my surprise, the veteran gangster stopped. I heard him breathing heavily as I lay battered, gasping, crying.

"Show your face around here again, and I'll fucking kill you."

He spat at me and walked away.

I watched him through heavy tears, remembering all the beatings I'd taken in prison. I thought of Walter in the club tomorrow night, telling Attica how he'd put Peyton "Deadbeat" Collard down, and how with each and every arrogant step he was carving clear distance between my daughter and a decent future.

I needed to be my old self. I needed the strength of the man I'd once been. I needed to fight for Skye. For her future.

The thought of my daughter put the fire in me, and every humiliation I'd ever suffered grew it, fanning the flames until it burned everywhere. I was mad. Hellfire mad, and there was only one way to put it out.

I had to kill the devil that set me aflame.

I reached under the dumpster and wrapped my fingers around cold steel. I wiped the tears from my eyes and gasped as a stabbing pain went from my ribs to my spine, and from there right into my jaw. Like a broken quarterback who knows he's got to make the play, I fought through the agony and used the dumpster to support me as I stood.

In his eyes I think I was so pathetic that Walter didn't even look back as he left the alley. But I wasn't pathetic. I would be the hero my daughter needed, and even though each step almost made me black out with effort and pain, I followed him.

I stuffed the gun into my waistband and reached into my pocket for the baggie of Sidewinders Attica had given me. Like the soldiers of old, I needed courage wherever I could find it. A grim task lay ahead. My shaking fingers pulled a couple of the fat yellow tablets out and I swallowed them. The alley spat me into the street, and I staggered across the sidewalk as the lights of a car flashed farther along Grand Canal. The road was graveyard quiet and the only other person around was Walter, who was walking toward the car.

I shuffled along the street now, faster, fighting the black edges that threatened to overwhelm my world. I felt electricity in my veins and had no idea whether it was the adrenaline of the hunt or the first effects of the Sidewinders. They couldn't work that fast, could they?

I put the baggie back into my pocket and pulled the pistol from my trousers. Hard grip. I wasn't going to drop it this time.

Walter opened the driver's door of his car. It looked like a BMW SUV, but everything was hazy. The logo seemed to be dancing across the hood as I got close. He must have sensed, because he turned, gave a disappointed look, and shook his head. "You should have stayed down."

He moved toward me, but I raised the revolver. "Don't."

The magic of the gun froze him instantly. I looked around the street and saw the lights of cars crossing the intersection to our south. Some of the surrounding apartment windows still shone with the glow of

TV sets. Night owls or early risers. In truth, I had no idea what time it was.

A life.

A lifetime.

I was going to take a life.

To make a better one.

But I couldn't just shoot the man here, could I? Too risky. Too many witnesses, and I didn't have my vigilante hood on. If I had learned anything from Batman, it was that all the best avenging angels cover their faces.

A plan congealed in my intoxicated mind, and I interpreted its greasy entrails. I could see words forming out of ethereal guts floating in front of me.

The pills were almost certainly kicking in.

"Get in," I said.

The words were big and heavy, and I had to guppy my mouth, stretching my jaw like a hippo to get them out.

He could gamble I'd be too slow, that I'd drop the gun, that he could overpower me, but it turned out Walter Glaze wasn't a gambler. He backed toward the door and eased into his seat. I kept the gun on him as I walked around the vehicle and climbed in beside him.

The leather seat felt like candy floss, and the interior smelled of flowers after a spring shower. My seat seemed to curl around me, hugging me, whispering everything would be all right.

I was high and getting even higher, but unlike the last time when I'd been sober, these pills were rising off a cloud of liquor. I was up with the kites and if I continued climbing would soon be in space.

"If you do anything—" Walter began, but I cut him off with a wave of the gun.

"Shut up and drive."

"Excuse me?"

"Stutter? Drive." I meant to ask did I stutter like in that movie I saw one time, but it came out clipped. Reality was cut wrong. Thoughts were quick and small, the world big and slow, taking on colors and shapes that belonged in a cartoon.

He got my meaning, though, and started the engine. "Where?"

A word came to me. It used to mean something. It used to make me feel good.

"Home," I said. "We go to your home."

CHAPTER 26

The Sidewinders were a beautiful way to fly. Weightless in a state without worry or meaning. Timeless. Streetlights, cars, buses, storefronts became long rainbows, and soon the city was lost to bands of light.

"What the fuck do you want?" Walter asked. "Who the fuck are you?"

I focused on him. Patterns danced across his face, reflected bands of light, maybe? Or shifting emotions made visible to me by the magic pills. I saw anger, that's for sure.

I kept the gun pointed at him.

"Never mind me," I replied. My voice was slow, too, and slurring. "Just drive."

"I have money," Walter said.

"You think you can buy me? I'm a child of light and I ain't for sale," I told him, but I look back now and see it was indignant booze and drugs talking. I was in that car because I'd sold my soul. I was no child of light.

He was on edge and watched the gun nervously.

Some of you might be wondering how I planned to get away with murder with my DNA in the car. Raised on *CSI*, you might believe in the all-knowing cop, but let me clue you in on something. For a while, I shared a cell with a man who'd murdered his entire family and driven from New York to Chicago covered in their blood. He'd disappeared, raised two new kids with his new wife, and was caught only when he beat a man to death in a bar fight and confessed to his old crimes, figuring he might as well go down for five murders as for one. Eighteen years he lived free and clear without Forensics coming to knock on his door. Gloves and clothes would be disposed of. DNA wouldn't matter much unless I tore my gloves or I bled on the seats, and I had no intention of doing either.

". . . family . . ."

The word invaded my thinking.

"I can't let you into my house," he said. "I have a family."

I couldn't say he sounded afraid. More resigned, but it was hard to be sure through the static of the pills.

"Did you hear me?" he asked.

A family?

Killing Walter was all right. I would make bank for my daughter, stop a gangster from gangstering, and get him back for the wrongs he'd perpetrated against me. But shooting a family was bad karma no amount of booze or drugs or holy contrition could undo. I was an opportunist, not an assassin. And certainly not a spree killer. Who did this guy think he was, making that kind of accusation?

"You don't know me, man," I found myself saying. "You think I'm a loser, but I'm not. I was like you. Not a thug, but a stand-up guy. I had money and a family."

Was I crying? Maybe. Slurring? Definitely.

"I want to help you," Walter replied. "I know people who can."

The gunshot came out of nowhere. Even the fog of booze and drugs didn't blunt it.

The sound startled me and set my heart pounding, and the car veered right and crashed into something solid.

I hadn't meant to shoot him, I swear. Not now. Not in the car at least. Certainly not when he'd been offering me kindness.

The gun had come alive and made the decision for me.

Looking back with a clear head, I realize I must have pulled the trigger by accident, but at the time, the smoking beast seemed to smile at me as my dazed eyes peered down at it.

Fuck.

We were stationary, buried in some crumpled parked cars.

Walter growled and turned on me. I had shot him in the head, but the bullet had grazed his ear and only made him mad. He punched me in the face and tried to grab the living, spitting gun.

Crack.

Crack.

Crack.

I saw the words burst into life and color and linger in the air after each bullet.

Walter stopped fighting and fell back against the driver's door, bloody craters on the side of his head.

I nudged his face with the hot muzzle of the gun, but his eyes were unfocused and still. I thought they seemed sad, as though his last memory was of all his cruelties. I shared his sadness. Speaking plainly, I had planned to kill him, but not like this.

This wasn't one of the scenarios I'd visualized, but some part of me managed to cut through the transcendent high. I reached into his jacket pocket for his wallet and removed his watch. A staged carjacking and robbery would work.

I got out of the car and saw we were in a deserted residential neighborhood. His SUV—it was a BMW—was smoking as it nestled in the wreckage of a couple of other cars.

I had no idea where he'd brought me, but I could see a well-lit, busy road in the distance, so I stumbled in the other direction toward darkness.

CHAPTER 27

Nothing about that night feels real. Sometimes when I close my eyes, I can still see Walter Glaze's featureless face watching me as we drive through the city. When I sleep, I meet him again, his eyes all sad and glassy after I'd shot him, head all cratered and bloody, but as time goes on the whole experience seems more and more like a nightmare. The newspaper and police reports tell me his death was real, but people make mistakes, right? If it wasn't for the fact that part of him is always with me, a specter of guilt attached like a cancer on my conscience, I might have been able to convince myself it was all a bad trip.

I can't bear to think about the moment the gun went off and changed so many lives. I wish it had been a nightmare, that I'd woken on my floor the next day, reeking of booze, having fantasized the whole thing after a heavy night on the depth charges and ketamine with Jim. But it was real. Walter Glaze is dead, and I guess you could say I killed him. Although I'd argue against that being the whole truth. Was it me or the bump in the road that jolted the trigger? Was it me or the drugs? The cruel prisoners who'd abused me when I was inside and given me such issues with bullies? Was it me or my patron? The person who planted the seed of murder in my mind. Was it me or Walter? The person who humiliated me and beat me up. If I'd shot him while he was kicking me, no court would have convicted me of anything other than self-defense, but time played a cruel trick, so a righteous killing looked like murder.

As you can see, I'm confused and still have problems accepting all the guilt for Walter's death.

But that night I wasn't even thinking about responsibility. I staggered away from the wreck, stumbling along dark streets, glad of the black clothes I'd chosen, which hid his blood, out of my head on whatever was in Attica's pills. I started at every sound and tried to focus on the world around me in case a cop car materialized. It was hard because I was, in the parlance of wasters everywhere, fully fueled. Months of alcohol abuse, drugs, broken sleep, bad diet, the bottle of Jack Daniel's, and Attica's Sidewinders all bore down on me like the tip of a stiletto worn by an elephant, applying unbelievable pressure, warping reality, setting my heart jack thumping and my brain cartwheeling.

At some point, those cartwheels took me into prison, and I pictured my life there, serving a new stretch for Walter's death. I saw my own murder at the hands of another inmate, a shaven-headed tattooed killer paid by Walter's shady associates to be an angel of retribution. I think I cried and laughed at blurred, kaleidoscope images of what had just happened. Walter spoke to me from beyond the grave, his ghost accusing me of killing the wrong man.

The gun was pointed the wrong way, his specter said.

I was still carrying it and glanced down to find myself tempted to join the dead. Even through the worst trip of a lifetime, I sensed danger. It would have been easy to turn the gun on myself, but I'd be killing part of Skye, too, and I couldn't do that.

I muttered, "You're a good man, a good man," over and over, like a mantra, and wiped the revolver clean of prints. I found a storm drain and tossed the weapon into the black mouth.

I lost track of time, but must have walked for hours, because when I finally regained some proper sense of who and where I was, the sun was rising, and I was less than a mile from home. Instinct had guided me to the closest thing I had to safety.

Paranoia was kicking in, though, and I imagined armed cops waiting for me inside the house, so I inched the door open so slowly it felt as though I might have been standing on the porch for an hour. When I finally looked inside, I saw the place was empty. A mess, but empty.

I went in and reached straight for a bottle of Jim Beam I kept for emergencies. I didn't even bother with a glass. I might have ditched the gun, but Walter was still talking to me, and I was eager to silence him. I swigged from the bottle until I felt the warmth hit my belly, and only when I knew I'd refueled and pushed the needle to max did I come up for air.

Walter was still talking to me, but now he was slurring his words, which didn't seem so bad, but still wasn't as good as silence. I took another drink and another and another. I needed to kill the dead man within.

CHAPTER 28

Police!"

Twin battle drums sounded. The thumping of a heavy fist on my front door, and the thunder of my heart trying to hammer its way out of my chest. Both woke me from oblivion and sent me into an adrenaline-charged state of panic.

I had passed out on my living room floor in the same black clothes I'd worn to kill Walter Glaze. Some assassin. Blood spatter? Hair? Gunpowder residue? I wasn't worried about them picking up samples from the car, but if they caught me like this, well, I'd watched enough TV to know I was a walking crime scene.

"Police." The voice was deep, almost a growl. "Open up!"

I got to my feet, and the sudden movement triggered a tide that crashed through my head in angry waves. I staggered with the weight of a hangover and the burden of a narcotic comedown. Maybe there was a sprinkling of guilt too.

Get out, I thought.

Get out.

Get out.

I stumbled to my bedroom and looked at my dress uniform laid out like a melodramatic costume, the ghost of an honorable life haunting me with the man I'd once been. I could never come back to this place. I took off my hoodie and tossed it into the corner. At least my T-shirt was clean.

I don't think my mind was functioning properly that afternoon, which might explain my odd choice. It might also cast some light on why it took me a moment to realize what the cold metal things were in my pocket. I'd ditched the gun but still had some bullets.

I ran to the bathroom and inexplicably dropped them into the toilet and flushed.

"Police! Open up or we're coming in."

My heart sank when I saw the bowl rapids calm and the shining bullets gathered like pebbles at the bottom of a pool. My mind wasn't in top gear, but there was nothing I could do now. I had to go.

I ran into the bedroom and went to the window. The hammering on the front door stopped, and I knew it would be a moment or two until the battering ram, so I turned the latch as quickly and quietly as I could.

I hauled myself onto the sill and slid out, working myself into position to drop onto the overgrown backyard.

"Freeze!"

I felt the barrel of a gun pressed into the small of my back.

This was it.

My life was over.

If you've ever rock climbed, or skydived, been in combat, or taken a bend too fast on a really powerful motorbike, you'll know that split second of regret when you wish you could undo the choices that put you in danger. In that moment I thought about Skye and how much I would miss her if I survived another incarceration.

"Jesus! You're a fucking blast," Jim said, and I turned to see my drinking buddy pushing his finger into my back. "Cops don't knock, man."

"Jim, you motherfucker," I responded. "You almost gave me a fucking heart attack."

"Guilty conscience?" he asked. "Innocent man has nothing to fear. Certainly can't be found climbing out of windows."

I glossed over the question, but as I dropped from the sill, I saw more than a glint of suspicion in his eyes. Did he know?

"What are you doing here?" I asked, brushing dirt off my clothes.

"Rick was worried about his best customer. I said I'd check you hadn't died. Looks like we weren't that lucky." Did Jim miss me? Was he short a drinking buddy? He'd never admit it.

"What time is it?"

"Five thirty," Jim replied, lighting up a cigarette.

I'd slept most of the day.

"Give me an hour," I said.

I realized I could really do with a drink to take the edge off the hangover and to blur the memories of the previous night, which were starting to appear in my mind. I didn't want another haunting by Walter Glaze.

"I'll have a couple lined up," Jim said, and I followed him to the front of the house.

He'd already had more than a couple. He was swaying and his breath was ninety proof. He hadn't had enough to stop him driving, though, and I watched him amble over to the Lincoln, climb in, and give a nonchalant wave as he pulled away.

I was on my way back inside when I saw the little flag was up on my mailbox. I walked over to the metal tube decorated with the faded stars and stripes, opened the flap, and reached inside to find a package about the size and weight of a house brick. The handwriting on the front was the same as the package that had contained the URL and thousand bucks.

My heart jacked up again, this time joined by nervous stomach acid that set me fizzing. I looked around to make sure I wasn't being watched and double-timed it to the house.

I fumbled with my keys but finally got the door open. I was breathing rough and heavy when I shut it behind me. I ran to the window and closed the tattered old drapes, and when I was sure no one could see in, I tore open the package.

The blue hundreds were instantly recognizable, and as I tore away the envelope, I realized I was holding more cash than I'd ever seen in my life.

CHAPTER 29

A down payment on a house.
A chance at a new life.

A college fund for a wonderful girl with big dreams of med school.

Years of financial security.

One hundred thousand dollars.

There will be folks reading this thinking one hundred grand isn't enough to put someone in the ground, to rob a body of life.

If you had the means and the opportunity like I did, what would your number be?

How much would it take for you to kill someone?

There are people who'll do it for fifty bucks. Hell, they'll bury you for free if you give them the wrong look.

What dreams would you trade for the life of a bad man? Because that's what money is. That's the con the millionaires and billionaires have played. Us poor folk think money is for essentials, to pay bills, buy gas, put a roof over our heads, but it's so much more. Dollar bills are dream tokens. You wanna be an astronaut? You can if your money's good. Want to live a longer life? Money can buy you more years. A life of luxury for you and your kin, doing only the things you love, eating and drinking only your favorites? Money is the key.

A hundred grand was enough to be sure Skye was safe whatever life threw at her. It was enough for me to finally get my life back on track.

Get a job. Toni was gone, in the arms of another man, but that didn't stop me being a good father. I could be there for Skye.

I sat on my dirty old couch, holding my new fortune and torn remains of the envelope, which was otherwise empty. As the dollar rush died away, questions swept in. I don't know why they hadn't mattered to me before. Maybe part of me hadn't believed something this good would really happen to a deadbeat like me.

Who was this money from? Whoever it was knew where I lived.

Why had he or she wanted Walter dead?

Was it one of Walter's rivals? Another crime boss? Why had this anonymous patron chosen me? Blood money usually came with trouble. Was I now in danger? And how did they know Walter was dead? Were they watching me?

The irony wasn't lost on me. These were questions a cop might ask. In a way, I think my investigation of Walter Glaze's death began on that couch, while I was holding the money I'd been paid to kill him.

I picked up my remote, and it took a moment for my ancient TV to glow to life. I trawled the local news stations for anything on Walter's death, and as I surfed the networks, I pictured an observant neighbor or some vigilant cop who might have evidence on me.

My heart skipped when I saw a file photo of Walter on KTLA. The anchor described the shooting in somber tones. It was, she told this edge-of-the-seat viewer, an apparent carjacking gone badly wrong. Another tick on the random crime chart to add to the background level of worry most Los Angelenos have about falling victim to a wrong-place, wrong-time predator.

I switched off the TV when they started talking about the victim's family and the fact that he'd died a block from home. I didn't want to think about Walter's grieving wife and kids. News was meant to be entertainment. Background to fill time between other shows, or work, or because you wanted a reminder your life wasn't all that bad. It wasn't supposed to be up close and personal. I wasn't meant to actually share the suffering of the victims, to imagine them grieving. They were supposed to be "oh, that's sad" anonymous figures of pity. It was intrusive, irresponsible journalism that wouldn't have made it on air twenty years ago. Thoughtless.

But they'd put the picture in my mind now, and I couldn't shake it. Little mini-Walters crying, hugging up to his wife. Or maybe husband? I had no idea. I didn't really know the man I'd been asked to kill. Just the bad things he'd done, and that was enough justification to feel good about the money in my hand.

Hold on to the evil you've taken from the world, I told myself. *Hold on to the fact no one else will suffer because of him. And hold on to the money. A hundred grand will do a lot of good for your family. Never mind Walter's. You did this for Skye.*

I saw my reflection in the dark TV screen. I couldn't see my eyes properly, just vague shadows, but I knew they were bloodshot and troubled. I could feel the blood thumping through them, making them almost bulge from my head. And no matter what I told myself, a sense of wrongdoing nagged at my soul, and I had no doubt it would show in my eyes.

I have a family, Walter's ghost said.

He was there at my shoulder, reflected on the TV screen, but when I turned, of course, I saw nothing. A figment, haunting my mind, tugging on my conscience like vermin picking at the wiring.

"I'm glad you're dead," I said out loud, but my words didn't sound convincing, not even to me.

You've killed before, and it took everything you loved and almost destroyed you. What price will you pay for all this? Walter's ghost wondered as I looked at my new fortune.

Walter Glaze never felt guilt. He swaggered through life with an easy conscience, untroubled by his evil.

Just like you, Walter's ghost said. *You're a murderer now.*

I didn't like my new companion. He was making me feel bad, confused. I needed to get away from him. I reached for my keys and wallet, then remembered a flash from last night.

Walter's watch and wallet.

They were in my front pocket. I took them out and put them on the table. Perfectly ordinary objects to the unknowing, but they seemed to darken the room, as though invoking his vengeful spirit.

I couldn't bear to look at them, so I stuffed them under one of the couch cushions. I counted out twelve thousand bucks, put the rest of the money back into the remains of the envelope, and shoved it under the cushion with Walter's relics.

I fished the bullets out of the toilet bowl, wrapped them in a garbage bag with the clothes I'd worn the previous night, took a military-grade shower, got dressed, grabbed the garbage bag, my keys, and the twelve grand, and left the house.

CHAPTER 30

I put the bag into a dumpster behind a convenience store five blocks away and kept walking. Walter didn't bother me for a while. Maybe it was the evening heat? Or the vehicles rumbling by as I shuffled along to Toni's place. The tires on asphalt, roaring engines, and rattling axles left little space for ghosts, but the noise managed to set off a thunderous headache.

It took me a little under an hour to reach Toni's, by which time the sun was a low red crescent just peeking above the horizon between the apartment buildings. I was sweating and tired, wrecked by the booze and drugs of the previous twenty-four hours, maybe straining under the weight of guilt too.

When I knocked, I heard muffled words spoken in irritation. Toni opened the kitchen door and looked at me like a hair in her soup.

"Peyton, you can't just show up here."

"Hey, Peyton," Jack said, emerging from within.

"You look like shit," Toni went on. "Skye isn't even here. She's at Laura's on a sleepover. Jack and I are having a date night."

I felt queasy.

"We're celebrating the good news."

I was clueless.

"I left you a message, Peyton," she said.

I pulled out my phone, and sure enough there was a missed call. Three in fact.

"Skye's results came back," Toni explained. "It's not diabetes." She beamed happy. "It's some bacterial kidney infection. The doc's given her the right antibiotics. She's going to be okay."

"What the fuck!" I blurted out.

One of the reasons I'd turned murderer was to provide my kid with security. Money for her long-term health. Now she just needed a few days on antibiotics. It wasn't my only rationale, but it had been a big one and it had just been knocked away, leaving me off-balance. I took a deep breath and tried to hide my confusion.

"You're supposed to be happy, Peyton," Toni said. "Jeez."

"I am happy," I assured her. "It's just a shock is all. I'm so relieved."

I really was glad Skye was going to be fine, but my words came out half-hearted.

He was still bad, though, I told myself. *All the other good reasons to kill him stand.*

"I'm happy," I said with more conviction. "I'm so happy for her, but I didn't come here to see Skye. I came to see you."

I reached into my pocket and pulled out a hundred and twenty C-notes. "Twelve grand. Everything I owe you."

Toni's eyes widened as she looked down at the money.

"Those look crisp. You rob a bank, dude?" Jack scoffed.

I wanted to grab the guy and throw him out. I wanted Toni and me to have a date night. I wanted to be the one to take off her dress, to wake up with her in the morning. I wanted her to love me again.

"It's thirteen thousand, Peyton," she said. "You missed the last two months."

I closed my eyes, sighed, and shook my head. Such a deadbeat.

"Of course. I forgot. I'll get it to you," I told her.

"Where did you get this from?" she asked.

"Back pay," I lied. "I was due some money from the army that got held up when I was inside."

Keep it vague, I told myself. *It sounds more plausible that way.*

"I thought you'd prefer cash."

Her eyes were full of questions, but she just kept shifting them between me and the money and didn't say anything. Desperate people do desperate things, accept desperate lies.

"Things are gonna be different now," I told her. "I'm gonna help you look after Skye properly. Put her through college."

Jack yawned like a lazy lion and put his arm around Toni's shoulder.

"That's great, man," he said, flashing a smile. "That's really great."

"Thanks, Peyton." Toni pressed her hand against my arm. It was a tenderness I hadn't felt from her for a very long time. "I appreciate it. I know Skye will too."

"We should open a couple of beers," Jack said. "To celebrate."

For a moment I thought he was talking to me, but his eyes were on Toni, and they both looked at me awkwardly.

"Right. Of course." I backed away. "Date night."

I turned and headed for the broken gate, jealous of the celebration that lay ahead. My blood money would ensure Jack Harper had a great evening.

CHAPTER 31

I didn't go to Rick's that night. In fact, I took a long way home so I wouldn't go anywhere near the place.

Be a better man, Walter's ghost told me as I trudged the poor streets of Lynwood. *Don't let me lie down in vain. Make a change. Be a better man.*

High on drugs, low in a hangover, Walter's ghost had seemed real to me, but now, passing the twenty-four-hour Laundromat, where a skinny woman in torn shorts, broken sandals, and a Nirvana T-shirt watched one of the spinning drums, it seemed as though I was listening to my conscience. A better self that might steer me to higher ground.

I'd paid Toni almost everything I owed her and had enough money stashed in my couch to start a college fund, maybe even hire a halfway decent lawyer to get me off the charges I was facing for trashing the sheriff's car. I couldn't risk ruining the opportunity for a fresh start by spending the money on booze.

I turned off the main drag, down Carlin Avenue, where decent folk lived behind barred windows. Even though it was only a few blocks away, this wasn't like my neighborhood. The locals hadn't woken to the American nightmare, and I could sense striving all around me. They believed "it" was possible, that if they worked hard and kept their heads down, they could achieve the object of their desires, their "it." The billboard life.

I wanted to be like them. I wanted a full jasmine bush in my yard giving off sweetness like the one I was passing now. As I headed south, the dwindling traffic died a little more. The city had entered that evening calm when sounds other than the growl of engines and rumble of millions could be heard, and scents rose above the bed of exhaust fumes to remind a body what this place must have been like before the city took over. There were birds singing and somewhere in the distance a dog barking and children playing.

They sound like my kids, Walter's ghost said.

Had he mentioned kids? Family, yes. But kids? Would I have killed a man with children? Even now, a day later, everything was a blur of happenings. Attica's pills had done me a favor. I could conjure up only flashes of events, and maybe soon the whole episode would be wiped from my mind. A clean slate to go with my new start. Maybe a couple more pills would jettison the last memories completely, and if I didn't know I'd killed Walter Glaze, who would?

The person who hired you, Walter's ghost said.

I didn't like this specter.

He was right, though. My patron would always know what I'd done. Someone would always see my shame, and I had no idea who it was. That made me kind of uneasy, and looking back, it should have bothered me more. I should have made it my business then and there to find the person behind the killing. The one who was really responsible.

I made it home and was very good. Acting out a scene from a movie I'd watched, I poured every drop of alcohol down the drain. It was tempting to take a few swigs from some of my favorites, but I resisted the lure even though I knew it would ease my pounding headache.

When I finished, I showered, packed away my old uniform, trying hard not to think about the oath of protection I'd made to earn it, and lay on my bed with the back window open. I could see the massive concrete pillars of the highway looming out of sight and heard the light traffic rumbling overhead.

The gentle bed of sound lulled me to sleep, and I dreamed of Walter Glaze. His ghost took me through my life and told me about each wrong

I'd ever committed, as though he was recounting a fairy tale. He didn't judge me, not as far as I could tell, but he was conveying a moral. At least that's what I thought he was doing.

I woke more rested than I had in years. My headache had gone, and apart from a grainy feeling behind my eyes and a dry mouth, I had none of the usual hangover symptoms that had greeted me each morning since my release from prison.

I'd made it through a sober day and genuinely saw this as the beginning of my recovery in every sense of the word. Walter's sacrifice would not be in vain.

The first thing I did was roll out of bed and check the money was still stashed in my couch. I found it next to Walter's watch and wallet, relics I forced myself to look at. I stood in my trashy living room and held them.

I'm going to make this worth something, I thought. *I'm going to do right by a dead man.*

His ghost had no reply, so I assumed it was okay with my vow. I put the relics back with the money I'd had from my patron and made sure the cushion was tightly over the treasure.

People who say money can't buy happiness have probably never lived a day with an empty belly. Food goes a long way to putting a smile on a face. Heat, too, when it's cold, and cool air when it's hot. Medicine for a child, a comfy chair for the old, these simple things can make a difference to folk, and only those who haven't known want take them for granted. I knew there was happiness in that money, but I hadn't found it yet and was troubled by heavy pangs if I thought about Walter's face in his moment of death.

You took so many moments from me, his ghost said. *You took them from my kids, my wife.*

There. See. It doesn't pay to dwell. I had to focus on the good things to stop the ghost coming back.

There was a clean room company that hired ex-cons as part of a second-chance program. It was based in Montecito, a good hour or two from my place, depending on the traffic. The work was dangerous, all hazmat suits and chemicals, but the pay was good—five hundred per day. The kind of green that could kick-start a new life. I'd need a new car to get up there and interview, and I knew exactly which one I wanted.

There's an auto dealer on Alondra Boulevard that specializes in cars with character. They had a gunmetal-gray '06 Range Rover Vogue front and center in their lot, and I'd eyed it every time I'd driven past the place. It was on at $8,999, but I got it for a clean eight after knocking the slick salesman down. The thick leather seats were weathered and cracked, but no less comfortable than the day it had rolled off the production line. There were 117,373 miles on the clock, but the BMW-built engine purred like new. These things could run for three hundred thou easy. And the stereo system sounded like my own private nightclub. Who needed Ultima?

I did, Walter's ghost chimed in, but I wasn't going to let him spoil this moment.

I took the car out to Montecito, and it handled the mountain roads like a dream. I passed the Hi-Finish, the clean room business, and took a picture of the number on the Now Hiring sign.

By the time I headed back to the city, I had a huge smile on my face. Maybe it was euphoria? Or perhaps it was pride? Whatever the reason, I thought it would be a good idea to go to Rick's. Not to have a drink. I was too smart for that. I just wanted to show Jim the Range Rover. I knew how much he loved cars, and he'd appreciate such a finely crafted machine.

You'll drink, Walter's ghost told me. *You'll drink and I'll have died for nothing, because you'll drink it all away.*

I won't, I told the cynical spirit.

I would show the ghost of the evil dead man just how much self-control I really had. I would show Jim the car and then go home.

I wouldn't have a drink.

Not even one.

CHAPTER 32

I drove into the parking lot and pulled up next to Jim's Lincoln, and for the first time in a long while I felt proud getting out of my car. I might seem like a strutting peacock for being so vain, but the Range Rover made me feel like a person, not an apology for one. I crossed the lot and entered the bar through the back door.

I passed the restrooms, which always stank of the misery of excess, and walked into the saloon. It was busier than usual, with a selection of regulars plus six guys I didn't recognize who were sitting at a table beside an old, empty cigarette machine. They looked mean, in heavy metal T-shirts emblazoned with the names of old bands engulfed in hellfire and surrounded by demons. The guys watched me as I walked to the bar and slid onto the stool next to Jim.

"Fuck happened to you last night?" he asked.

He was slurring badly, and his eyes were thickly glazed.

"Sorry, man. I had to deal with a crisis over at Toni's."

"Women!" He raised his beer glass, which was three-quarters empty. "Where's your drink?"

"I'm okay right now, man," I replied. "I just came to show you my new ride."

"New ride? New ride needs a celebratory drink. A christening." He leaned across the bar. "Rick, this man got a new ride. We need a couple of chargers to celebrate."

Rick nodded and set to work.

"I'm okay, really," I said. "I just wanted you to see it."

Wiser folk than me say misery loves company, and it certainly felt that way when Jim said, "You ain't going square on me, Peyton?" His eyes went distant for a moment but suddenly sharpened on me. "I hate squares."

If you've ever been around addiction, you'll know the addict wants someone to share their decline. The drunk probably won't buy you drinks but will put a friendly arm around your shoulder while you pay for your own. The crack smoker won't pass the pipe but wants you out there hustling for your own rocks. And if you try to leave the life, haul yourself out of the decline, they don't like it. Not because they care about you or might miss you, but because if you change, you'll hold up a big mirror and force them to look their reflections in the eye and ask what's keeping them down. What is it that prevents them from climbing out of the hole just like you?

"Really, Jim, I'm okay," I tried.

"You don't refuse a friend who's bought you a drink. Not if you want them to stay friendly."

I nodded, reluctantly picked up the shot Rick deposited in front of me, and dropped it into the beer glass next to it. Rick was too smart to ever judge his customers or give any indication of disapproval, but I could have sworn I saw pity in his eyes.

Jim watched me with a fierce glare as I picked up the beer glass and necked it. I'd drunk hundreds of the things, but even as the cool liquid spilled down my throat, I realized this one felt different. It was the end of a fledgling way of life.

I told you, Walter's ghost whispered in my mind. *You killed me for nothing, Deadbeat.*

After a day of living clean, I suddenly felt dirty. And people who feel bad about themselves are more likely to seek comfort in drugs and alcohol.

Which is what I did.

I don't remember much after my fourth drink.

There's me and Jim staggering into the parking lot and him having a good poke around the Range Rover before declaring it a "fine automobile," but not a great one like his Lincoln.

I still don't know whether I told Jim about Walter Glaze or bragged about my new wealth, but my only other memory of that night is loudly proclaiming drinks were on me, and buying a round for everyone in the bar, and smiling as a few folks toasted my health. The six tattooed heavy metal demons didn't join the toast, which should have been a warning, I suppose.

CHAPTER 33

The universe was ending. At least that's what it sounded like as I came around from oblivion. There was an epic bang, and, disoriented, I realized I'd somehow made it home and had crashed on my own bed.

Sleep pulled my eyes shut, but more banging and crashing dragged me to my feet, and I stumbled out of the room still high and very drunk. I made it into my living room as the frame around the front door splintered, sending chips everywhere as the lock came away. The door flew open and six men wearing Donald Duck masks stormed my home.

I don't know why they'd bothered with cartoon faces, because their T-shirts gave them away as the heavy metal demons from the bar.

They rushed me before I could say anything. Two of them grabbed my arms and forced me onto my back. A third guy came flying in with a heavy fist and landed a punch in the gut that knocked the wind from my lungs. I groaned as the pain finally cut through the booze.

"Where's the money?" the fourth guy asked, reaching into his pocket. He had the deep, rasping voice of a man who'd smoked a truckload of cigarettes.

The last two men stood either side of the front door, watching the street. They kept glancing back at me with the air of people who were expecting something bad.

I told you, Walter's ghost said. *You blabbed. You got drunk and opened your big fat mouth, and now you're going to make sure I died for nothing.*

Had I been that stupid? Had I bragged about the eighty grand still concealed in my couch? I couldn't remember. It was very possible I'd told Jim within earshot of these monsters. Why had I gone to the bar?

Because you're a deadbeat, Walter's ghost replied.

The fourth guy, Rasper, produced something black and oblong, and when he stuck it against my neck and delivered fifty thousand volts into my spine, I realized it was a stun gun. I don't know if you've ever taken a Taser or a stun like that, but if you haven't, consider yourself lucky. Pain hit me like a lightning bolt and sobered me up in an instant. I lay on the floor, convulsing like a dying fish, gasping, writhing as the charge ran through me from teeth to testicles, down to my toes.

Rasper took the stunner away from my neck, but the white light and searing agony took more than a moment to fade.

"Where's the money?" he asked.

Four Donald Ducks crowded my vision, two holding me down and the other two threatening violence. It could have been a bad trip had it not been for the very real pain.

"Pocket," I replied.

There was a chance they didn't know about my big payday and were just here for my walking-around money.

The third guy, Thumper, reached into my right front pocket and fished out the remaining cash I'd taken to the bar—about three hundred bucks.

Rasper shocked me again, and this time I could have sworn I saw my mom and dad waving me on, beckoning me to join them in the hereafter.

But they disappeared as the agony waned.

"Don't fuck with us, Collard," Rasper said. "You know what we're here for."

Pain is one of the most difficult things to describe. When a doctor asks, "How much does it hurt?" what do you say? Your eight might be someone else's one. They might have a genetic desensitization to pain that makes it difficult to feel anything but center-of-the-sun searing agony.

Even in literature it's hard to convey degrees of suffering, but when

I tell you I saw my dead folks calling me, I hope you get the sense this wasn't a run-of-the-mill experience. Just imagine someone scraping a blunt knife down your exposed spine and scorching every cell in your body.

I couldn't face another, and even though my mind filled with memories of Skye and I knew I'd be betraying her future as well as my own, I answered Rasper.

"It's in the couch."

Rasper patted my cheek before backing away to search under the cushions. He found the torn envelope and Walter's wallet and watch.

He examined everything.

"Nice," he said before pocketing them. "Let's go," he said to his crew, and I groaned as the duck duo released me. All five henchducks followed Rasper into the street.

I fought back tears until I was sure they'd gone. When I heard their car pull away, the flood came and I lay on the floor, sobbing like a baby. I'd killed a man to improve my daughter's life, and now I had nothing to show for it.

The change in my fortunes had been brief, and I was now back to my normal role.

That's right, Walter's ghost told me. *You're a deadbeat.*

CHAPTER 34

My dad was an alcoholic. I don't talk about it much because misery should be left in the past, right?

The American dream is built on reinvention. The pilgrims became new people when they settled a stolen world. We reinvent ourselves every time we move to a new city or change jobs, hoping that this time we'll be the person we aspire to. My dad never reinvented himself. He was born and died in Skokie and was blue-collar through and through. He was one of the few people whose past, present, and future self were the same. My mom said he'd been different when they'd married, but I'd never met that guy. I knew only the cruel drunk.

Maybe if he'd traveled, he wouldn't have used the bottle as a way of escaping whatever demons tormented his day-to-day. My mom always tried to feign normalcy, and I guess me being an only child helped. I was portable, easy to ship out of the house to friends and family before the liquor monster came home. His drink of choice might have been beer at one point, but by the time my first memories formed he was on to the black nectar, Jack Daniel's and Coke, and later he ditched the Coke.

On our wedding day fourteen years ago, when my high school sweetheart looked as beautiful as I'd ever seen her and I still thought the world might give me a good life, my dad outdid himself. We were twenty-four and I was home from deployment in Afghanistan. We'd planned the wedding for almost a year and had booked South Park Church and the

DoubleTree on Skokie Boulevard for our reception. We were getting married in our hometown, so everyone we knew was invited, and even though my mom had finally left my dad three years earlier, she wanted him there. She always prayed for his redemption. Maybe she knew how much I longed for a decent father.

People say I look like him, and that scares me, particularly when I think about how I've veered toward his path. Booze bared his flaws, so I could see there was much to dislike. Especially about the way he treated my mom. He never hit her, but he coerced her and made her fearful of life with and without him. I hated him for what he did to us, but I loved him, too, and now that I've slipped into my own deadbeat rhythm, there's more love than hate. Or if not love, then sympathy at least. Bitter experience has taught me how easy it is to fall so far.

I don't know why Mom wanted him at the wedding. I don't know if she hoped he'd finally be the dad I needed, or if she felt obliged to defend him against my darker emotions, but she pressed for his inclusion, so I invited him on the condition he'd behave himself.

He showed up in a purple velvet tux because "a man's gotta see off his only son in style," and not only did he fail to behave himself, after spending the whole day drinking and being the loud, aggressive guy everyone pretends isn't there, he got up to dance and leered over Toni's girlfriends. After half an hour of attempting the running man, the hop step, and other classic dance moves, his alcohol-soaked, pickled heart gave out and he collapsed and died in the Versailles Conference Suite in the Double-Tree on Skokie Boulevard in front of the mobile DJ booth.

Our wedding came to a sudden end, and instead of going on honeymoon to Catalina, we had to cancel our reservation to help Mom pay for the funeral. Toni and I made a promise we'd get a honeymoon one day, but something always came up and we never did.

I buried my dad two weeks after Toni and I exchanged vows. Hardly anyone came to his funeral. He died a lonely man, having alienated most of his friends over the years, and my last memory is of him gyrating suggestively behind Angie, a disgusted woman half his age.

I tell you this not for sympathy, but so you know I fully understand the impact booze can have on people's lives. It's a wrecking ball that keeps swinging. Toni and I never really celebrated our wedding anniversary because of what happened to my dad. His passing always hung over us.

If you asked me to pick between his death and the robbery committed by the six Donald Ducks, I'd say the robbery was worse. Dad's death brought an end to a miserable existence and traumatized those few who loved him, whereas the theft of my blood money robbed Skye, a total innocent, of a better future.

CHAPTER 35

I cried for a while and regretted my decision to pour away all my booze. I lay there feeling sorry for myself, my mind spinning through "what-ifs" and "if onlys" until exhaustion finally freed me from despair and I fell asleep.

It was late afternoon when I finally woke. I knew because golden sunlight was filling my living room, streaming through the open front door. I wiped my raw eyes and looked around the wreckage of my living room. There on the floor near me was a photograph, face down. I picked it up and regretted it the moment I saw the image. It was of Walter Glaze. The picture must have fallen out of the wallet Rasper had taken along with Walter's watch and my money.

He had his arm around a woman with a beautiful smile, and they stood behind a pair of boys who were clearly their sons, and an older girl, their daughter.

I wondered what kind of gangster carried such sweet keepsakes with him. The boys were younger than Skye, but the girl was about Skye's age, and I couldn't help but puzzle over how they were feeling. Skye would miss me. Even after all my mistakes, I knew I still had a place in my kid's heart, and maybe it was the same for Walter. They wouldn't know their father was a villain, would they?

I couldn't let these kids suffer for nothing, not Walter's sons and not my Skye, who deserved her college fund.

I had to get that money back.

I stood, staggered to the door, and headed out. A few steps into the warm afternoon, I remembered to shut the door, but the lock was broken, so the best I could do was pull the door shut. I didn't much care, there was nothing else in the house worth stealing anymore.

By the time I got to Rick's, adrenaline, shame, and anger had burned away most of my hangover.

The bar was officially closed, but Rick's car was in the lot next to my Range Rover. I'd been too drunk to drive and had left the keys with Rick. I found him inside, stocktaking.

"You look like you could use a drink or three," Rick said. "But I can't serve you this early. Here are your keys."

He tossed them at me, and I fumbled the catch.

"Thanks," I said as I stooped to pick them up.

He was nice enough. Cynical, jaded maybe, but no more than you'd expect from a man who'd heard every sob story going. Part counselor, part therapist, he managed to make people think he cared while maintaining the passionate disinterest essential for anyone whose job involved pumping people full of stuff that wasn't good for them. He was friendly without ever becoming anyone's friend. The enigma everyone knew. He had a small beer belly that hung over the top of his belt, and his thinning hair made him look older than his years.

"I just wanted to ask you about some guys who were in here last night."

His face fell. "The metalheads?"

I nodded. "I hit turbulence. Or rather the turbulence hit me."

Rick shook his head slowly. "I'm sorry to hear than, man. Frankie Balls is their leader. Guy with brown curly hair and the Metallica T-shirt. I don't know who the others are, just that they're dealers and gangsters. Bad news."

"Why have I never seen them before?"

He shrugged. "No idea, man. But whatever happened, let it slide. They're a known quantity in Compton. Bad news. Even the big gangs won't touch them."

"Where do they hang out?"

"Peyton . . . ," he began.

"I'm not going to do anything stupid. But I can't let it slide."

He shook his head and smiled knowingly. "Frankie owns the pool hall on Raymond Street."

"Thanks," I replied, heading for the door.

"Be careful, Peyton," he called after me.

"I'm just going to talk," I assured him, but I started trembling as I left the bar.

I knew I wasn't going to get my money back without a fight.

CHAPTER 36

I took the Range Rover from Rick's parking lot and drove to the heart of Compton. Raymond Street is split in two by South Central Boulevard, and I found the pool hall tucked behind a mall on the east side. My neighborhood was seedy, and Rick's would have been described by a hustling realtor as "authentic," but Raymond Street was downright dangerous. I knew that from the bars and shutters on the windows of every small, single-story home. Residents imprisoned for their own safety while criminals roamed free.

The pool hall was in a grimy whitewashed two-story warehouse on the bend near the mall parking lot. It was approached by a driveway that ran beside a little bungalow that had been painted electric blue. A sign stuck to the wall of the warehouse read Ocean Beach Pool, which must have been some kind of joke, because there was neither ocean nor beach anywhere to be seen.

I parked a short way up the street, in front of a house with a small porch where a couple of old guys were drinking from unlabeled brown bottles. They didn't say anything and just watched me walk away from the car.

Were they a vision of my future? Would I end up on the porch of some run-down house, day drinking? How many bottles were they from a life on the street? How far did I have left to fall?

You can go all the way, Walter's ghost said. *I believe in you.*

Fuck you, I thought, but the spirit was right. I had all the wrong potential.

Keep mouthing off, smart guy, the ghost said. *I've got company down here. Keep shooting your mouth off and I'll cut her loose.*

I knew instantly who he was talking about.

The girl.

I'd spent years binding her, smothering her spirit deep within me. I didn't want her back haunting me. My very first victim had almost killed me with her whispers of guilt.

I'm sorry, I told Walter's ghost inwardly. *Please don't.*

My plea was met with silence, so I walked on, aware that I had to get my money back. But I was scared, and my stomach started shooting acid into my throat as I neared the warehouse. It flipped when a couple of painted guys eased themselves out of the front door of the electric-blue bungalow beside the driveway. Young, muscled, wearing shorts, vests, and dark shades, the message was clear: *this is our land.*

They said nothing and eyed me as I started along the driveway. I felt their sour looks on my hot shoulders as I walked the curving, dusty track. I moved toward the bungalow's yard so the peeling slats would obscure me, but when I looked back, I saw the two men fall in behind me, lumbering like a couple of fighters on their way into a ring.

Keep tumbling, Walter's ghost said. *You haven't got far to fall. You're almost at the bottom.*

I could turn around now and pretend I'd come to the wrong address, but Skye would lose her future and I'd be an inch closer to a life on the street.

And I'll have died for nothing, Walter's spirit chimed in. *Death is one thing. Death at the hand of a deadbeat, that's just a crying shame.*

I couldn't stop my feet marching toward the warehouse entrance.

The two-story building was like a church, with a steep gable roof. The walls were streaked dirty gray, and the windows that overlooked the track were cracked. There were a dozen cars parked in a yard at the end of the track. Souped-up old trucks and muscle cars, the kind driven by men who want the world to have a clear gauge of their strength and virility. A small porch extended into the yard. It was covered with graffiti, scrawled words and images, some obscene, all designed to send a simple message: *keep out.*

You've probably realized I'm not a brave man. I served in the army, true, but for most of my time I was a master builder who stayed well away from combat. I made things that killed people or stopped them being killed. I built bridges, defenses, things other people used to wage war, but I wasn't a warrior myself. Until prison, I managed to go my whole life without a proper fight, not because I let people walk over me, but because I never allowed myself to be in a position where their boots could touch my back. I skirted danger, avoided confrontation, and kept out of trouble. Did that make me a coward? I think it made me smart. But it certainly didn't make me brave. Now here I was standing outside a place of violence, about to confront the men who'd stolen everything from me. Seeking conflict was the opposite of everything I'd ever done, but if I didn't go in and face these men, Skye's future would be lost, and I'd probably end up on the street after a long spell inside for the thing with the sheriff's car.

I had thought about trying to get hold of another gun, but if I went in there playing the action hero, there was a better than even chance I'd be the one chewing a bullet. I figured my best hope was to try to strike a bargain, let them know my daughter's future was at stake and agree they could keep some of the money.

Even gangsters have souls, right?

The two tattooed thugs were close now, their presence pushing me on like a steer being corralled by a couple of wranglers. I was sweating, but not because of the heat, and my gut was pulsing with acid. My legs were weak and my hands trembled.

Do it for Skye, I thought.

I ignored a handwritten sign on the door that featured a skull above the words Members Only and pushed it open.

I stepped into a large room with a double-height ceiling. Less a pool hall, more a gang hangout, Led Zeppelin's "Ramble On" was playing for a dozen or so guys who all stared at me as I made my reluctant incursion. Stained, torn couches lined the walls, a couple of battered pool tables stood in the center of the forty-by-twenty-foot space. Behind them was an old restaurant bar that didn't quite fit the corner it had been built into, obviously salvaged from somewhere else. Mean faces watched me, betraying histories of blood and violence. I saw the six men who'd been at Rick's, the ones I assumed had robbed me. They sat on stools by the bar, a Donald Duck mask on the counter behind them.

Outwardly, I kept my cool as I walked across the room toward them, but inside I was as nervous as a frog in a pit of snakes. The two thugs from the bungalow entered the building behind me.

"Private club," the barman said. Like the others, he was dressed for a metal concert and covered in ornate tattoos that featured too many skulls. "Get the fuck out."

"I'm—" My voice broke a little, so I cleared my throat and took it down a few notes. "I'm looking for Frankie Balls."

"He don't live here," one of the men by the Donald Duck mask said. I recognized his voice. He was Rasper, the man who'd electroshocked me. Everyone else watched him for cues, and he had the air of a leader. Vicious, but a leader nonetheless.

I guessed he was Frankie Balls.

"I don't want any trouble," I said.

"What you don't want don't count for shit," Frankie replied, rising from his stool. The men around him did likewise.

"I had some trouble yesterday. That was enough for me. I was robbed. Some men took my daughter's college fund. She wants to be a doctor." I grew increasingly nervous as the thugs from the bar fanned out around me. "Like I said, I don't want any trouble. I was hoping the guys who took the money would find it in their hearts to give most of it back. Keep, say, twenty percent for their trouble."

"Twenty percent?" Frankie asked. "That's a pretty sour deal for guys who already have one hundred percent. Why would they give anything back?"

"To help a kid who doesn't deserve this," I replied. "Thirty percent if it makes it any easier. Thirty percent and a chance to do something good."

Somewhere in these men there had to be a kernel of decency. I had to believe that like me they'd just taken a wrong turn in life. I had to believe it for Skye. But even as the naive thought flared, I knew it was a delusion told by a desperate father who'd walked into the lion's den. Square folk don't know what desperation really does to a person, but if you've ever felt desperate yourself, you'll know why I stood there trying to reason with monsters. I had no other hope. Looking back on that day, I wonder at just how low and desperate I was, because standing in the midst of thugs and villains pleading with them to return stolen money was one of the stupidest things I've ever done.

Frankie smiled. He looked like an evil version of *Escape from New York*–era Kurt Russell, complete with wild long, straw-blond hair and manic eyes.

"Good? What the fuck does good have to do with anything? Do you think the world is good?" he asked. "Has it been good to you?"

I knew it was the kind of question that didn't have a right answer, so I kept my mouth shut and felt a little sick at the growing sense of foreboding.

"The world isn't good, friend," Frankie said.

I didn't see who threw the first punch because it came from behind and sent me stumbling forward.

"This is from the gospel of Frankie," he said as he drew back his fist. "Life is pain."

He hit me hard enough to knock me down, and then they all joined in and after a few seconds of dazzling agony, I passed out.

CHAPTER 37

They sent me to see Freya Persico. She existed only in the minds of those who'd loved her and the guilty subconscious of the man who'd put her in the earth before her time. She was beautiful, and according to those who posted about her on social media, she was good and smart and kind. A pianist who used to play in old people's homes as a child to entertain her elders, a young philanthropist donating money and time to environmental causes, an organ donor whose death gave new life.

I wish I could take back the day she died, not just for her but for me, Toni, and Skye most of all. Freya Persico changed everything. She's with me now and forever, the girl I didn't know, her face haunting me. She has a ghost, too, but it never speaks. It's locked somewhere deep inside me where the pain lives, a place that rots me from within. Walter threatening to release her had terrified me.

She reminded me of Liv Tyler from her *Lord of the Rings* days. Elfin features, dark hair, but no alabaster skin. Freya was tanned, and as I staggered from my car, my head whirling like a carnival ride and my stomach ready to toss up my celebratory lunch and too many drinks, I saw her half out of her overturned car. She was in a navy-blue, ruby-red, and chalk-white bikini, her toned body twisted in ways that would have been impossible in life, her lips pulled back by friction, her smashed teeth gleaming white beneath the dark drops of blood. Her eyes, so bright and shining in the moments before the crash, now like glass beads, forever distant.

She'd had friends in her convertible 3 Series, but I don't remember their names. They'd all survived the crash, maybe because they'd been wearing their seat belts. Trust fund kids, like her, they'd never had to worry a day in their lives. Not until they encountered me. Freya had been the same, from money. Her mother had died when she was a child, but her father, Joseph Persico, the guy I'd prayed to from the mountain above his huge estate, was still alive. I thought about the reclusive man often and found myself making pilgrimage when drunk because I lacked the courage to face him and apologize for the pain I'd caused.

I went to Freya's funeral when I was out on bail. I kept a respectful distance, standing in the shade of a cypress tree where I spent the whole time crying. Her dad wasn't there. I don't know why. Just her friends, three of them still carrying the marks of their injuries from the crash, and others all sad and bereft.

Freya joined me in the shade of that cypress tree, wearing a long white dress. She didn't say anything, just smiled at a joke I couldn't hear. She took my hand and held it gently, and as I watched her body being buried, I knew she'd always be with me, eating away at everything I was, everything I did, like some beautiful cancer.

And then we were somewhere else. The sudden dislocation of a dream took us to Walter Glaze's car. It was night, that night, the night I shot him. Only he wasn't driving. She was. And she was smiling and laughing just as she had been the day I'd killed her. But I never heard her above the roar of engines and rumble of our tires on the PCH, so here in Walter's car she was silent.

She looked at me and I wanted to say sorry. I wanted to take it all back, but I couldn't.

Once again, I was startled when the gun went off, and a bullet hit her head and sent it smashing into the window, which exploded, showering everything with glass. The car went into a violent spin and then flipped and tumbled along the road.

We rolled, crashing and grinding as though in a stone wash, being smashed against concrete with each flip.

Finally, we stopped, and I snapped to and found myself out of the car. Only it wasn't Walter's Mercedes anymore. It was Freya's BMW again, and I was in the median of the Pacific Coast Highway where broken pieces of glass and mirror glinted in the late-afternoon sun. Her friends were upside down in the wreckage, unconscious, but she was out, twisted on the road.

Poor girl, Walter's ghost said.

He was beside me now, looking down at Freya.

I wanted to scream at the horror of everything I'd done, but no sound would come.

You can never leave, Walter's ghost said. *In this life, we'll always be with you. In the next life, we'll always be with you. We're there now. Waiting. Waiting for you, Peyton.*

CHAPTER 38

There isn't a passing day I don't regret what I did. I wish I could go back and relive my time.

I'd left the army and taken a job with St. Clair Engineering, a specialist technology firm. I would get a huge jump in salary with stock options, and with all that came the potential for admission to the golden California lifestyle: sailing boat, chalet in Aspen, beach house in Malibu.

Eric Andersen, an old buddy from army training, had introduced me to the firm. He was one of their lead designers, and he invited me to the Sundown Inn to celebrate my new role.

I wish I'd never met that glad-handing, good-time fool. Maybe I'd still be in the army now, on my way to a fat pension and a solid second career, but I was seduced by riches. We had a delicious lunch outside on the terrace, but Eric kept plying me with drinks and goading me to have more, even though the waiter refused to serve us at our table.

The waiter was a good man and had taken our grumbles and gibes without complaint, but he'd held firm and refused us a second bottle of champagne because we were driving.

The barman, nothing more than a blurry figure in a shirt and waistcoat by the time I met him, didn't have any such scruples and served until I could hardly see straight.

I don't know what I was thinking. I was high on life, on the prospect of success, and believed I was going to be untouchable, that I deserved a good time.

I found out only later that after walking me to my car, Eric had returned to the restaurant, handed the waiter his car keys, and hung around until an Uber arrived.

Meanwhile I, the greatest fool to have cursed this planet, headed south along the PCH, steering for LA, where my beautiful wife and child were waiting at home.

Each mile covered under the influence was a betrayal of both of them, and when I finally crashed into Freya Persico, I also killed the family we'd once been.

I became a deadbeat that day. I wasn't a murderer, but I was a killer, and the punishment for my crime was seven years in maximum security. I served a little over three, which was about the limit of what I could take.

All the misery in my life, all the adversity I face, my whole rotten world stems from that day. A few bad choices robbed me of my light and destroyed my family forever. I put a promising young woman in the earth, and for that I can never forgive myself.

CHAPTER 39

The real world freed me from hell, and I came around to find myself lying on my back on the sidewalk in front of the blue bungalow on Raymond Street. I had one of my feet in the gutter.

They hadn't even bothered to hide me or dump me any real distance from their lair. A gnarly old dog with a rope around its neck entered my field of view and sniffed my crotch. I tried to brush it away, but when I moved my arm, pain froze me. Then a filthy hand holding the other end of the rope leash came into view, followed by an old, bearded, dirty face. Sun worn and craggy, the dog's owner looked as though he'd lived many years on the street.

"You okay, fella?" he asked, revealing a mouthful of brown teeth. "You looked pretty beaten up."

I grunted, got to my feet, and staggered to my car.

You killed me for nothing, Walter's ghost whispered.

For the twelve thousand bucks I'd given Toni, plus the money for the Range Rover, I countered inwardly, but the dead man was right, I'd lost everything else to weakness.

I would have cried if my eyes had any tears left to give. I was too sore and swollen for sorrow. What kind of idiot had I been to walk into a place like that and try to appeal to the better natures of men who had more in common with jackals than humans? I'd been desperate, but desperation is the barroom buddy of stupidity.

The drive home took twice as long as it should because I had to pull over a couple of times to wait for the pain to subside and catch my breath. Finally, I pulled into my driveway and climbed out of the car into dust bowl heat. My legs buckled as I staggered toward the house, but I kept myself upright by veering toward the mailbox and using it as a leaning post. I knocked my elbow against the little raised flag and saw the tail of a package poking out of the hatch. I looked around to make sure there was no one else on Edgebrook, took it out, and stumbled into the house as fast as my battered, weakened legs could carry me.

I went through the broken front door and grabbed a wooden chair from the living room, put it against the door, and lowered myself onto the seat with gasps and groans. Once I'd settled into a position that made the pain bearable, I took a couple of deep breaths and tore open the package. I reached inside and found two thousand-dollar bundles of fifty-dollar bills. I understood the significance immediately. This wasn't just money; it was a life.

At the bottom of the package was a slip of paper with a web address. I typed the URL—a mix of numbers and letters again—into my phone and was once again taken to a page that contained nothing but an audio recording.

I pressed the sideways play triangle, and the machine voice that had given me my first set of instructions said, "You proved yourself with Walter Glaze. I know I can trust you, and you know you can trust me. Farah Younis works for Ruben, Dozal, and Taft. She's a San Diego lawyer who launders money for arms brokers and drug dealers. Two hundred thousand dollars for her."

CHAPTER 40

What would you do?

That's two questions really.

Would you—the person sitting in your favorite chair, lying in bed, on the train, bus, or relaxing in the bath—kill a bad person if doing so would make the world a better place for someone you love? Maybe you're sitting by the pool outside your mansion or lying in a super-king bed in your ten-thousand-dollar-a-night hotel suite as you read this, and two hundred grand is chump change. Maybe you've never felt hunger pangs because you had to decide between feeding yourself or your children. Or had to climb through the kitchen window to avoid the heavies your landlord sent round to collect the rent. Maybe you're not familiar with the deadweight of a handful of overdue notices warning you of repossession, prosecution, or imprisonment. How you want to cry when you see the penalty interest and charges added that mean you'll likely never escape the suffocating burden of debt. They say food tastes sweeter when you're hungry. If you've never wanted for money, you'll have no idea what I'm talking about. You'll never know how good a few folding bucks can feel. Your morals will remain intact, and you can look down on the rest of us scrabbling for survival on your leave-behinds, fighting over the scraps from your billboard life.

I didn't have the luxury of moral certainty, so after I'd showered, cleaned up my wounds as best I could, and got changed into fresh clothes, I went to Toni's for some advice.

I needed peace of mind. Thinking about death in the abstract is easy. Words on a page. Ideas in a head. But I knew from Freya Persico and Walter Glaze that taking a life had taken part of mine too. My stomach rolled acid every time I thought about pulling the trigger on someone else. And this target was a woman. Maybe I should say *victim*, but that would reinforce the idea I was doing something wrong, whereas *target*, a word used for terrorists and criminals, put the wrongdoing firmly on the other party. It might have been latent sexism, a product of a late-twentieth-century childhood, but for some reason the death of a woman seemed to carry more weight than that of a man. Walter Glaze had deserved to die, but did Farah Younis? I hadn't checked her out yet, because I realized I needed to be more careful about searches that could be traced back to me. If I went ahead with this, I couldn't pretend to be an accidental killer. I'd be a very deliberate and careful one. And two would be a series.

A serial.

Jim Steadman had already absolved me of sin, but he was an immoral man. I needed absolution from someone I respected and wanted my ex-wife and high school sweetheart to bless my transition from deadbeat to assassin. Or to prevent it, if that's what she was minded to do.

If I'm honest, now that I had prospects that could put a roof over our heads and money in our pockets, part of me was also hoping for a reconciliation. I thought I still loved her. She'd moved on, but I was still stuck basking in memories of the past. If she'd asked me to hit the straight and narrow, I'd have put thoughts of killing in my rearview and squared up solid. She told me she wanted the twelve grand only if it was legal, but would she feel the same way about two hundred? Everyone had their price. Was this Toni's?

I parked near Toni's building. Body aching, I winced and bit my lip as I shuffled toward the broken gate. I could give you a long list of organs and limbs that ached or flashed with pain, but it's probably easier for me to say the only parts of me that didn't hurt were my teeth. Movement and touch were my enemies, and even the soft cotton of my faded blue Quiksilver T-shirt set my ribs aflame.

A normal person would have gotten medical attention, but a US hospital would have relieved me of my two grand faster than any pistol-toting crack addict. I had to hold on to that cash. I couldn't leave it in the house with the front door broken, so it was in the Range Rover's locked glove compartment.

I knocked on Toni's door and groaned as I settled. I'd taken a couple of Advil, but nothing stronger because I wanted to be sober for this. So, the sharpest edge of agony was blunted, but the bulky hammer remained.

There was no answer when I knocked on Toni's back door, so I knocked again. I pulled out my phone and tried Toni's number.

"What is it, Peyton?" she said without ceremony.

"I need to talk."

"We're out with Jack," she replied. "He's taken Skye and me to the Reel Inn."

Was she deliberately trying to wound me? The Reel Inn was a fish place out near Topanga Canyon on the Pacific Coast Highway. It was one of my favorite restaurants and had been a regular haunt of ours during the happy years.

"Oh," I said.

"We'll catch you another time," she responded.

"Toni, I really need to . . . ," I began, but I realized she'd already hung up.

The only decent person I could turn to wasn't there for me. I was alone.

Feeling sorry for myself, I leaned against her kitchen door.

You ain't got no one except the spirits of the folks you killed, Walter's ghost told me. *Loser is as loser does.*

What does that even mean? I thought, but there was no answer.

CHAPTER 41

I didn't have anywhere else to turn, so I eased myself into the Range Rover and drove across town to Bel Air Road. I parked at the head of the trail, and, using my cell's flashlight, climbed the mountain to the spot that overlooked Joseph Persico's home.

The old man didn't know I carried his daughter's ghost with me, or that he gave me absolution each time I visited, but that's okay, he didn't need to know. We weren't linked by life. We were bound by death, and I found peace just being out here, close to him, paying my respects, my every breath an apology for what I'd done.

I asked him for guidance and let my mind drift. As I stood on the rocky hillside, looking down at the beautifully lit garden, the trees swaying in the evening breeze, a single word formed in my mind: *vigilante*.

Life is not as sacred as we think. There are plenty of legal reasons a person can be killed, and even more if one rolls in the gray areas of life. What about a father who kills the man who murdered his child? It's not legal, but is it just? Revenge speaks to some ancient part of us, hence the popularity of revenge stories and vigilantes in fiction. The vigilante takes revenge for all of us, acting when we don't have the courage to do so, righting wrongs the system can't handle.

In the hands of a Marvel movie director, the dramatized version of my life might cast me as the avenging angel.

Seeing myself in a new light, I thanked Joseph Persico for guidance and walked down the mountain.

After I left Bel Air Road, I drove south to Koreatown and found an internet café I'd passed a few times on the corner of Western Avenue and 11th Street. I didn't know anything about Farah Younis beyond where she worked, so I needed to do the research.

I parked in an almost empty lot at the back and entered the windowless building through the poster-covered glass doors. There were a few kids gaming, but it was easy to find a machine in a quiet corner where I could have privacy. I paid the bored attendant for an hour. I didn't want an in-depth trawl showing up on my phone, and the café didn't appear to have any cameras, so there was no way for the cops to tie me to time and place. The attendant stank of skunk and would probably forget my face the moment I left the building. I won't lie, I was a little excited to find myself starting to think like a vigilante. Batman, Year One, before the cops realize he's a good guy.

A site called the *San Diego Intercept* was the most useful source of information on Farah Younis. A long investigative piece suggested she laundered money for drug cartels working out of Mexico and Colombia, and that she was linked to arms dealers in Ukraine and Pakistan. I found a few other mentions of Farah, a corporate law firm vanilla LinkedIn profile, and some photos of her and her family posted on Facebook. She had two boys and was married to a young, athletic man who was as handsome as she was beautiful. The Facebook tag identified him as Sammy Younis, local restaurateur.

If it hadn't been for her twisted character and the misery inflicted by those she worked for, this would have been a difficult kill. Mother, wife, intelligent, loving, and beautiful. Her official persona had every right to life, but the truth of her corruption and wrongdoings meant death would be easy. The *San Diego Intercept* marked her as evil, and why wouldn't I rid the world of someone who helped spread pain and misery? Especially if in doing so I could buy my way into the billboard life of the dream-makers and fakers. I didn't have the worry of Skye's medical bills pushing me on, but there was still the question of a good life for her and for me. Didn't we deserve something better?

The answer was obvious, so I shut down the computer, got to my feet, and started the next stage of my journey toward becoming a vigilante.

CHAPTER 42

I went back to Rudy's, the pawnshop on Compton Boulevard, and got there as he was shutting for the night. Rudy sold me another gun, and this time I went for a Glock 19. It cost me a thousand bucks, but I knew it was a reliable, commonplace weapon.

I didn't know Rudy, but I lost what little respect I had for the guy. He sold me a box of ammo to go with the gun, no questions asked. Who buys two illegal handguns in less than a week? Criminals, that's who. He might tell himself I was a careless gun owner who lost his first piece, or that I was starting a collection or some other lie to help him sleep easy, but we both had enough years behind us to know people didn't buy one illegal firearm, let alone two, unless they were into some pretty shady stuff.

"I got robbed," I blurted out, trying to dispel any unuttered suspicions. I didn't want him blabbing foul ideas to the cops if they ever came calling.

"I'm sorry to hear that," he replied with the sincerity of a corrupt insurance salesman.

"Broke down my front door and took everything, including the last piece."

"I see. You get the door fixed?"

I shook my head. "Haven't had the time."

"I have some padlocks," he told me, shuffling off to the counter on the other side of the store.

He sold me a couple of padlocks and a hinge and gate setup for busted doors and told me they were popular with people who were behind on their payments and got unwanted visits from cops or repo heavies.

It was almost ten thirty by the time I pulled into my drive on Edge-brook, and the street was deserted. I grabbed the padlock and security set and headed for my house.

I wish I could say my spidey sense had tingled, but I was blind to danger as I walked through my unlocked front door to find Frankie Balls seated in an armchair a few feet away. I wished I hadn't left my new gun in the glove box.

"Peyton Collard," he sneered. His rasping voice was like nails scraping my spine and set me on edge. "Army man. Tough. I can tell because you're on your feet going solid even after the beating we gave you."

How did he know I'd been in the army? Had he overheard me and Jim talking at Rick's one night? What else did he know about me? I hated him and wanted nothing more than his death. My hate must have shone like the midday sun, because he produced a huge revolver from behind his back and placed it casually on the arm of the chair.

"Where you been, Peyton?" he asked.

"Errands. I had to run some errands."

"You come into any more money?"

I shook my head.

"You've had a rough couple of days," he said, getting to his feet. "You might not be thinking straight." He stepped forward and put the muzzle of the revolver to my temple. "Sometimes it's good to clear the mind."

I trembled as I looked into the eyes of this psychopath.

"Don't be afraid, Peyton. We're old friends," he said.

Was he telling the truth? Had we met before? In prison maybe? I didn't remember him, but then life had been so traumatic, much of that first year inside had been wiped from my mind.

"I get why you're fearful. You've been robbed and beaten up these past couple of days, and that's hard on a man. But you know what it tells me?"

I hesitated. I didn't want to shake my head with a gun pressed against it. I could smell alcohol, body odor, but the psychic stench coming off this nutcase reeked stronger than Florida swampland. His eyes were pitiless.

"You need protection. You need someone who will look after you. I'll do it for fifty percent of whatever you bring in. I want your money. Give it to me. Give me your money. Do you understand?"

"I don't have any money," I said. "You took it."

He slapped me. "Man with eighty grand ain't gonna stay poor for long. When you get more, you give me half."

I didn't respond.

"If it helps you sleep easy with the arrangement, think of us as business partners. You're front office, doing whatever it is you do to bring in the big bucks, and I'm back office, making sure no one, namely you, gets hurt by anyone, namely me. You follow?"

He withdrew the gun, and I nodded uncertainly.

"I'll be seeing you, partner."

And with that he pushed past me and was gone.

I took a deep breath of relief, sank into the armchair, and watched him cross my yard. There was the roar of an engine, and a black Escalade stopped in front of Frankie, who jumped in. The car shot away.

I knew that man would hurt me whether he got any money or not. I'd already decided to kill Farah Younis, but this encounter made it imperative. I needed a new home, a new place somewhere Frankie Balls wouldn't find me.

CHAPTER 43

I woke the next morning still aching from the beating Frankie Balls and his crew had given me, worsened by a crick in my neck from lying on the back seat of the Range Rover. I'd driven south to San Diego and spent the night on the edge of the city at Ocean Beach. I'd bought a burger from Hodad's and ate it on the weathered old shore wall that overlooked the Pacific. Watching the sun set, I'd tried to quiet my misgivings about what I was about to do and was only partly successful. My crimes, past, present, and future, troubled me as I spent a fitful night in the car.

I went to the Midway District, an industrial neighborhood, and found a vacant lot near the train tracks. I parked next to a pile of rubble that might have once been an old warehouse and relieved myself. An early morning freight train rumbled by, and I glanced over my shoulder to watch the cars clitter clatter along the tracks. A bladder lighter, I returned to the Range Rover and headed downtown.

Farah Younis was a partner at Ruben, Dozal, and Taft, a heavy-duty law firm located in the heart of San Diego on Columbia Street. I took the long route there, winding south past downtown, along Harbor Drive by a huge convention center, which was gearing up in advance of Comic-Con. Gigantic posters hung from the exhibition halls, and banners had been draped down the sides of the surrounding skyscrapers, advertising upcoming Marvel and DC blockbusters, most of which featured vigilante heroes of one form or another killing bad guys by the hundred. I longed for the black-and-white morality of a superhero, because in their world there was no doubt I'd be a troubled good guy with a shades-of-gray backstory on a righteous mission of silver screen justice, but in this life I was a flawed human trying to navigate the lesser evil.

Satisfied I'd established myself as a sightseer taking in the city's landmarks should I be picked up on any traffic cameras, I turned north for the city center. I didn't enter a destination in the Range Rover's GPS but managed to use the onboard map to find my way to Columbia Street, a wide avenue of low-rise office blocks and baby skyscrapers.

Ruben, Dozal, and Taft was located in a brand-new six-story white stone, black glass block with an underground parking lot. It was the kind of place that cost serious dough, and I wondered whether Farah's partners knew she was crooked. Maybe they were too?

There was a parking structure across the intersection with West C Street, directly opposite the building, and I found a space on the fourth floor that gave me a great view of Farah's building and the entrance to the underground parking garage. I settled in for a stakeout, and the radio kept me company with the local DJ's rambling chatter and an easy listening playlist.

Facebook had given me photos of Farah Younis, so I knew exactly who to look for, and sure enough, she showed up for work a little after eight, driving a red BMW X5 into the underground garage. She wound down her window to present her security pass.

I wanted to hate her, but she looked like a decent person in her photos. No devil horns or fangs to mark her out as a wrongdoer. She had dark hair, olive skin, bright eyes, and a broad smile. But they say Hitler was kind to animals, which goes to show the most evil of us can have moments of humanity.

Once her car was out of sight, I relaxed a little and settled. She'd likely be inside for a while, and I wasn't there to kill her. Not that day. I wanted to make sure she was in town, not away on cartel business, and I needed to figure out where and when she was most vulnerable. I was determined not to repeat the fiasco of Walter's death, and my old military training, hidden in the recesses of my mind, was retrieved and revived to help with more methodical preparation. I was an engineer at heart, and every good engineer will tell you success is all in the planning.

I spent the day in the parking structure apart from a short bathroom break and trip to the deli. There were people around in the morning, but after lunch it got too hot, and the streets emptied.

Finally, soon after seven, the red BMW rolled out of the garage and headed south. I left the lot and caught up to it. I followed Farah through the city, paying no attention to my surroundings, focused on my target like a lion on a gazelle. We drove northeast for half an hour until we reached Carmel Valley. It was dark by the time we left the I-5, and five miles from the interstate, Farah turned onto an access road that led into a private estate. The houses rivaled anything in Bel Air. I slowed as I passed the mouth of the access road and saw the guards at the gatehouse raise a candy-cane-patterned barrier and wave her in.

I took the next right through the gates of a small neighborhood park. The play equipment was deserted, and the parking lot was empty, except for me.

I grabbed my gun and ski mask from the glove compartment and climbed out of the Range Rover, groaning a little as my injuries acted up. I pocketed my gun and pulled on the mask as I shuffled my way across the park to the high wall that edged the private estate. The thick structure was constructed of rough, uneven gray stone and was covered with No Trespassing and 24 Hour Security notices. I reached up to the capstones, lifted myself to peer over, and saw a perfect California garden encircling a huge Craftsman house with pitched roofs and a large overhanging porch. The estate was exactly the sort of multimillion-dollar hideout where I would have expected a mob lawyer to live. Secluded and protected, somewhere hard for enemies or law enforcement to reach.

I was a soldier again, and this was my mission.

I groaned when I dropped into the garden on the other side of the wall, but didn't have time for pain. My heart thumped adrenaline, numbing my aches, and I crept quickly through the garden bushes toward the house. There was a family inside, seated at a dining table. It wasn't Farah or her husband and kids, so I moved on to the next property, which was deserted. I climbed a wall to get into the neighboring grounds and hugged the bushes and trees as I stalked through the private estate, marveling at the lives these people had. Huge homes, swimming pools, lush gardens, existences free of worry or want, living high on the mountain like Greek gods, untroubled by the events that might plague a typical American life. Would they ever miss a payment on an overpriced, ancient car? Be considering murder for the price of a small condo in a bad neighborhood? No, if there was murder planned in these homes it was on an industrial scale: the pharmaceutical executive who calculates a profit while knowingly releasing a dangerous drug, the investor pushing to open a new oil field while the planet chokes, the defense CEO selling arms to foreign lands.

As I crept through this modern Olympus, I grew to resent these people and everything they had, and by the time I spotted Farah's red BMW in the driveway of an enormous double-fronted mansion, I was truly in the grip of envy.

An architect's dream, her two-story home was mostly glass, which was stylish and impressive, but also very helpful for would-be vigilantes who wanted a window into her life.

I went to the back of the house, where I got a CinemaScope of a chef's kitchen through a run of folding glass doors. Farah was in there with two boys and her husband, who looked as though he'd just stepped from the Hilfiger catalog in beige slacks and a checked shirt with rolled-up sleeves. He was standing at the stove holding a pizza, and Farah was by the door, kicking off her heels. Her floral summer dress swirled as she swung one of her boys into a pickup hug, before depositing him at the long dining table. She tousled the other boy's hair and kissed his forehead. It was a silver-screen-perfect family scene, and I was green jealous.

Hitler was kind to animals, I reminded myself.

You're a murderer, Walter's ghost chimed in. *You're doing this for money, and not that much either. A deadbeat gutter killer.*

This woman wasn't Hitler. She ran some gray deals for some bad people, but she was a mom and wife, and those kids would be cut up by her death. Would the pharma exec who signed off on a bad drug sleep so easily at night if they had to stalk the gardens and see the lives of their victims? Faraway death was easy. Up close like this was hard.

I resented a world that forced hard choices on me. I told myself I resented Farah Younis's blessed life, which had been paid for by the misery of others. I told myself I resented everything she stood for, but did I really believe it? Was I doing this for justice? Or for money? Did it matter? Both were good motives. Money was bad only if motivated by greed, but I wanted my payday for Skye.

And she wants hers for her kids, Walter's ghost said.

Then at the very least we're the same, I responded inwardly. *And if it's my kid's happiness over hers . . .*

Weighing my dilemma in those stark terms, one thing was very clear. She had to die.

CHAPTER 44

You want to make parole, you have to learn to talk the talk about rehabilitation and reconciliation. I spent a lot of time in the prison library reading what social scientists have to say about the dangers of alienation and the disempowerment of men who feel so frustrated they turn to violence. Domestic violence, sexual violence, gun violence—you name it and it can be linked to some grant-funded academic theory that recasts the perp as the victim and the true victim as the unlucky bystander in some grand exercise that seeks to absolve the individual of responsibility. It was their mom's fault for working two jobs and never being around. It was their dad's fault for slapping them around too much. Their teacher's fault for being hard on them at school.

I was about as alienated as anyone could be. I'd lost the social and professional network of the army, I'd been sucked into the criminal justice system, been robbed of liberty, livelihood, wife, child, and the only people who offered me any comfort were a drunk and a barman, until a stranger made an assassin of me. Assassin sounds so much better than serial killer, but even after all that bad luck and strife, I'd never put the blame for my actions on my drunk dad, browbeaten mom, or society.

The responsibility for my crimes lies with me alone. And with my mysterious patron, I guess. I should have been clued to the fact this person was no benefactor and probably didn't have my best interests at heart, but like a starving dog whose eyes are fixed on a treat in the exterminator's hand, I had sight only of the money and was missing the bigger picture.

Still, even if I was blinded by my patron's money, he or she didn't coerce me into anything. I became an angel of death willingly. I was the one who woke the following day. I was the one who pulled out of the oceanfront parking lot where I'd spent the night, drove through San Diego, and rolled into a concrete parking structure on G Street. I took the ski mask and gun from the glove compartment and stowed them in the pocket of my hooded top. I was the one who left the structure and hailed a cab. I was the one who saw the words *Believe the hype* scrawled on the side of the parking structure as the young Armenian driver pulled away. I was responsible for getting him to drop me off at West Ash Street, three blocks from Farah's office. It was I who walked those three blocks and who hid in the doorway to the fire stairs beside the barrier to the underground parking lot. I was the one who pulled on the ski mask and lay in wait in the shadows.

Society didn't do anything.

It was me.

A victim of circumstance.

A moment of madness.

I couldn't stop myself.

You made me do it.

You provoked me.

I wasn't thinking straight.

The excuses we make for ourselves are endless and made meaningless by contrition after the fact.

I could have turned away at any point, gotten into my car, and driven home. But I didn't. I'd convinced myself Farah Younis was a bad seed and that I had two hundred thousand reasons to make the world a better place. Looking back, I can see that greed and a feeling of righteousness had merged into an ugly motive.

So, I stood in the doorway, hidden by shadow, checking my pistol, craning forward to peer past the lip of the wall whenever I heard a car pull up to the barrier. I was ready and willing to gun down a complete stranger, and society didn't put me in those shadows. I put myself there, and not a day goes by when I don't wish I'd been somewhere else. Anywhere else.

Regrets aren't excuses. They are an expression of the torment a mind suffers after perpetrating a wrong. I don't want absolution or sympathy. If anything, I want you to hate me, so you come away from this cautionary tale determined not to be like me. You can live a good life and make the world a better place and leave regret to fools like me.

Finally, a little after seven, I heard a car pull up to the barrier, and I leaned past the lip of the doorway to see Farah Younis in her red BMW. I checked my mask and edged out of my hiding place. As I walked toward the passenger side of her X5, I raised my gun and wrapped my finger around the trigger. The old ways were coming back to me. Soldierly ways. But I was still anxious.

My nerves had become hornets, and they were wild now. My stomach was full of them, and my head was buzzing. The stress and horror of what I was about to do had set off the whole hive. They pricked my palms with sweat and flew around my legs, making them tremble.

Farah must have sensed movement, because she turned to look at me as I brought the muzzle level with her head. Her eyes went galaxy wide, and she fumbled with something.

Do it, the devil inside me said, but I couldn't pull the trigger.

Do it.

Do it.

There was a crack like a huge firework had exploded, and the passenger window shattered. I ducked as a bullet zipped through the air and hit the concrete behind me. The hive went nuts as I realized Farah Younis was shooting at me.

Fucking mob lawyer, the devil spat inside, *you should have put her down.*

I ran round the car, as Farah floored it and forced her way through the barrier. An alarm sounded and I opened fire, shooting out the X5's rear window. I kept shooting as the car gathered speed down the ramp, and a bullet tore through Farah's headrest and into her skull, sending her head snapping forward and a spray of blood and brains all over the windshield.

I was almost sick as the BMW crashed into a parked Bentley coupe.

I shot out a camera that was pointed into the garage, stumbled down the ramp, and hurried to the crash to find Farah Younis most definitely dead, her face resembling a Hollywood makeup artist's prosthetic, a mess of blood and bone. One lifeless eye looked directly ahead. The other was missing.

I was beautiful, Farah's ghost lamented.

He did the same to me, Walter's ghost chimed in.

I was sickened to hear their words inside my head and horrified at what I'd done.

I still am. There is no glory in murder. It is abhorrent and I deserve to be punished, but self-preservation is a powerful instinct.

I fled the scene, back up the ramp and onto the street.

I slipped the gun into my pocket, and when I was three blocks away, I slowed to a walk. A block farther and I took off my mask. Another two and I hailed a cab. I was still shaking when I got in and told the driver to head for G Street.

I caught sight of a shambling deadbeat reflected in the rearview mirror. I looked as degenerate as ever, more so because there was something missing from my eyes. A spark, vital energy, some part of me had been taken with the life of Farah Younis.

You really are a killer now, Walter's ghost said.

For sure, Farah's ghost agreed. *A stone-cold killer.*

CHAPTER 45

The most dangerous gas station in the world is the Shell on the Coast Highway just outside San Clemente. It might not be a hazard for most folk, but it was for me. I pulled in with the Range Rover running on fumes, my hands shaking, body trembling, head buzzing. I'm pretty certain I'd cried for at least part of the drive out of San Diego, but I can't be sure whether I dreamed those memories later. I have the image of me smacking the steering wheel as I went north up the coast, angry at myself and what I'd done, but again I can't be sure I didn't imagine it to make myself feel better with the idea of murder. I was still human if I expressed remorse and regret. I wasn't a monster.

Farah's death had messed me up, that's about all I can be certain of. I wish I could get rid of the memory of the event itself, but I don't think I'll ever forget Farah Younis and her one-eyed face looking blankly at a blood- and brain-spattered window.

I'll always be with you, her ghost said as I pulled up to one of the pumps.

I ignored her and noticed the gun and ski mask were still on the passenger seat beside me. Acid flooded my stomach as I shoved them inside the glove compartment. I was shaking so much it took me a full two minutes to get the cap off the gas tank.

As the pungent gas infused my lungs, I gradually came back to reality and took in the world around me. I was on a four-lane road that followed the curve of the coast north into San Clemente. Cars lined up at the Jack in the Box drive-thru next to the gas station, and across the street was a laundromat with a large mural of a merman painted on its side wall. Next to it was a single-story red building with a black roof. Blooms Irish Pub.

I didn't even pretend to try to resist. A quick drink would settle my nerves.

I topped off the tank, paid cash, and parked the Range Rover outside the pub.

When I walked in, I saw I wasn't the only one who'd be enjoying a prelunch drink. It was 11:15, and I'd pretty much blanked what I'd done between killing Farah Younis and pulling into the gas station, because I was only about fifty minutes north of San Diego. Had I driven around aimlessly? Had I parked up and shed tears?

Did you kill someone else? Walter's ghost asked. *Have you got a taste for it?*

I wanted these spirits gone, but I knew there was no way to exorcise them. I'd tried to get rid of Freya Persico's with drink and drugs, but she was still in me, near my heart, turning it rotten, silently judging everything I did. I'd bound her deep within me, and even though she was silent, I knew she was still there.

These dead were part of me now.

There were five men in the place and a woman behind the bar. The men were all in sneakers, socks, knee-length shorts, polo shirts, and baseball caps. It was like a uniform for sad, red-cheeked, overweight souls who'd once hoped life would give them so much more. The bartender had long brown permed hair, a lined face, and dead eyes. No one smiled when I entered. A couple of guys didn't even bother looking up from their pool game. The others sat solo on stools by high tables around the bar. There was a dining area, but no one was eating yet. There were tiny windows in the side walls, but the place was mainly lit by artificial light, and, with sunshine more or less banished, it was the kind of trough where a body could lose track of time.

"Hey, fella," the bartender said. "What can I do you for?"

"Can I get a table?" I replied, nodding at the dining section.

"Sure," she said. "Follow me."

She grabbed a menu and stepped out from behind the long bar. The pub carried a wide selection of whiskeys and beers from the old country, each colorful bottle and pump handle promising me relief.

I ordered a beer and Jägermeister and finished them both quickly so I could order refills when the stack of pancakes was delivered. I picked at my food but kept drinking steadily until I was well and truly relaxed. The tremors had stopped, and if I concentrated hard, I could pretend to forget why I was there.

But flashes of Farah One-Eye and Walter the Startled kept reminding me why I was day drinking. If you want to know how ordinary folk feel about murder, let me tell you: terrible. There's no glamor in death. No action-movie heroism. Guilt chews you up until there's nothing left of your soul, just a mangled mess that might have once been something divine.

Everything that happened after midday is a blur. The place filled up with lunchtime trade, that much I remember. There were people at the tables around me, eating, drinking, talking, and laughing. Families, friends. Faces come back to me sometimes, but nothing distinct. I was far gone by that point.

I was on my way back from the restroom when I made my catastrophic error. I stumbled and reached out a hand to steady myself. My fingers caught the back of someone's head. A tiny, rat-faced man whirled around, an angry, drunk glint in his eyes. His T-shirt was now soaked with beer he'd spilled on himself. "You fucking clown."

It wasn't the friendliest of introductions, but even wasted, I didn't rise to his hostile bait and tried to voice an apology, but all that came was a mumble.

"What the fuck did you just say?" he asked, getting to his feet.

I tried to tell him I didn't want any trouble and patted him reassuringly, but my words were indistinct, and my pat came across as a shove.

He swung and caught me with a left hook that sent me flying into his table, knocking over his two friends' drinks.

As I clattered to the floor in a shower of beer to the tune of smashing glasses, his friends rose with the same furious looks.

We soon got into it immediately and were rolling around the place, crashing into tables, smashing things, and brawling up mayhem. There I was, swinging one against three. I think I was holding my own, although it's hard to tally the winners and losers in a drunken ruckus like this.

The cops had a different take, and when they arrested me, they made remarks about having saved me from an ass whooping. I got put into the back of a cop car, under arrest on all kinds of charges I was too wasted to comprehend. While I was driven off to jail, my Range Rover stayed in the parking lot of Blooms Irish Pub with a red-hot murder weapon nestled in the glove compartment.

CHAPTER 46

I lay awake in the holding cell at the San Clemente station house for much of the day and night, slowly sobering up, certain I'd breached my bail conditions for the thing with the sheriff's car, waiting for the moment the cops found the gun in my glove compartment.

Which is why I wasn't surprised when one of the younger cops came in and called my name. This was it. I'd be marched to some interview room and quizzed about my role in Farah's death.

"Yeah," I said, getting to my feet slowly, trying to control my nerves and minimize the crashing pain of my headache.

"You're getting out of here," the cop said, unlocking the tank gate.

For a moment I thought I hadn't heard right.

"Excuse me?"

"You're being released."

Suddenly everything seemed sunshine bright. I shuffled forward unsteadily, dazed and bewildered. I deserved to be punished. Why was this fresh-faced officer releasing me? He was betraying every principle of the oath he'd sworn to uphold the law. Was it a trick?

He let me through the gate, and we walked along a corridor lined with offices, an equipment store, and a briefing room until we reached the booking area, which looked completely unfamiliar to me.

An older cop at the desk gave me back my phone, car keys, and wallet. He didn't seem happy about my release, but I wasn't going to tell the guy I agreed with him.

If this is what passes for law and order in the United States, then we have truly lost our way, I thought.

I signed a couple of slips of paper, and the older cop eyed me coolly. "You can go."

I nodded, still a little surprised and uncertain, and turned for the door. The clock on the wall said 8:43 a.m. If I got my hustle on, I could be back in LA by lunchtime.

I staggered out of the station house into bright day and felt the tender kiss of a cool ocean breeze. I was on a hill, high above the surrounding buildings. Palm trees lined the approach road, and there were more lush trees on the streets to my west, which fell away in tiers as they approached the ocean. The vast blue of the Pacific met the sky in the distance, and as I squinted at the beauty of the scene, I couldn't help but think I'd died in that barroom brawl and somehow gotten a ticket to someone else's paradise.

There was movement to my left.

"Mr. Collard?" a woman said.

I turned to see the speaker lurking in the shadows just beside the entrance. She was about five-six, slim, with black hair pulled into a loose tail. She wore boots, linen trousers, and a dark blouse.

"Maybe," I said, suddenly aware of the mucus filling my mouth.

Had I been sick at some point? I needed a glass of water.

"My name is Detective Rosa Abalos of the Los Angeles Police Department," she replied, and her words were like sparks from a cattle prod and shocked me out of my stupor. "I'm investigating the murder of Walter Glaze."

CHAPTER 47

Looking back on that moment, I wished I'd had the savvy to ask, "Who?"

But I just stood in stunned silence and tried not to look guilty as my heart skipped to about a thousand beats per second.

"We interviewed people who were in Mr. Glaze's nightclub the evening he was shot, and your name was given to us by Attica Douglas," Rosa said. "I ran a search, and guess what? I found you were in custody, so I called down here and convinced the chief there was no point holding you. The pub isn't pressing charges, nor is the man you assaulted, and given the other charges you're already facing—"

"I'm not a criminal," I replied, maybe a little quickly, because I realized I'd interrupted her. "This has just been a difficult year."

"Difficult few years," she said, stepping closer. "Your life seems to have been one bad decision after another."

Tell her what you did, Walter's ghost said.

Yeah, tell her, Farah's spirit chimed in.

"It's just a run of bad luck." My guts were being wrung out like sheets in an old laundry.

How do innocent people behave? I wondered.

"You haven't asked who Walter Glaze is."

I knew it.

"I think I saw the news a few days back. About the shooting."

"I see."

I think I was meant to fill the silence that followed, but the criminal justice system had taught me some hard lessons, one of which was to be economical with words, so I didn't oblige the detective.

"The chief said you were arrested at Blooms Pub. I'm guessing your car is back there."

Gun, Farah's ghost whispered. *She'll find it.*

I pictured the pistol nestled in the glove compartment, tucked beneath the ski mask.

"Let me run you down there," Rosa said. "We can clear up a few things on the way."

"That's okay," I replied, backing away. I was sweating in the morning heat. Or was it flop sweat? "I don't want to cause you any trouble."

"It's no trouble. My car is just right there." She gestured at the lot to the side of the building. "I came all the way down here to talk to you. You'd be doing me a favor."

I knew the way this went. If I didn't take the easy offer, she'd have a couple of uniforms pull me in for questioning when I reached LA, and if they did a roadside stop, they might have cause to search the vehicle. At least this way I could keep her from the car or make a run for it if things went askew.

I nodded reluctantly, and she smiled and started toward her car, a late-model dark blue Chevy Tahoe.

"The passenger door sticks a little," Rosa said as she unlocked the car. "You gotta give it a good pull."

She got behind the wheel, and I did as instructed, but instead of sticking, the door came away easily and I winced as I fell back unexpectedly. The gift of pain from last night's fight, as well as the beating from Frankie Balls and his crew, was now renewed.

"Well, what do you know?" Rosa exclaimed. "You okay there? You look like you're in pain."

Had that been a test? Was she trying to ascertain the extent of my injuries?

"I'm fine," I said. "Just an old back thing from my army days."

She gave a noncommittal grunt as I sat beside her. I made a point of slamming the door as hard as I could, but if my disrespect for her car bothered her, she didn't show it. She just smiled at me, started the engine, and pulled away.

It didn't matter how much chilled air she pumped into the car, it felt oven hot, stifling, and bitter, and I just couldn't stop sweating.

"What took you to Ultima?" Rosa asked as we went under the freeway.

"I don't know," I replied, squinting as we emerged from shadow into bright California sunshine. The tops of the palms that lined the road were an emerald green against a cobalt-blue sky. "I'd heard some good things about it."

"From whom?" she fired back as she pulled a left and joined the on-ramp that led to the freeway.

I hadn't been expecting the question, so it took me a beat to answer.

"My buddy Jim."

"Surname?"

"He doesn't like cops."

"What's not to like?" She flashed a smile. "We're having a friendly conversation here, aren't we?"

"Steadman," I replied.

"Regular there, is he?"

I shook my head. "I think he went with another buddy one time. Probably doesn't even remember it now. He can party pretty hard."

"I see."

That was the second time she'd said those words and she managed to make them sound like "you're damned guilty, you murdering freak."

She drove on in silence, following a semi that proclaimed it was delivering beds and mattresses. I longed for the huge vehicle to stop suddenly so we'd crash into it and die in a flaming fireball. But I wasn't that lucky.

"Did you know Walter Glaze?" she asked.

I shook my head. "I met him that night. Attica introduced us."

"She says you got into it with Glaze."

"We had a moment." I tried to smile, but I was pretty sure it came across as the kind of grimace a hyena might give before it was eaten by a lion.

"Enough to want to kill him?"

"Are you kidding?" I scoffed. "I wouldn't hurt a fly."

"You were in the army, right?"

"Yeah, but I wasn't at the business end of a gun. Engineering Corps. I built bridges and things."

"Weren't you just arrested for fighting?" she asked.

"For defending myself against three men."

She didn't seem convinced but said nothing and pulled off the freeway. We weren't far now. I just had to hold my nerve.

What if she finds the gun? Walter's ghost asked.

It's game over, right? Farah's spirit answered.

The specters of those evil people put a picture of that gun in my head, and I couldn't stop thinking about what would happen if Rosa found it. I felt sick.

"You okay?" the manipulative detective asked.

"Yeah. Just had a bit much to drink. I'm not used to it."

I was so relieved to see the pub up ahead and almost punched the air when Rosa pulled into the parking lot and came to a halt beside my Range Rover.

"I believe this is yours," she said.

I nodded. "Thanks for the ride."

I opened the door and made to leave, but she grabbed my arm.

"Mr. Collard, when you get back to LA, please make sure you stay where we can find you in case we have any follow-up."

Did I gulp? I think I gulped.

She smiled. "Don't look so nervous. It's just routine."

"Routine?"

"Yeah. Routine."

She held my gaze. If this was a shakedown, it was the most subtle, expert shake I'd ever experienced. I couldn't underestimate this cop. She was either incredibly dumb or supersmart, and wise money would take odds on the latter.

She let go of my arm, and I climbed out and shut the door.

Moments later, I was in my Range Rover, heading north on the San Diego Freeway.

Every time I looked in the mirror, I saw Rosa Abalos in her Chevy Tahoe. She was somber, as though my every breath was a disappointment to her. The rear windshield of the Range Rover was made of opaque privacy glass, but I couldn't shake the feeling Rosa could see into my soul and was judging me.

She followed me all the way to Los Angeles.

CHAPTER 48

Ticktock, Walter's ghost repeated for most of the journey.

Farah's spirit was silent, but I sensed she was pleased justice was near.

I drove five miles below the speed limit to ensure Rosa had no excuse to pull me over and search the car. Every lane change, every turn, switch of direction through an intersection made me feel sick because I knew I had to execute all of them perfectly. If I drifted, or got too close to another vehicle, if I messed up at all, I'd give Rosa cause for a stop and search.

So, I spent ninety minutes sweating in the ice-cold air, trembling, and fighting waves of nausea.

I hoped Rosa Abalos would ditch me when we reached LA, but she stayed on my tail all the way home. I thought about going somewhere else, but everywhere carried a risk of discovery of the gun. At least I had certain constitutional rights on my own property. I didn't know exactly what they were, but I knew she couldn't just march up and stick her head into my glove compartment.

After fighting my way through the LA freeway traffic, I finally made it to Edgebrook, pulled into my short driveway, and killed the engine. As I climbed out of the freezing car into the roasting dry heat, I saw two guys I recognized from the pool hall emerge from a custom Dodge Charger. They wore low-slung jeans and tight vests and were covered in tattoos that broadcast their street names, Cutter and Curse. Cutter might have been human once, but his shaved head, scarred face, and bitter eyes spoke of a journey of violence that had turned him into something else. Curse looked as though he'd been born wrong. No scars, but one of those people who chill the spine with malevolence.

As they crossed the road, heading for me, Rosa stopped directly outside my house and got out.

"Detective," I said loudly. "This is a surprise."

Cutter and Curse were almost at the start of my driveway, and they changed course the moment they heard the word *detective*. They hurried along the sidewalk away from my house, eyeballing me over their shoulders.

"I wanted to make sure you didn't run into any more trouble," Rosa said.

She had no idea she'd probably just saved my life.

She knows it's you, Walter's ghost said.

It's hard to look innocent when something inside you is constantly reminding you of your guilt, but I tried my best. My eyes settled on Cutter and Curse, who had settled outside Mrs. Barrera's house, a little tumbledown about fifty yards away from mine on the opposite side of the street. They were both smoking and trying to look nonchalant, but the appearance of innocence was definitely out of reach for these stone-cold killers. They kept murdering me with their eyes.

"You got some mail there," Rosa said, heading for my mailbox.

The little flag was up, and she lowered it before reaching inside to retrieve my mail. I could see bills and junk, but none of that mattered. My eyes were locked on the thick package she'd pulled out. I recognized the print and the envelope, which was about the size of two house bricks. My patron had sent me payment for Farah Younis, and it was being delivered to me by a cop.

Don't open it, I willed her.

Open it, Walter's ghost countered.

Open it, Farah's spirit said.

"You know what, let me grab that," I said, walking over. "Thanks."

"You're welcome, Mr. Collard. It's heavy. What is it? Books?" she replied as I took my mail.

"Yeah," I said, flashing a smile. "A couple of engineering books. I'm trying for a job."

"Well, I'll be seeing you around."

I turned for my house and opened the padlocks Rudy had sold me.

My front door was still broken, so I had no way to stop a home invasion if Cutter and Curse were so minded, because the padlocks were on the outside. I glanced back and saw the men watching Rosa in her cruiser. They would pounce the moment she was gone. She started her engine.

"Detective," I yelled, hurrying toward her.

She rolled down her window as I drew near.

"We've had a couple of robberies round here recently. My own place was broken into," I said. "Those men look like they might be casing houses."

I made a show of pointing at Cutter and Curse, and they tossed their cigarettes and started walking away. A dumb move that made them look even guiltier.

"Thanks, Mr. Collard. I'll check them out," Rosa said.

She pulled away and swung a U-turn, and when they saw the maneuver, Cutter and Curse sprinted into Mrs. Barrera's front garden and disappeared down the side of the house.

While Rosa got on her radio to ask for backup from a local patrol, I jogged to the Range Rover, jumped in, tossed my package onto the passenger seat, reversed down my driveway, and raced off.

CHAPTER 49

Having a cop sniffing around wasn't good from either a practical or psychological perspective. How would I learn to forget these traumatic memories if some detective was always shining the guilt light on them? Would Rosa cotton on to my involvement in Farah's shooting? I thought I'd been so careful, but I hadn't counted on Attica linking me to Walter Glaze.

I tried to wrangle the thoughts as I headed west, toward Hollywood. Frankie Balls had turned my home into a no-go zone with his thugs doorstepping me. I had a cop on my case and still had the gun I'd used to shoot Farah. On the positive side of life's ledger, I had a package from my patron that I assumed contained two hundred grand, which was enough dough to solve a lot of problems.

The gun was easy. I went farther west, out to Malibu to the land of the billboard folk. I parked on the PCH, wrapped the Glock in the ski mask, and walked down a long staircase to the beach. There was hardly anyone around, so I found myself a clear stretch of sand and dug a deep hole with my hands.

The sun was falling toward some distant spot in space, and I enjoyed its warmth against face. Very few people passed me. The occasional jogger or dog walker, but this wasn't the sort of place folk made eye contact. The beaches attracted the homeless and crazies, and no amount of Silicon Valley or high Hollywood money could stop the public right of access to these sands, so the millionaires and billionaires had to put up with folks like me ruining their endless Pacific views.

When the beach was clear and the hole was over a foot deep, I wiped the pistol with my ski mask and dropped both into the dark shadow at the bottom. Some guy with a metal detector might find the gun, but I had wiped it clean of prints, and soon the sand and salt water at high tide would degrade it. I was counting on the hope that no one would remember all the people who'd sat or passed this spot. I scooped all the dug sand back into the hole, and when it was well and truly patted down, I got to my feet, brushed myself off, and walked back to my car.

The sun was touching the horizon by the time I reached the top of the staircase, and the cars on the PCH had their headlights on as they roared past. The glare of their beams was almost blinding as I made the walk north to the Range Rover. It didn't bother me, though, because I'd lightened my load and shed one weighty problem. When I was behind the wheel, I finally checked the contents of the package Rosa had pulled from my mailbox. It was stuffed with hundred-dollar bills, and I really didn't feel the need to count it.

Two hundred thousand bucks.

A bright future for Skye. A new one for me.

I put the package into the glove compartment and locked it. Strobing light filled the Range Rover's cabin as cars raced by, and with each flash and flare, I thought I could just about see the ghosts of Walter and Farah reflected in the rearview mirror. I convinced myself they were on the back seat, but when I turned, there was no one there.

Just me, and my guilt staring back at me.

A new life.

Worth the price? Farah's ghost asked me. *You saw my family. You saw my kids, my husband, and you destroyed them.*

Worth the price, I told myself. *Rid the world of bad people. Do good for me and mine.*

I pulled out my phone and started working on another of my problems. I searched Trulia for rentals in Laurel Canyon and found a beautiful two-bedroom cottage tucked in a little plot near Kirkwood Drive. The surrounding estates were huge, but according to the satellite map, this place had a small garden, which might explain why it was on offer at six thousand a month. I'd always dreamed of living up in the hills, high above the city. My pilgrimages to the mountain behind Joseph Persico had cemented that desire. His place was beautiful and peaceful, and I wanted peace more than anything.

I sent the realtor an email asking to see it as soon as possible. If people like Walter Glaze and Farah Younis could have seats at the best table, so could I. A new place would also keep me away from Frankie Balls and his gang, and it would never occur to them that I'd moved straight from that deadbeat neighborhood to the high hills.

CHAPTER 50

When I woke, I found a message from the realtor inviting me to see the rental at 3:00 p.m. I spent the day killing time, driving around, daydreaming about a better life. I reached Laurel Canyon at two thirty and spent twenty-five minutes cruising the neighborhood before going to meet the realtor, a guy called Jay Nerfons.

He was the kind of man who would split folk right down the middle. Some would want to punch him because they'd see his cheesy smile and easy charm as sure signs of his insincerity. Others would look at the trinkets of a billboard life, his Porsche, designer suit, sharp shoes, shades, and aura of wealth and success and assume he was the Answer Keeper, the sage who held the secret to a happier life.

Me? I just wanted the two-bedroom cottage that was my gateway to a better world.

He pulled in through the open gates a little after me, and we both parked in the small drive. The cottage was made of gray stone and stood one and a half stories high. The upper gable end had been covered with wood panels that had been painted grass green. The house was close to the road, and the property boundary seemed to have been carved out of the grounds of the neighboring estate. The garden wasn't much bigger than a tennis court, but that was fine by me because I wasn't much of an outdoorsman anymore.

Jay Nerfons strode across the drive like a demigod.

"Peyton," he said. "Nice ride. Classic."

He gestured at the car of poor dreamers and eccentric millionaires. I was holding the package full of money and suddenly realized I was 20 percent of the way to being in the latter category.

"I love her," I replied, trying my best to sound as though I belonged. "Magnificent machine. I've had her a while and just can't bear to let her go."

He nodded. "What brings you to this neighborhood?"

"I split from my wife," I replied.

"Sorry to hear that," Jay said.

"What sort of references does the landlord need?" I asked.

"One character or employer," Jay replied. "The owner asks for one month security and two months' deposit, so she's pretty flexible as long as she's holding the tenant's money."

I nodded gratefully. I didn't want someone who'd make me jump through hoops.

"Let's take a look inside."

He opened the door and took me into a decent living area.

"Nice big living space down here and two bedrooms upstairs either side of the full-size bathroom. You should take a look." Jay gestured toward a staircase that stood opposite the front door.

I climbed the hardwood stairs and came to the half-story landing, which looped back from the top of the stairs and took me to a bathroom at the front of the building. The bedrooms lay on either side and lost height at their edges as the eaves of the roof ate into their space. There were a couple of double beds and some closets. It was low-key by comparison to most of the homes in the hills, but it was more than enough for a deadbeat.

Looking back, I'm not sure whether I was in my right mind at any point during those months after my release from prison, but what I did next seems particularly crazy. I took twenty-five grand out of the package I was carrying and crouched down by the closet in the east bedroom. I removed the drawer at the bottom and shoved the package inside, pushing it right up against the back. I kept checking over my shoulder, but there was no sign of Jay as I slid the drawer back into place. Given the cops and villains on my tail, the money would be safer well away from me, and I couldn't think of anywhere better than my new home.

"What line of work are you in, Peyton?" Jay asked when I went downstairs.

"I'm between jobs," I said truthfully. "But I have substantial savings." That wasn't a lie either. "Three months, right? One month deposit, and two up front?" I confirmed.

I had more than that stuffed into my pockets.

"That'd do it," Jay replied.

"Then I'll take it," I said with a smile.

I'd just bought myself a whole new life.

CHAPTER 51

Everything in the square world takes time. Even a cool guy like Jay Nerfons expected a legit bank transfer, not dirty bundles of cash, and tellers give the side-eye if you deposit unusual sums into your account, so you have to go little and often.

It took three days to put enough money into my account for the security deposit and first month's rent, and I did it by visiting branches all over LA, so no teller saw more than five hundred bucks. Jim had agreed to act as my character reference.

In the meantime, I was homeless, traveling around with some of my cash, sleeping in the car, and trying to find the courage to go back to my old place to grab some things that had sentimental value. My old laptop with Skye's baby photos, a Best Dad T-shirt Toni had bought on our daughter's behalf one Father's Day, and my uniform and medals. But I knew Frankie's men would be casing the place, and if they caught me I might not escape again.

When you want something real bad, every second is an hour and every hour a week.

I spent my days sitting in the Range Rover, willing my phone to ring, and finally on the afternoon of the fourth day, the call came. My money transfer had cleared and my testimonial from Jim had checked out. Jay Nerfons, real estate's golden boy, would be at the property with my new keys the following morning.

My plan to leave my old life behind was coming into focus, but I was insufficiently Buddhist in my attitude to stuff. I wasn't prepared to let it go. So, I waited until two in the morning and went back to my old neighborhood.

I parked a couple of blocks from my old house and walked the still streets, checking for any sign of Frankie's crew. I figured they'd have given up by now, and it seemed I was right. There was no sign of them anywhere, so I crept into my garden and opened the padlocks that secured the front door.

It creaked as I pushed it open, and I held my breath waiting for disaster. Nothing happened, so I went inside. The place was as I'd left it—a mess. I didn't dare turn on the lights, and crept around the house, gathering the few things that were truly precious to me.

As I made my way toward the front door, I was sure I heard a noise coming from Skye's room. A shiver ran up my spine and set my skin tingling. I stopped and listened but couldn't hear anything other than the light traffic speeding along the freeway high above the house. I started to think I'd imagined the noise and got moving again.

I swear I almost wet myself when the roar came, and a figure lurched out of Skye's bedroom yelling, "Get out! Get out, motherfucker!"

We tussled, grabbing each other's arms, and when my fingers touched bare flesh, I realized the terrifying man wasn't wearing any clothes.

"Oh, Peyton, fuck, it's you," the man said, and he stepped back and switched on the light.

It was Jim, and he was buck naked and swaying. He was completely wasted.

"Where the fuck have you been? I came by to check on you after Rick's tonight," Jim said.

"Naked?" I asked. My thumping heart was settling back to normal rhythm.

"I climbed in the back window. It's broken, by the way. Saw the bed and wanted a sleep," he slurred. "Man needs to be comfortable. It's uncivilized to sleep in clothes."

"Cover it up," I suggested as he leaned into Skye's bedroom and switched on the light.

I walked over and turned it off.

"What the fuck!"

"We need to keep it dark," I explained, switching off the hallway light too. "Frankie Balls is after me."

"He responsible for the padlocks?" he asked, feeling around for his clothes.

"Yeah," I replied. "Broke in and robbed me a few nights back."

While he stumbled, fumbled, and cursed his way into his clothes, I picked up my bag of stuff and headed for the living room. As he joined me, doing up the buttons on his jeans and setting his jacket on his shoulders, I heard an engine's roar outside. I ran to the living room window and saw Cutter and Curse in their modified Dodge Charger right outside.

"What's up?" Jim asked.

"They're here. We have to leave. We can go through the back window. Where's your car?"

"Dunno," Jim replied, peering out of the window. "Rick's? I probably walked here."

His eyes narrowed.

"Come on," I said, urging him toward the bedrooms.

"Jim Steadman doesn't run from nobody."

He reached beneath his jacket and pulled a pistol out of an underarm holster.

"What the hell?" I declared. "Don't."

I tried to stop him, but he brushed me off and staggered to the door. He pulled it open and fired the first shot without any warning. The loud bang set my ears ringing.

"You motherfuckers are trespassing," Jim yelled. "And I'm standing my ground. The dead gotta take responsibility for their own funerals from here on."

The first shot had been high in the air, and it had stopped Cutter and

Curse in their tracks. The next barrage was aimed at their feet. Or as well aimed as could be expected of a lunatic drunk.

Frankie Balls's men sprinted to their car as bullets hit the ground around them. I saw lights go on up and down the street as Cutter and Curse jumped into the Charger and escaped into the night.

"Pussies!" Jim yelled after them.

I rushed over and urged him out. "We gotta go."

He registered faces at some of the neighboring windows. "Okay, okay. Don't fuss me," he said. He stumbled down the steps into the garden. "Did you see those punks run?"

"I did. Thanks, Jim. You saved my hide."

"Damn right I did."

I padlocked the front door, set my bag on my shoulder, and hurried toward my car. "I've got to run, Jim. I'll see you at Rick's."

He was shuffling across my garden, wasted, the alcohol probably combining with fresh night air to renew his buzz. He looked around vacantly. "Make sure you do. Man's got no business drinking alone when he's got friends."

I started across the garden toward my car but saw something in the gutter near where the Charger had been parked. I ran over to take a closer look. It was a gun, a 9mm pistol. The word *Beretta* was clear in the orange glow of the nearby streetlamp. Cutter or Curse must have dropped the weapon when they panicked and ran. I crouched to pick it up and started running.

I was breathless and sweaty by the time I'd covered the two blocks back to my car. I don't know why, maybe it was a subliminal need to be close to someone familiar, but I soon found myself on Skye and Toni's street. I parked a short distance from her building, and once the adrenaline had left my system and my heart had settled, I fell asleep in the driver's seat and had nightmares about what Frankie Balls and his men might have done to me if it hadn't been for Jim.

CHAPTER 52

I used to see her every night. Her smile so wide, her eyes so alive, hair whipping around to form doodles in the air. Never moving, I experienced her like a slide set, one beautiful moment at a time. The moments I wished I could take back. The moments before the accident. Freya Persico.

She came to me that night. Except she wasn't her—carefree Freya. In the way dreams do, people, times, and places had changed, and it was Farah driving with Walter in the passenger seat. They didn't smile as I drew alongside them.

They were judging me.

Waiting for my mistake.

Waiting for the fall.

"Fuck! Peyton!"

I woke, groggy and disoriented. Toni's face dominated my vision, and for a moment I didn't know where I was. I went back to the night Toni and I had first made love when we were in high school. She was so beautiful. I'd never wanted anyone so much.

I tried to caress her face, but glass stopped me, and I realized I wasn't with my teen sweetheart. This was present Toni, and she banged on the car window, staring at me, her face a map of anger rather than ecstasy.

"What the fuck are you doing here?"

She stormed away, and I wiped my face and stumbled out of the car and jogged to catch up.

"It's not what it looks like."

"Not what it looks like?" She stopped and faced me. "I get up to put out the trash and see my wasted ex parked down the street, sleeping in his car. It looks like you're fucking stalking me, Peyton. That's what it looks like."

"That's why I said it's not like that," I replied.

"Are you a stalker now, Peyton? Is that what you are?"

"No. Of course not. I just ran into some trouble and had to spend the night in the car—"

"Oh, Peyton—" she cut me off.

"Don't 'Oh, Peyton.' It's okay. I'm moving house. The new place is amazing. You'll really—I mean Skye will really like it."

"A new place?" she asked. I was familiar with her "bullshit tone," which was deployed whenever she thought I was lying. "And that's your car?"

She pointed at the Range Rover, and I nodded.

"I'm getting the keys from the realtor today," I said. "It's in Laurel Canyon."

"So, you live in the hills now, but you're sleeping in a car outside my home?"

"I'm not outside. Not directly anyway."

"Outside my home," she continued. "But you have a place in Laurel Canyon?"

"I know it looks bad and sounds crazy, but it's gospel," I replied. "Come by later. I'll send you the address."

"Sure, Peyton. You do that. I'd love to see your home in the hills. I pray this isn't some trip," Toni said seriously. "I really do. I hope you're going up, Peyton, getting your life back together. Not falling the other way."

"You'll come out and see the place and make your own decision about which way I'm heading."

She still didn't seem convinced, but after years of disappointments, I couldn't blame her. She continued toward her building, and I went back to my big car and my better life.

CHAPTER 53

Jay Nerfons was a king. No, a god. I say that without fear of being accused of blasphemy, because no man could have transformed my life the way this magnificent critter did. His bone-white smile, bronze skin, and golden hair were waiting for me with a set of keys that glittered silver in the bright sunshine.

He offered to show me around, but I didn't want that. I paced nervously while he rounded out his good-guy patter, watching the keys dangling from his fingertips the way a velociraptor would eye loose entrails. Thunder filled my chest, and I could hardly take a wholesome breath. It was as though I was pulling off a heist.

I knew I didn't belong there. Sure, I'd paid my money and signed the lease, but gutter dwellers like me aren't meant to ascend to the billboard life. We stay far below, and over time life grinds us further, crushing us down, down, down.

Jay Nerfons was saying something about my security deposit, and the golden sun was catching him at an angle that bleached his hair and skin, making it seem as though he had a burning white aura. About right for a man who was my deliverer.

He finally stopped talking and handed me the keys, and I felt such blessed relief that my dream was becoming real, that my good fortune would not be snatched from me at the last minute, and, most importantly, that I could do right by my daughter.

"You take care now," he said, walking to his Porsche.

"Thanks, Jay," I replied as he slid behind the wheel. He screeched out of the driveway—my driveway—with a casual wave and a parting thumbs-up.

I looked at the keys and could hardly believe they were real. There were three of them. One for the front, one for the back, and one for a lock as yet undiscovered. Jay had probably explained it, but I was too jacked on adrenaline and optimism to have paid him much mind.

After trying the wrong key, I got the front door open.

This was it.

My new life.

I stepped inside. There was a musty smell I didn't remember from before, but it was nothing an open window wouldn't take care of. The place was smaller than I recalled and was getting stuffy in the late-morning heat. I checked my phone; 11:03 a.m., a time that would always be significant as it marked the death of the old me.

You're just passing through, Walter's ghost said. *Nothing meaningful is built in blood.*

The old me might have died at the moment, but Walter was still on board. I shook my head, eager to be clear of the spirit that was trying to ruin a banner experience.

The worst punishment is to eat nectar and taste ash, Farah's ghost whispered. *Your new life will be as your old, deadbeat.*

Part of me knew these voices in my head couldn't be real, but why would my subconscious turn against me in victory? I didn't want to think about the money that had brought me here. Good people and bad die every day, some through ill health, some because of bad luck, but others die because a government chose not to ban cigarettes twenty years ago or because some federal worker set a high-risk threshold of deaths per million for a pesticide, or some corporation concealed a product safety issue. Was I any worse than any of these? Was I more at fault than a soldier with a rifle? A drone operator taking out a wedding party in some distant desert? A politician deciding the fate of millions with the flourish of a pen? I didn't think so.

You had it coming, I told my unwelcome guests. *You weren't innocent. If I hadn't finished you, someone else would have.*

It didn't matter what I told them, suddenly my new home didn't seem so inviting and perfect. The walls appeared to shrink inward with the pressure of guilt. My new life started to feel like my old.

"Fuck this," I said aloud. "You're not going to take this from me."

I couldn't let some misguided sense of remorse suck the sweetness out of my success. Guilt was the business of fire-and-brimstone Sunday-school preachers, not the new me.

Toni saved me from my cursed reflections and steered her old gray Civic through my gates. Skye sat beside her, all wide-eyed and full of wonder as she took in my new place. I watched them through the living room window before stepping outside.

"Peyton, this place is crazy," Toni said as she exited the car.

"It's awesome, Dad," Skye agreed as she joined us, and her beaming smile lit my world.

She'd wandered over to the mouth of the driveway and was peering along the street at the big estates. You could see only the rooftops of a couple of mansions from my place.

"And look at the mailbox," Skye remarked, running over to a cabinet built into one of the stone columns that supported the gates. The letter slot was on the front of the column so the resident wasn't even disturbed by the arrival of mail. "It's like something from a castle."

"How did you do this?" Toni asked.

"I got my disability payout," I replied, glossing over so much ugliness. "Come inside."

I took them into the living room. I'd opened the French doors to air the house, and the place was full of the scents of flowers and herbs growing in the surrounding gardens. Some of the beautiful smells came from the colorful plants in my tiny patch of California.

Skye was open-mouthed, and Toni turned to me with something approaching admiration.

"I'll be honest, when I saw you sleeping in a car, I thought you were heading for the bottom, but this—"

"Dad, this is amazing," Skye interrupted, and I'm not too modest to say I felt a swell of pride.

"Go check out your room," I replied, pointing at the stairs.

She ran up, leaving me alone with Toni. There was a time when I might have tried to use my newfound success to try to win her back, but even a deadbeat like me could see my ex was with Jack now, and that was okay. I was happy for her, truly. She deserved better than me, and he clearly couldn't be any worse.

"How are her symptoms?" I asked, referring to the diabetes scare that had helped make a hard decision easier.

"Mostly cleared up," Toni replied. "It really made me think about what matters."

I nodded.

My connection with Toni was limited to being a good dad to our daughter, and it was in that mode that I pulled out an envelope I'd stuffed into the back pocket of my jeans.

"I want to give you this," I said, handing it to Toni.

I hadn't bothered sealing it, and she looked inside immediately.

"Jesus, Peyton." Her eyes widened. "How much is in here?"

"Twenty thousand. Put it away for her. It's the start of a college fund."

"Disability?" Toni asked with more than a hint of skepticism.

I nodded. "It's good money."

"I'm happy for you," she said with a gentle smile that reminded me of better times. "You deserve some luck."

She was right. I was owed some good luck to even out all the bad. And even the shady source of my fortune couldn't overshadow this bright day. Farah Younis and Walter Glaze were a couple of villains who deserved nothing better than the ends I'd given them. Here, in this place, I was putting my reward to good use, building a better future for my daughter.

"I've been worried about you," Toni went on. "I'm glad life is coming right for you. Skye needs her dad."

She slipped the envelope of cash into her purse as Skye rushed downstairs.

"It's awesome, Dad."

"Did you pick a room?" I asked.

"Can I have the one that overlooks the backyard?" she replied.

It was the master suite, but I didn't need anything fancy. Even the smaller of the two bedrooms was better than anything I was used to.

I nodded, and she squealed with delight.

"Come look," Skye urged. She didn't wait for us to follow and raced up the stairs with a "Come on."

It had been a long time since I'd seen her so excited and happy, and it felt good.

My kids will never know this, Farah's ghost said, but I wasn't going to let specters spoil my day.

My daughter's face told me I'd done right. Toni felt it, too, because she was smiling like a lottery winner.

"Listen, Pey," she said. "Can you do me a favor? I've got a job interview and Jack is out of town tomorrow. No one else can step in for me. Can you pick Skye up from school?"

Just like that, I'd become reliable and trustworthy. Sort of. She had run out of other people to ask. But last resort was still a resort, and it was a start. A chance to prove myself.

"Where's the interview?" I asked.

"It's for an admin role at an entertainment agency in Beverly Hills. It's a big pay raise if I get it. Gotta keep up now that you're setting a new standard."

"Sure," I said with a swell of pride. "Happy to."

"Thanks." She smiled again.

"Come on," Skye yelled down.

"We'd better go before we get in trouble," I suggested, and Toni started up the stairs.

I followed her, feeling more human than I'd felt for a long time.

CHAPTER 54

Life is measured in landmarks—births, exams, qualifications, jobs, marriages, deaths—but sometimes the smallest waypoints give us a better sense of how things have changed. Take the Monday after Toni and Skye had come to visit. I'd be bringing my kid home for the first time and wanted the place to be better than awesome, so I went to the mall and bought new bedsheets, cutlery, and kitchenware, and found myself in the hand appliances section of a cookware store, looking at the cheese graters. I smiled at the mundanity. I hadn't owned a cheese grater since before my prison years, but here I was standing in the Perfect Chef in the Farmer's Market in my surf shorts and neon palm tree T-shirt, looking every inch the normal functioning human as I adjudicated between graters. In the end I went for one designed to look like a turtle with serrated blades built into its shell. It wasn't the most practical, but Skye would find it cute.

I paid cash for all my purchases and stopped for a long lunch at a Brazilian grill in the Farmer's Market. I had chargrilled seasoned beef, surrounded by my bags of shopping, watching the world, basking in the feeling I belonged. I was no different from those eating and chatting around me and was well on my way to reclaiming my place as one of the functioning folk. Only this time I'd be up in the clouds, living billboard, not down in the mud where I'd spent so long. I wasn't sure how long I'd stay in Laurel Canyon, but I could afford at least the year I'd signed up for, more if I went for the clean room job. But that was tomorrow's problem. Today I could just enjoy feeling normal.

A little after two, I grabbed my stuff, went to the parking structure, and put all the bags into the Range Rover trunk, before climbing in and starting my journey south to Centennial High School to fetch Skye.

The sun seemed to shine more brightly, and the sky was a deeper shade of blue than I'd seen for a while. The city, which had lost its luster long ago, was regaining its high polish. From the low buildings that spread along the broad avenues and boulevards that all appeared to have been freshly licked with paint, to the bowing palms and lush trees that sprung here and there from the sidewalks. The people, usually so hostile, now seemed familiar, like they might be old friends from way back when.

I stopped behind a black BMW M5 at a set of lights on South Central Boulevard, a couple of blocks from the school, and not far from my old place on Edgebrook, and I got the shock of my life when someone started banging on the passenger window of the Range Rover.

I turned, ready to step on the gas, but saw a familiar face.

"Let me in, Peyton," Jim said. He was mad as hell.

I popped the central locking, and he climbed inside as the lights changed.

"What the fuck have you been doing?" he asked.

I followed the BMW when it started to move. My heart raced, and I took a quick look at him to see his face traffic-light red.

"Why have I got the cops coming around asking me what my car was doing in Venice the night before some guy got shot?"

Thrusters took my heart rate up by a factor of ten, and I suddenly understood his anger.

"Don't bring me into whatever it is you've been doing, Peyton," he said. "I won't do any more time for anyone. Fucking cops."

My mind was whirring. I was no good to myself or anyone else in a state of panic, so I took a couple of deep, calming breaths. When had Jim been in prison? It didn't surprise me, but he'd never talked about it.

"What the fuck have you been doing, Peyton?" He eyed me closely.

I didn't answer. I couldn't. Jim wasn't a straight shooter, but he wasn't a murderer, least not as far as I knew, and with the police tapping him for answers, I couldn't trust him not to tell them something that would let him cut a deal in exchange for hooking me.

"I know cops," Jim went on, "and this one is a digger. Like a terrier, she'll keep going till she unearths the rat and takes him off in her jaws."

I shuddered, imaging giant teeth closing around me.

"What did you tell her?" I asked.

"It speaks," Jim observed. "I told her the truth. Most of the time I'm too wasted to know who the hell is doing what. Anyone can take my car any night of the week. My keys are on the counter half the time."

"Thanks, man," I said. I took a couple of easier breaths.

"I didn't do it for you," he replied, his voice colder than a penguin's behind. "Pull over."

I signaled and stopped in a turnout.

He climbed out and glared at me. "Keep me clear of your shit, Peyton, or God help you," he said before he slammed the door and stalked away.

The smell of his stale booze breath hung in the car as I drove on. He wasn't a friend, at least not in any real sense. He wasn't worried about me or the fact I might have murdered someone. He was stirred only by his own skin and keeping it out of prison, which struck me as kind of selfish.

I had a new life now, and I had to do whatever I could to protect it. That meant staying away from people like Jim Steadman and the alcohol-soaked gutter in which he lived.

CHAPTER 55

"Dad, you're going the wrong way."

I blinked and saw the familiar streets of Lynwood. We were almost at my old place on Edgebrook. The house I'd left behind. The house being watched by Frankie Balls. I was so preoccupied by Jim's words and the possibility of the detective linking me to Walter's death that I'd been on autopilot.

"Sorry, kiddo," I said. "Got a lot on my mind."

"That's okay," she replied with a fake smile.

I signaled right and took the next turn, and soon we were heading away from the liquor stores, body shops, and motels and rising into the hills where the billboarders lived.

Skye chatted the whole journey, and this time I tried listening. She told me all about her day and about being called out by her teacher for not listening. But she didn't miss a beat and immediately recounted the teacher's words to the class. She was smart like that. She had a better brain than me. She'd make a fine doctor. She was kind, too, like Toni before I screwed up our lives.

We pulled up at the cottage gates. I was about to jump out, when Skye said, "Let me do it."

Before I could answer, she climbed out of the Range Rover and drew back the gates, which I didn't lock. The fancy homes had remote barriers, so I wasn't quite a fully paid-up billboarder yet.

Just a fraud living among them, Farah's ghost said.

I ignored the dig. These spirits weren't real. Just defects of my mind. Echoes of sins troubling the sinner, as the old pastor used to say when my mom still believed in God enough to drag my reluctant young feet to church.

Skye waved me through, and as I crawled forward, I saw her go to the mailbox built into the gate column. I parked in front of the cottage and got out of the car.

"You got mail, Dad," Skye said, and I turned to see her holding a package.

My head started thumping and my heart stuttered. It was from my patron. I recognized the envelope and writing. The man or woman who'd hired me to kill Walter Glaze and Farah Younis had found me.

"Let me take that, honey," I said, hurrying over.

I grabbed the package and ignored her puzzled look. Was my stress showing? Did I seem weird? Probably, but one of the advantages of having a track record as a drunk is everyone gets used to unpredictability. Even if she suspected something, she'd know better than to question it.

I steered her inside the cottage.

"Wow, Dad," she said when she saw the big TV and cushions and throws and other touches I'd added since her last visit.

The place was starting to look like a home.

"Nice, hey?" I said. "Kick back and relax. Turn on the TV."

"Kick back and relax? Who even says that?" She smiled, grabbed the remote, and flopped backward onto the couch.

I walked to the kitchen and tore open the package, wondering how my patron had got my new address. Inside I found five bundles of twenty-dollar bills wrapped with $1,000 paper belts. There was another URL printed on a piece of white card. If past experience was anything to go by, the person named on the audio recording would be worth half a million dead.

There's a name for people like you, Walter's ghost said.

Serial killer, Farah's specter whispered.

Assassin, I told myself. *Vigilante. At least find out who it is. See why they deserve to die.*

And find out who's paying you, Walter's ghost said. *So you know who turned you in when the cops finally put the bracelets on.*

The spirit was right. I was exposed. My patron knew enough to send me away forever. In contrast I knew nothing about them.

I drifted toward the archway that separated the kitchen diner from the living room and watched Skye flicking through the channels.

Half a million could set her up right and buy me out of my trashy life forever. I'd become a fixed billboard, not some gutter dweller who was hanging on to the high life by his fingertips. There would be no going back with that much money. What harm would it do to find out the name of the next target?

The noose is tightening, Walter's ghost said.

The spirit was almost right. The noose wasn't tightening, but I had to be careful. I couldn't access the URL from here, not with Detective Rosa Abalos on my tail.

"You hungry, kiddo?" I asked Skye. "How would you like an In-N-Out burger?"

CHAPTER 56

I'm a rotten father. I mean termite-infested, weather-lashed, Florida swamp shack rotten. On the outside, I was being a good father. I was heading east along Santa Monica Boulevard, and Skye was sitting beside me munching the last of her French fries. We'd eaten at the In-N-Out on Sunset, and for a while I'd been able to pretend I was a regular dad out with his daughter for smiles, a burger, and a shake. But I wasn't a regular dad. I was using the meal as an excuse to get out of the house to clue myself up on my next target.

"Where are we going?" Skye asked.

"I just have to run an errand," I replied. "It won't take long."

We were in one of the oldest Los Angeles neighborhoods, a mix of redbrick warehouses and deco buildings sprinkled with modern stores and mini-malls. It seemed darker here. Fewer billboards, streetlights, and signs illuminated the people on sidewalks who were little more than shadows against the lit-up storefronts. We crawled by bondage and fetish stores, cut-rate medical centers, and pop-up churches advertising salvation with handwritten signs. God was only passing through, a fly-by-night tenant for as long as the failing economy kept rents cheap.

"Mom says you want to be a doctor."

She nodded and ate another couple of fries.

"That's really cool, Skye."

"Dad, no one says *cool* anymore." She smiled and shook her head with the mock pity kids are so good at.

"Why a doctor?" I asked, smiling back.

She went from clown to judge in an instant. Her face fell, and she reminded me of the old guy in black robes who put me in jail for the accident. All somber and responsible.

"Where are we going?" she asked.

"Is it a secret?" I countered, still smiling.

"No. I just don't want to talk about it now. We're having fun." She smiled, but it was forced.

"Okay. Cool," I replied, and she went from judge to clown with a genuine grin.

"Not cool," she said. "So where are we going?"

"I just don't want to talk about it now." I was mocking her, but it was also the truth.

"Okay. Also not cool," she replied. "But cool. People are entitled to space. Secrets even."

I guess she'd reached the age at which she could surprise me with her maturity, and this was one of those moments.

People are entitled to space. Secrets even.

I was using my entitlement to research another target.

Victim, Farah's ghost said.

"Bill, Laura's dad, googled you after we met them in the park," Skye revealed, and my heart sank as I imagined another of Skye's friends distancing herself. According to Toni, it had happened a lot during my trial.

"I'm sorry, kiddo," I said.

"It's okay," she assured me. "He told Laura he felt sorry for you. Said it must have been a traumatic experience. That you'd paid your debt, which meant society had to forgive you."

I wanted to buy Bill a beer.

"You know I forgive you, too," Skye said, and I choked up. "I know you're not a bad man, Dad, not like some people said."

"What people?" I asked, suddenly wondering about my daughter's pain. Had the isolation she'd experienced come with bullying? Had people judged her for my crime?

"It doesn't matter," she replied softly. "I know you'd never hurt anyone deliberately."

The lump in my throat grew.

"You're a good man," she went on. "At least you always try to be. It was an accident. Just one of those bad-luck things. It made life hard for everyone. I'm sorry it happened. It must have been difficult."

"It was," I told her. "What makes you so sure?"

"Sure of what?" she asked.

"That I'm a good man?" I choked back heavy sorrow.

"Because you're my dad," she replied. "And I know in my heart I came from somewhere good."

My eyes filled, and I wiped away the welling grief I felt for the man I'd once been. The man she still believed in.

We drove the rest of the journey in silence, and I pretended not to notice her concerned looks.

"An internet café?" Skye said as I turned into the lot behind the windowless building on the corner of 11th Street. "Is it a museum?"

"I just need a new USB drive," I replied, unbuckling my seat belt. "I won't be long."

I turned on the radio so she'd have company and stepped outside, simultaneously proud of her and ashamed of myself. The sun was long gone, but the glow of the city edged the rooftops and caught the underbelly of a jet making its descent into LAX as I crossed the lot and went inside.

I paid the front-desk employee, who directed me to a terminal at the back. I passed kids playing games, making use of the café's bandwidth for a zero-lag experience their parents probably couldn't afford to give them at home.

At the terminal, I typed the URL into the browser search bar. The screen went black for a moment before an audio file appeared. I turned on the ancient, dust-covered speakers and leaned in.

"Father Richard Gibson of Sylvia Park," the familiar machine voice said. Clinical and robotic, it told me nothing about my patron, other than that they were careful. "He's a retired priest. A serial abuser of children. He's worth half a million."

I exhaled sharply. I'd been right about the bounty on this target, but this was a change of direction. Walter Glaze and Farah Younis had been mob-affiliated, and I'd assumed my patron was connected to that world somehow. Maybe the parent of a drug addict who'd overdosed? A cop who had the evidence but couldn't bring a case to court? But an abusive priest suggested someone with a broader vigilante mission. I wondered who it could be and why they'd chosen me. Was it someone I knew? Jim didn't have this kind of money, did he? Someone from my army days who knew I'd bottomed out after the accident?

I ran a search for Father Richard Gibson of Sylvia Park and found a couple of news articles about a former priest turned artist who did atmospheric paintings in oil that were reminiscent of Edward Hopper. The isolation and loneliness of guilt, maybe?

I clicked on one of the articles in the *SoCal Herald*, a local paper, and saw a photo of a kindly looking old man in a zigzag pullover standing next to an easel. Gibson had sad eyes, but I wouldn't have called them evil. In fact, with a few extra pounds and a fluffy white beard, I thought he could have had a second career as a store Santa.

I went back to the search results and scrolled down. More articles about this man who'd turned from priesting to painting and how grateful he was that God had given him a talent he could use in his retirement. I went to the second page of search results and found what I was looking for in a backwater bulletin board called the Opus Insider, a chat set up for the victims of church abuse. There anonymous posters alleged a Sylvia Park priest had assaulted them as children. One of the posters had written, "Completely unrelated, I hope Father Richard Gibson is doing okay wherever he is." The other poster had replied, "LOL," and made liberal use of the angry emoji.

The thread hadn't been active for six months, but it was still up. Gibson would have had ample time to protest his innocence and demand its removal if he in fact had a clear conscience.

A priest.

A man trusted by the community to do good.

To be the instrument of the divine on earth.

I imagined how the parents of these abused children would feel, and a fatherly rage kindled as I thought of Skye wandering into Gibson's path. I could rid the world of wickedness and make half a million dollars in the process. It wasn't even a difficult decision.

I closed the browser, cleared the cache, and shut down the computer.

You go, killer, Walter's ghost said. *You're going to murder a priest with Detective Abalos on your case?*

Maybe I'd grown overconfident, or maybe the thought of becoming a semi-millionaire had blinded me to the risks, but I wasn't worried about Rosa Abalos, in spite of the poison of self-doubt the specter was dripping into my mind.

Outside, I crossed the parking lot, thinking about Gibson, and climbed into the driver's seat.

"Let's go home," I said to Skye. "You can pick a movie for us."

"Where's the USB?" she asked.

"They didn't have any," I replied, making use of the expertise drinking had given me in lying. "That's what took me so long. He was checking in the back."

Skye frowned but didn't say anything else. I started the car and headed for home, where I could pretend to be a good father after this brief interlude preparing for murder.

CHAPTER 57

Toni picked up our daughter just before ten. Skye left while I was sleeping, so I woke on the day of my arraignment sober and alone.

I didn't mind being sober, but I didn't like being alone.

I showered, grabbed some dry toast, jumped into the Range Rover, and drove south to the Compton Courthouse. The modern white building was broken up by black stripes and looked like a giant air filter, inhaling wrong and exhaling justice. It was a monument to countless lost hopes and broken dreams.

I entered the building determined not to do time for driving into the sheriff's car. I would not have my hopes stolen or my dreams broken.

I met Mitch Hoffman outside the courtroom, and as we stood in the huge space surrounded by stagnant air and the serious whispers of lawyers, defendants, witnesses, and press, I reappraised the guy. A drowning man might be glad of a rotten hunk of timber tossed his way by the raging sea, but I wasn't drowning anymore, and I could see the flaws in this piece of flotsam. He was nervous and shifty, with eyes that never met mine. My initial assessment was wrong; this man was not like George Costanza. He was like someone who'd been bitten by a radioactive Costanza and acquired a manyfold magnification of his defects.

"So, they've offered two years minimum security if you plead guilty to assault and criminal damage," Mitch said. His voice was as feeble as an old man's punch and inspired no confidence.

"I'm not going to prison," I replied.

"If you fight this and are found guilty at trial, you could get fifteen years," Mitch protested. I'm doing him a service because his voice wasn't capable of protest. I'm inferring intent. And he still didn't look me in the eye.

The American justice system is not for the faint of heart. It's for wealthy gamblers. You have to be rich to afford a decent lawyer, and you have to be willing to gamble because only a nerves-of-steel adrenaline junkie would turn down the certainty of an easy two against the prospect of a hard fifteen.

"I'm not going back to prison," I repeated, and Mitch nodded wearily.

"Okay, okay," he said. "I'll see what I can do. I think you're making a mistake, by the way, but it's your life. We'd better go in."

He shuffled toward the courtroom, and I followed a few paces behind so no one would think we were together. I was in a better suit than my lawyer, who wore a brown two-piece that was frayed at the hems and looked as though it might have belonged to his Depression-era grandpa. His shoes were scuffed and his heels badly worn at a diagonal.

The courtroom was a drab place with cream walls and wood paneling. We sat near the front and waited twenty minutes for my case to be called. The judge was speeding through the arraignments, keeping the wheels of justice turning as one defendant after another was crushed by an expedient guilty plea. When my docket was called, Mitch and I took the hot seats, directly opposite the gnarly old judge who'd long since surrendered the battle against old man hair. It sprouted from his nose and ears, and his eyebrows were as wild as any jungle. His jowls sagged like an ancient and faithful mutt's, but who was going to tell a judge with power over liberty he looked like horseshit?

The clerk read out my name and the charges, which immediately deepened the furrows on Old Hairy's craggy face.

"How does the defendant plead?" he snarled once the clerk had finished.

Mitch got to his feet. I noticed his hands were trembling as he fumbled with a blank piece of paper.

"Erm . . . your honor, we've erm . . . that is to say, the defendant pleads guilty."

It took me a moment to realize what had just happened.

"What the actual fuck," I said. I couldn't help myself.

"Excuse me?" Old Hairy exclaimed.

"I'm sorry, your honor, I didn't mean to cuss, but my lawyer got it wrong." I turned to Super Costanza, Mitch. "You got it wrong, didn't you?"

The hopeless attorney in his New Deal grandpa's suit gulped and nodded. "I haven't been to trial in years. I'm out of practice." He leaned close to whisper. "And no one fights a case like this."

"Your honor," I cried out. "Surely this is a mistrial or something."

"It's not a mistrial, Mr. Collard, but it is certainly grounds for an investigation of your counsel's competence," Old Hairy said. "I assume you'd like to make a complaint."

"Please don't," Mitch whispered.

"I would," I replied, and quickly added, "your honor."

"Perfectly understandable, and in the circumstances, I imagine you'd like to avail yourself of new counsel."

"I most certainly would like to avail," I replied.

Mitch crumpled beside me. This was an abject and very public humiliation. The prosecutor, a shark in a shiny suit, was laughing and nudging his junior, a serious woman in her early thirties. She didn't share her boss's amusement.

"If you cannot afford a lawyer—" the judge began.

"I can, your honor," I interrupted. "I can afford a lawyer."

"Well, in that case we'll push the arraignment . . ." He trailed off and looked at the clerk.

"A week," she suggested.

"We'll give you a week, Mr. Collard." Old Hairy nodded indulgently, like he was Santa Claus and had just handed me a neatly wrapped gift.

"Thank you, your honor," I replied.

I was glad Mitch had fumbled such a simple job. I should have thought about firing him sooner. I could afford one of those expensive OJ lawyers, the kind who can get a person off a smoking-gun, blood-spattered-shoes murder rap. Might also be useful if Rosa Abalos started to get too close.

I had the money to make these charges vanish, and if I took out the pedophile priest, I'd have plenty more to beat a murder rap too. And it was hardly murder in any case. Killing the priest wasn't even in the same league as Walter Glaze or Farah Younis. I'd have done it for half the price and wouldn't have lost a second's sleep over it either.

Look at what you're becoming, Walter's ghost said.

Righteous, I replied inwardly. *That's why you're in the ground.*

I swaggered out of court full of myself. I wasn't tied to losers like Mitch Hoffman anymore, and soon I'd be a fully paid-up billboarder. But you know what the book says about pride. Well, my fall was waiting for me right outside the courtroom. Three of them, dirty and brutish. Cutter, Curse, and Frankie Balls, oozing menace like a trio of festering wounds.

"You think you can give us the slip?" Frankie asked. "You've got five days to get me another fifty thousand. Or we're gonna put you in the hospital. Think on that."

He narrowed his eyes and stared me down before he and his heavies stalked away.

CHAPTER 58

You ever felt so out of place your skin was crawling, trying to get away from you? That was me in the office of Anna Cacciola, one of LA's most famous criminal lawyers. We were on the top floor of a sixty-story white skyscraper that stuck out of the ground like a giant tombstone and loomed over the Avenue of the Stars, down the street from Fox Studios, where the billboard fakers and dream-makers worked their magic, making big-dollar tentpoles for the silver screen. Anna's building had been picked up and dipped in a pot of money. It oozed from the walls in abstract art, flowed from the floor in gallery sculptures and museum furniture. It hung in the cool air and rich fragrances that came from well-placed bouquets and plants. This was less a place of business, more a palace of opulence and grandeur.

Even with my recent wealth and elevation, I didn't belong here, but my new lawyer most definitely did. She was in a brown tweed skirt and white blouse. Her shoulder-length blond hair framed her perfect oval face, which had been painted just so. She was beautiful, but her looks weren't what mattered; I was here for her mind.

Anna Cacciola was the polar opposite of Super Costanza Mitch Hoffman, and when I looked at her sharp eyes and no-nonsense expression, her "all about the business" demeanor, I saw the light of freedom ahead of me.

"So, I get the picture," Anna said from the other end of the couch.

She had her back to the magnificent view of the City of Angels and the Hollywood Hills. "I see you're a veteran. Were you deployed overseas?"

"Yes, ma'am. Afghanistan. Two tours."

"So, you are a war hero?"

"I helped reconstruct some bridges. Other work I can't talk about."

"Great." She smiled. "We can say this top secret work left you mentally scarred."

I shook my head in disbelief. She was planning her chess gambits with pieces of my life.

"Stories make the world go round. The ones we tell ourselves, which are usually lies to make life bearable, or to justify the choices we've already made, and the ones we tell others to get the outcomes we want. And in this case, we want to hear the words *not guilty*, so I'm going to major on your service to your country." She paused. "Which I thank you for, of course."

"I got posted out here. The corps has an operations center on Wilshire near the one-ten. We bought a tiny house near Silver Lake. About four years ago, I took my ETS and got a job in the private sector."

"ETS?"

"Expiration term of service. Honorable discharge. I had a job lined up with St. Clair Engineering. Big pay raise, options, change-of-life stuff. I drove out to Malibu to have lunch with a buddy. Kind of a celebration."

I hesitated. I hated telling this story. It showed a weak and reckless side of me, but what bothered me more was the thought Freya Persico's ghost might escape through the retelling. I'd spent many long, hard months wrapping her up and locking her away somewhere dark within me.

"I had one too many drinks. I don't know why. Excitement at a new life. The madness of big numbers, all that money. The American dream coming true. Maybe it was just too much for me to handle? I made the mistake of driving home and hit another car on the PCH. Flipped it. A young woman, the other driver, was killed. I served a little over three years for a DUI and involuntary manslaughter."

Anna sat back and brought her hands together as though she was about to lead us in prayer.

"I see."

The silence that followed was overwhelming. There wasn't even the hum of an air vent. Money can buy true peace.

She clapped her hands, startling me. "Your prior experience has given you post-traumatic stress disorder. We can bring a psychiatrist as an expert witness to testify you are triggered by police officers or any other authority figures. That you weren't in your usual frame of mind. The mind of a law-abiding war hero, whose only mistake has been paid for."

You have a ton of unpaid debts, Walter's ghost chimed in, but only I could hear him, so I ignored his words.

Anna smiled triumphantly. "I'll need fifty thousand dollars up front against earned fees, and we'll take it from there."

The rich don't solve problems like the rest of us. "How much are we talking in total?"

"Hundred, maybe a hundred and fifty thousand, all in," she replied. "Depends on the judge and prosecutor."

We want to believe we live in a world of laws, but when we get caught on the wrong side of the line, we think we should be the exception because we're good people. Poor folk don't often get the chance to escape transgressions, but the billboarders have the great lubricant. Money greases America's wheels, making life a smooth ride for those who can pay.

"That okay?" Anna asked.

I nodded.

A priest was going to have to die so I could go free.

A mean old pedophile, I corrected myself. It sounded okay in the abstract, but I was going to have to figure out a way to kill the old man without giving the cops anything to go on. And I'd have to pull the trigger on another life. Good or evil, that was never easy.

"You'll need to answer a money-laundering, source-of-funds questionnaire. Ethan, my assistant, will email it along with our client agreement."

She looked me up and down. My courtroom suit didn't speak to an easily accessible hundred and fifty grand.

"Where will the funds be coming from, Mr. Collard?"

"Savings," I replied. "My savings."

CHAPTER 59

My dance with Frankie Balls and his thugs outside the courtroom had shaken me. They weren't going to forget, and why should they? I was easy money. And then there was Detective Rosa Abalos and her fishing expedition to hook me and put me in the tank for Walter's death. The cop and the gangster put years of worry on me, but I walked out of Anna's office a younger man.

Clear the charges against me, kill the priest, and take my payoff to some secret hideaway where I could live a better life far from Frankie and Rosa and all my other troubles.

After lunch, I drove up Bel Air Road, following the winding street past the estates and houses nestled in the hillside. The sky was a deep azure, striking against the rich greens of the tropical gardens.

I parked the Range Rover at the head of the trail near Joseph Persico's house and hiked up the mountain to my place of penance. I looked down on his beautifully designed contemporary villa, set in its perfectly landscaped grounds complete with citrus trees, high cedars, and flowers and plants of every kind, and thought about the paradise it might have been if it wasn't for me and my recklessness. There might have been grandchildren one day, scattered around the garden, losing themselves in its many nooks as they played hide-and-seek like so many windup toys.

I told myself not to dwell on such things. The past and all the infinite futures it might have spawned were gone. There was just now and what was to come, and in this moment of potential, I wanted Joseph Persico's blessing. I wanted him to know that I was doing everything for Skye, for the children she might birth, and that from the death of another would come life. I wanted absolution for killing a priest, and as I stood beneath the unblemished sky, I was struck by the thought that no one, neither priest nor pope, should be able to use their position to conceal their crimes. Grateful for the revelation, I nodded my appreciation toward the reclusive man in his huge house and walked back to my car. I drove the short distance to Laurel Canyon and home, where I shed my courtroom clothes and ran a bath.

I pulled myself out of the water, cleaned and reborn, and put on a pair of black jeans and a black T-shirt. I took the gun I'd found outside my house the night Jim had shot at Cutter and Curse and went to my car.

I wish I could say I felt trepidation at what I was about to do, but there was no doubt in my mind. Not the slightest hesitation. The priest was an abuser and had no more right to live than any evil creature. I'd killed Walter and Farah for less. This death would be like a vaccination. I would inoculate society against Gibson's poison, and I just wanted to get it over with quickly.

I followed Topanga Canyon Road up from the shimmering ocean through the high mountains. Gibson didn't have a mansion. Google Earth and Street View told me he lived in a 1950s rectangular home built out of faded aluminum panels on a lot off Deerhill Trail. I stayed clear of his street and instead drove along Cheney Drive, not named after the trigger-happy former vice president, but taken from the family that used to own the ranch in the nearby mountains. I followed the road to the end and parked at the head of a deserted trail. I took a pair of black leather gloves from the compartment, climbed out, and concealed the pistol in my waistband.

Twilight was on its way, leaving the paths through the rugged terrain clear of joggers and walkers. I'd used Google Earth to memorize the route from the trailhead to Gibson's place and started my journey over the mountain. I felt more like the military man of old, planning and executing my operation.

The stars glittered overhead and lights from distant homes dotted the valley by the time I turned off the trail and made my way across a short stretch of scrub to the low fence that marked the start of Gibson's yard.

He had a lovely place. Way smaller than the surrounding properties, but better than anything I could have ever dreamed of as a high-flying engineer. Had the Church bought his silence?

I climbed the fence into a neat garden and walked through an orchard of citrus trees toward the aluminum bungalow. The property was too far inland to have an ocean view, but it was still paradise high above the city in the mountains, close to the stars and heaven beyond.

The lights were on inside, and I could see Gibson in the back of the house. He was standing before an easel, concentrating and painting his next work.

Anger surged through me. I'd made a mistake, run someone off the road, and hadn't been able to function as a normal human because of the guilt I'd experienced—and here was this monster, painting, untroubled by his conscience.

I crept toward the house, confident the contrast between the darkness outside and the light inside would blind him to my presence. I reached for the pistol and held it tightly. My heart raced out of habit, but I was experienced now, and Gibson deserved what was coming.

I slowed as I reached his porch and inched toward the glass door that led into his artist's studio.

I was close. Too close. He must have seen a flicker in the glass, because I registered his head turn toward me and his puzzled look. I moved from slow to fast motion, reached for the door, and was grateful the handle gave when I turned it.

"Who are you?" he asked as I stepped inside. "What are you doing here?"

He registered the gun and his eyes widened.

"Take anything you want."

"You're going to pay, old man. You're going to pay for what you've done."

His confusion deepened. Was he really so detached from the consequences of his actions? Or just playing stupid?

"What I've done? What do you mean, what I've done?"

"The kids, old man. You should have known better. You were a priest."

He raised his hands and pleaded, and my stomach turned a little more at the sight of his feigned innocence. "I don't know what you're talking about. You've got the wrong person. Please. Please don't do this. I've never hurt anyone."

If I hadn't known better, I might have believed him, but instead the stench of his bullshit only sickened me. I thrust the pistol forward, and he started weeping.

"Please," he spluttered. "Please. Our father who art in heaven . . ."

I was no believer, but I couldn't bear the sound of this evil one praying to a godly force to save him. I shot him twice in the head and his eyes went blank as he fell.

As I turned to leave, I caught sight of what he'd been working on. It was an oil painting of a young girl with her back to me, sitting on a swing, staring out over a high horizon that was unmistakably somewhere in these mountains. The Pacific glinted in the distance. All around the easel were reference photographs of the little girl, and Gibson was in some of them. She was a relative, perhaps? Or the child of a friend who had no idea of his wickedness.

It was a beautiful image, but I was relieved for the girl.

She would no longer be in harm's way.

CHAPTER 60

I'd like to tell you that I felt sick, traumatized by guilt, but I crossed the mountain, returned to the Range Rover, and drove away from Gibson's execution with the calm resolve of the righteous. Evil is a stain on the world, and it felt good to wipe some of it clean.

The moon shone on the creases of the valley, making silver ghosts of everything around me, and I admired the beauty of the world as I drove along Topanga Canyon Road toward the ocean. When I reached the intersection with the Pacific Coast Highway, the water stretched ahead and touched the hem of the blanket of stars, and that's when doubt whispered at me.

Were those the eyes of a guilty man? Walter's ghost asked.

You've got the wrong person, Farah's spirit added.

You did have the wrong person, Gibson's specter said, and I wanted to cry. *I've never hurt anyone.*

"You were a drug dealer," I said aloud to Walter. "And you laundered money for cartels," I told Farah. "And you were worst of all," I said to Gibson. "You abused children."

Did I? Gibson's ghost replied.

The question was devastating. I'd set myself up as his judge and executioner, but what if I was wrong? What if I'd killed an innocent man?

What if we were all innocent? Walter's spirit asked.

"Shut up," I said.

Then you're just a murderer for money, Farah's ghost whispered.

"Shut up," I repeated, but their sour words had washed over me and were getting me drunk on guilt.

I'd seen evidence of Walter's wrongdoing with my own eyes, but what if he'd later repented of his crimes and settled into a new life as a good man? Did I have the right to punish him for a self he might have already killed? Our histories are grains of sand on an infinite beach, and in the end, aren't all our wrongs washed away by the sweep of time? I looked up at the stars, the only true witnesses to the countless wrongs perpetrated here on earth, and they neither remember nor care about any of it. The torture and murder of innocents in centuries past, now just footnotes in rarely thumbed textbooks. Weren't perps and victims equally forgotten? Had I robbed Walter, Farah, and Gibson of the chance of redemption?

But then I wouldn't have gotten my five hundred grand, and when it came down to it, all my rationalizations about being a vigilante and fighting evil, all my cockamamie ideas about guilt and justice, I was killing for money. Farah's ghost was right, the payday mattered. It was a future for my daughter and me.

A vengeful father caught in the heat of retribution might have driven straight home, but I wanted an alibi, a reason that might explain my presence in the neighborhood. I'd driven to the coast for an evening walk in the hills and dinner at my favorite fish place, the Reel Inn. The military man was finally shining through, using his training and strategic thinking to execute targets. But without the uniform, I was just an assassin. A monied serial killer.

I pulled off the PCH and went inside the Reel Inn to order grilled sea bass from the counter. It was too late for civilized folk to eat dinner, so the place was quiet. I took a booth by the front window and watched the traffic on the highway, and the ocean shimmering in the moonlight.

Once finished with my meal, I hung around until the place closed and made sure plenty of people saw me in that booth before I left and drove east toward Laurel Canyon.

My headlamps lit up the road into the hills, and all was tranquil until I reached my front gate and my twin beams shone upon a blue Chevy Tahoe.

Detective Rosa Abalos stepped out of her vehicle, and I considered speeding away, but she'd seen me, and running would make me look guilty.

Realizing the gun was still in the glove compartment, my heart thrashed around like a fish on a hook.

I fought the urge to panic and showed nothing but calm as I lowered my window and slowed to a halt by my gate.

"Mr. Collard," Rosa said. "We need to talk."

CHAPTER 61

I parked on my driveway and got out. Rosa hovered by the gate line, waiting to be invited onto my property like some vampire, but I wasn't going to make that mistake, and walked over to her.

"Nice evening?" she asked.

I didn't reply.

"You been anywhere interesting?"

What did she know? Was she in on this somehow? She'd turned up to spring me when I'd got arrested on my way back from San Diego, but had she really seen my arrest flagged? Was it possible she was linked to my patron? Was she my patron?

"Why are you here, Detective?"

"I'd like to ask you a few more questions. Can we go inside?" She gestured toward the house and took a step forward.

I shook my head. "I don't think so. And you can stay off my property." Magic words. Cop vampires can't trespass without cause. She took a step back.

"Okay. I can talk from here. It's a warm night is all, and I wanted you to be comfortable."

"I appreciate your concern, but I don't have to talk to you. I'm tired and I want to get some shut-eye."

I started toward the house.

"You say you don't know anything about Walter Glaze," she said. "But have you ever heard of Farah Younis?"

It took a ton of self-control to maintain my mask, but inside a storm was raging. How had they linked the deaths so quickly? Had I left incriminating DNA at the scenes? Or been picked up on camera?

The reckoning, Walter's ghost whispered unhelpfully.

If they had hard evidence, a battalion of cops would already be hauling me in for booking. I stopped and turned slowly, casually.

"Never heard of her. What's she got to do with Walter Glaze?"

"Farah Younis is a lawyer who was shot in San Diego," Rosa replied. "The day before I secured your release from San Clemente. Were you in San Diego?"

"Yeah," I responded.

Gun in the glove box.

Cash in a strongbox in the house.

Fibers.

DNA.

Who knows what other evidence all over me, my car, and my place?

I started sweating.

"I've got a thing for good food," I said. "I drove down to Hodad's for a burger."

"A burger?" Rosa asked in a tone that made me think we were actors in a bad soap, each going through the motions of their role, neither convinced by the performance of the other.

This wasn't a simple fishing expedition. They had something that tied Farah to Walter, but did they have anything on me?

"Hodad's is a top five all-American burger joint. I'd just bought this car and wanted to stretch her out on a road trip."

"I see," she said. "And were you ever in the downtown area?"

"I might have driven through. I went into the city because it seemed a shame not to tour when I'd gone so far."

"But you don't know Farah Younis?"

I shook my head. "I don't. Sorry. Can't help you. How did you get my new address?"

"Your ex-wife," Rosa replied.

Toni. I told her she shouldn't give anyone my details.

"Why?" Rosa asked. "Are you hiding? You should know you can't hide from the LAPD. Not for long anyway."

I scoffed, but I didn't feel jovial. "I'm not hiding. Just interested in knowing since I haven't sent out my change-of-address notices yet."

She smiled. "It's a nice place. Step up from the old. You come into money?"

"Savings," I replied. If she did some digging, that tale wouldn't hold.

"Savings," she repeated. "I wish I could learn how to put some money aside, but a cop's paycheck doesn't go far these days. Certainly doesn't reach the hills."

She eyed me coldly for a moment, but I didn't give her a response. Not even so much as a twitch. Instead, I looked her up and down, all disappointment and pity. If I didn't have the right to judge Walter Glaze, Farah Younis, or Richard Gibson, what right did this collection of cells, this body of flesh given purpose by a flawed soul, have to judge me? What was she anyway? A cop? A meaningless title given to her by those in power to legitimize their view of the world and protect their interests over mine. If Anna Cacciola did get me assessed by a psychiatrist, they wouldn't have a problem identifying a heavy-duty problem with authority.

I see you, cop, I thought as I stared at her. *I see you, flawed like the rest of us.*

"Well, thank you for your time, Mr. Collard," she said at last.

"No problem."

I watched her get into her car. I walked to the gate and closed it as she started her engine and drove down the hill toward the city.

What right did she have to come here asking me questions? Making me feel like a wrongdoer? In a hundred years no one would care about what I'd done, and in a thousand no one would even know. Morality was a question of perspective. Justice a matter of who had power. I had the power to rid the world of evil, and that made me just.

As the gate clicked shut, I noticed the mailbox wasn't fully closed. Skye must not have shut it properly. I walked over and checked inside the small metal locker to see another package from my mysterious patron.

It was the largest yet.

CHAPTER 62

Five thousand hundred-dollar bills.

More than enough to put a kid through med school and pay for a slick lawyer to spring a man from criminal damage charges. I should have been happy. I'd done a good thing, ridding the world of an abuser, and made myself a demi-millionaire in the process. I'd cleared enough to reengineer my life and transform myself from broken deadbeat into successful dad.

I slept well that night, exhausted by the spin of recent events, comforted by my newfound wealth, and I woke late the next day and took a leisurely drive across town to reach Anna Cacciola's office in time for our 1:00 p.m. appointment. She arranged for us to have sushi while her paralegal, Daniel, a gawky guy who was awkward in his own skin, took my statement about the events that led to me crashing into the deputy sheriff's car.

Naturally I presented the truth, the whole truth, and nothing but the truth, as a veteran with post-traumatic stress, made worse by his time served in prison and his lifelong distrust of authority figures. It was a well-constructed sob story built on the scaffolding of Daniel's leading questions, designed to give the judge an easy out when he released me back to society.

"Thanks for the sushi," I said when we'd finished.

"We should be thanking you," Anna replied. "You're buying."

I didn't say anything. I just smiled and made a point of eating the remains, including an eel roll that I didn't even really like.

"Is there anything else we can help you with?" Anna asked.

I knew it was her polite way of kicking me out, but my rear end remained on her expensive couch. I eyed the paralegal, and Anna got the message. She was sharp, just like that detective.

"Daniel, why don't you get started on the transcription?"

He nodded and took his phone, which had been used to record my deposition, and headed for the door.

"How can I help you, Mr. Collard?" Anna asked when he was gone.

"I don't know why or how, but this detective has got it into her head I might know something about a couple of murders," I replied, trying to be as nonchalant as someone asking a cabdriver for directions.

"I see," Anna remarked.

"I was wondering if there was any way you could find out why they think the deaths are connected and what puts me in the frame?"

You can't hide guilt from someone like this, Farah's ghost whispered.

"What are the victims' names?" Anna asked.

"Walter Glaze and Farah Younis," I replied.

"And the detective?"

"Rosa Abalos."

"I'll see what I can find out," Anna said. "Is there anything else?"

I shook my head. I'd killed three people. Four, if you count Freya Persico, but somehow this slick lawyer managed to intimidate me.

I left her office, wondering whether she now suspected me of murder, and by the time I handed my stub to the garage valet, I remembered it didn't matter. She'd represented actual murderers, people she knew were guilty. What did it take to have such a barren conscience you could stand before a judge and argue a real killer was innocent? But I wasn't about to start moralizing. I didn't care if she was a villain at heart. As long as she helped me beat my charges and avoid any trouble with the law, Anna Cacciola was fine by me.

Now, some of you might whisper, *hypocrite*. Hadn't I killed Farah

Younis for aiding and abetting bad guys? True, but isn't life all a question of perspective? Anna Cacciola was helping me, and I'm not such a bad guy, am I? I mean, you know me well enough to judge that by now, right?

I started home, but when I reached the intersection with Sunset Boulevard, I took a right by Gil Turner's Wine and Spirits and then swung another right into the parking lot of S&J Solutions, an office supplies store that boasted the fastest internet connection in town. I suspected that might be stretching the truth, but I was pretty sure it would be good enough for me.

I wanted to see if the internet could clue me in on a connection between Walter Glaze and Farah Younis, something I couldn't do from home or my phone.

A few minutes later, a smiling assistant with a name badge that said Millie showed me to one of a dozen computer terminals that were tucked behind the office chairs and desks section. The machines were new and quick, but I was the only person using one. The assistant returned to the front counter, so I didn't have to worry about keeping my screen hidden from prying eyes.

I searched for Walter Glaze and Farah Younis and got no hits on them together. Instead, I got a mix of results on them as individuals. Most of the top hits were news articles about their deaths, which made me uncomfortable, so I scrolled down and clicked through to later pages. But I couldn't escape the news.

The article summaries read like obituaries, sharing tales of charity work, community volunteering, and social work. Farah ran a youth scheme helping disadvantaged kids get internships at San Diego's law firms, and Walter Glaze had established a music scholarship for aspiring DJs.

I scrolled further, looking frantically for *The Gray Letter*, *LA Exposé*, and the *San Diego Intercept*, the sites that had told me the truth about the people I'd been asked to kill.

But I couldn't find them.

Hot fire crackled over my skin, prompting cold flop sweat as I realized the sites had been deleted from the internet.

All of them.

Gone.

I searched for the Opus Insider, the message board that mentioned Gibson—

Sickness gripped me. I glanced around at the colorful signs offering 20 percent off reams of paper, filing cabinets, chairs, and desks, and they all seemed to dance and bend around me as though the world was whirling, maybe even melting. But at some level I knew the world was fine.

I was not.

Opus Insider just presented a 404 error, site not found.

You fucked up, Walter's ghost said.

No, I replied inwardly. *No.*

Yes, Farah's spirit joined in. *You were played.*

Someone's used you, Gibson's specter whispered.

I felt sick with guilt and grief and anger and fear. The websites that had convinced me these people were bad had been shells. I had been manipulated by lies, radicalized into murder, taught to hate by a carefully curated fiction.

My sickness turned to horror as I clicked through to the news articles about the murders of Walter Glaze, Farah Younis, and Richard Gibson, and realized with pangs of uncontrollable anguish that I'd murdered three very decent people.

CHAPTER 63

What the fuck?

What the actual fuck?

Infinite fucks spat from a galaxy of horrified mouths couldn't convey the scale of my horror. A pit opened in my stomach, and it was so dark and powerful it sucked away my sense of self and whatever shreds of morality I'd clung to. I sat in the office supply shop, scrolling, searching, flitting from page to page, scouring the internet for the slightest reason these three people should have been killed. Instead, I found goodness, generosity, and virtue. All qualities I lack. All of which I'd ignored when I'd needed a reason to kill.

Life stings, Walter's ghost said. *But it makes sweet honey for people like me.*

Someone played you for a fool, Farah's spirit added.

A fool rushes in, Gibson's specter said. *A wise man waits until . . .*

"Shut up!" I yelled before putting my hand over my mouth.

I hadn't intended to speak the words out loud, but I wasn't in control of myself. The pit in my gut had formed a vortex and, like the eye of a hurricane, had set my world swirling. I felt lightheaded and sick and wanted to be somewhere else. More accurately, I wanted to be someone else. Someone who hadn't taken three lives. Someone who had done his homework. Someone who wasn't such a deadbeat.

Deadbeat, Walter's ghost said.

Deadbeat, Farah's spirit agreed.

Deadbeat, Gibson's specter joined in, and three voices filled my head, chanting the word again and again and again.

It got louder and louder as the pit in my stomach grew denser until, like a black hole, it drew everything into a single point, creating a storm of memory, perception, and emotion that sent my world into chaos. I could hardly think straight, let alone see or hear.

Deadbeat. Deadbeat. Deadbeat.

What would you have done?

You discover the foundations of your new world are built on a sink-hole of lies. You realize as you search the easily manipulated digital world for shreds of your decency, you're the bad guy.

The villain of the piece.

No vigilante here.

Just a slayer of innocents.

A murderer.

A serial killer.

What would you do?

If you're sitting there thinking you'd turn yourself in, you've probably never served time. You've never felt the cruel heel of bad fortune grind into your neck.

I did the only thing I could do. Something that had been drilled into me by months of bad habit. Years, if you include the instructive lessons I'd had from my father.

When I'd caught my breath and recovered my senses enough to stand, I went to Rick's and got blind drunk.

I mean "vomiting, sick in the mind, closer to hell than earth, teetering on the edge of death" drunk. I didn't care about Curse or Cutter or Frankie Balls. I didn't care about the LAPD. I just wanted the memory wipe Rick had given me so many times.

My mom had taught me to run away from problems. We leave the house until they've passed out, and when they're defanged, fists un-clenched, and snoring, we creep in and take the sleep train to the clean-slate morning. My dad had taught me different: life is pain, the cure is found at the bottom of a bottle.

And that night I went searching, but no matter how many bottles I emptied, the pain didn't seem to go away, so I kept searching and searching and searching.

Jim was in good spirits and happy to see me. I'd caught him after just the right number of drinks, so he was pleased to join me on my quest for a cure. We did lines and pills in the restroom, and even later he didn't become angry, bad Jim. He just grew slurry and maudlin.

I think we talked about family. That's the only reason that would explain why I came around in his car, heading along Rosencrans Avenue toward Toni's place.

I remember being there, outside her apartment, the stink of vomit rising off my shoes, the night sky a dull orange, broken by only a couple of starry pimples.

I remember Toni's fire-red face as she woke the neighbors with her shouting. Skye's wounded eyes, peering out of the living room window, tears sliding down her cheeks. Jack hauling me away, and him and Jim tussling, but I don't know how Jim ended up on his ass, or how I wound up behind the wheel of the Lincoln, driving to a place in Carson.

Jim used the hem of his shirt to wipe a bloody gash on his temple and directed me left and right and straight ahead. We didn't hit anything or anyone, but my attorney says I should remind you this is a work of fiction, so even if your car *was* parked in the vicinity of Wilmington Avenue and was damaged that night, no bills will be payable because this is all make-believe, right?

Jim's destination turned out to be a cathouse on Calstock Street. *Cathouse* was his choice of words, not mine.

I don't recall much, just that we seemed to be real loud on a dead-quiet street. The home of felines was a bungalow on the corner. Red bricks and red tiles, but no red lights in the windows. If Jim hadn't slurred his assurances they knew him here, I would have thought we were about to wake fine residents who would run us off their property.

Once inside, I vaguely sensed this was no ordinary home. There were women in a living room that reminded me of my grandma's place. Jim flashed money around. Maybe.

But my strongest memory that night had to be of me and a woman in her thirties, alone in a sad little bedroom. Felicity, that was her name. She wore the shortest dress I've ever seen and matching underwear that covered little, but her eyes were too sad to hide, even beneath my fog of booze and drugs and her many layers of makeup. Her sadness made me feel at home. Something familiar and strangely warming. Like a good rum.

We didn't have sex. She let me lay my head in her lap and stroked my hair as my eyes fluttered shut. I had thought she'd ditch me the moment I fell asleep.

After all, I deserved no better.

CHAPTER 64

"Hey. Wake up."

Bitterness hit me as I swallowed the residue of vomit that coated my mouth. I opened my eyes and took in the depressing bedroom at Jim's cathouse. Black-and-white framed photos decorated the wall opposite the bed. One showed a nude woman in a Panama hat, posing in what I guess was meant to be an erotic way. In another picture she was in a chair with her legs crossed, and in the other she stood like an Instagram model, one knee in front of the other, leaning forward slightly and pushing her breasts together with her arms. I think the images were supposed to be classy, but they made the room feel even seedier, and they clashed with the rainbow zigzag pattern of the bedspread.

My head throbbed as I turned to see Felicity sitting next to me. She'd changed out of the tiny red dress and was in skinny black jeans and a T-shirt that had the word *Vibes* emblazoned in graffiti script.

She'd removed her blond wig to reveal her natural auburn, which had been cut short. Her eyes were a clear amber and seemed a little less sad than I remembered.

"Your buddy paid for the room until ten," she said. "It's ten thirty."

"Jim?" I said, almost choking on the word. "Jim?" I tried again after clearing my throat.

"Your friend's gone," she replied. "He got into a fight with his companion. They threw him out. Wanted to get rid of you, too, but you were out like a baby, and I didn't think you'd be any trouble. You can usually tell the bad ones."

"Thanks. He's an asshole, but—"

"When you get to know him, right?" she interrupted.

"No. He's an asshole, but when he drinks, he becomes a sour old bastard."

We both smiled.

"I thought you were going to defend him," she said. "That's what men usually do. Like you're all members of the same fraternity or something. Guy comes in here and gets rough and his buddies are all, 'You must have provoked him. He's a family man.' And they never ask themselves whether they really know their friend at all."

"You get many family men in here?" I asked.

"You have no idea. You a family man?"

I shook my head instinctively and immediately regretted it. I could feel my brain bouncing off my skull. "I mean, I have a kid, but we're divorced. Me and her mom."

"Do you remember what you told me last night?" she asked.

Panic shook off my headache, and I sat up and tried to fight the wave of nausea that washed up from my treacherous gut. Had I confessed to the murders? Had I spilled what was troubling me? I tried to focus on her face, but my eyes were defective, weeping and my vision vague.

"You don't remember, do you?" she went on. "Don't worry, I'm used to it. Men come in here to satisfy an animal urge, and when they're done most of them want to forget the animal ever existed."

"What did I say?"

"I'll tell you if it comes true," she replied.

"Listen, can I buy another half hour?" I asked.

Her face fell a little.

"I don't mean . . ." I trailed off. "I mean, I'm not even sure I can stand, let alone . . ."

She brightened.

"It's three hundred bucks for room and companion," she said.

"For thirty minutes?" I couldn't help myself and wondered how much Jim had handed over for the two of us.

"The owner gets fifty," Felicity said. "I make five hundred an hour, which is just enough for my pocketbook, but way too little for my soul. This one's on me, though. I'll fix it so you can stay for another hour." She got to her feet. "You look like you could use some kindness."

I laughed. She was right; I needed kindness, but not money. I reached into my pocket for my billfold.

"Please don't go," I said, peeling off a trio of C-notes. "I don't want to be alone."

She looked at my money, then at me. I leaned over and placed the money on a bedside cabinet next to a bowl of condoms and a large red vibrator. Should I have been embarrassed? I was too hungover to know.

"I've got to be somewhere, but I can give you thirty minutes," Felicity said, returning to sit on the bed.

"Thanks."

We sat for a few moments, her looking bored, me trying to fight the spin of the earth and resist the urge to vomit.

"This is fun," she said, her voice flat.

"Sorry," I replied. "I'm not great company right now. How did you end up here?"

"How did *you* end up here?" she fired back.

"Nicely done." I smiled. She was sharp, and I guessed her line of work had taught her not to take any shit.

"Thank you."

"Do you enjoy it?" I asked.

Her face crunched in disgust. "No. Not that. Don't ask me that. It's too clichéd. And it's rude. Would you ask a stranger about their sex life?"

"No, but I would ask them about their job."

"Nicely done," she replied.

"Thank you."

She thought for a moment.

"Did you enjoy everyone you've had sex with?"

"I thought we weren't allowed to ask that," I countered.

"But you know the answer."

I nodded. "I guess so."

"So, you never need to ask the question. Guys do it to exert power, not because they're really interested."

"What do you do when you're not here?"

"I'm studying to be an accountant." She registered my expression. "Don't look so surprised. Lots of the girls here have their eyes on better things, but if you come from a poor family, screwed around at school, and don't have connections, where else are you going to make five hundred an hour?"

"I guess. I just don't see you as an accounting type. That's all."

"What the hell is an accounting type?"

"You're too—"

"If you say I'm too pretty I will punch you in the mouth."

I thought she was joking but couldn't be sure, so I fell silent.

"I know you think I'm pretty because you kept saying so last night."

"Is that the thing?"

"No, that's not the thing," she replied. "But it's related."

"Why won't you tell me?"

"Be patient," she said. "And tell me why women aren't allowed to be pretty and smart."

"Nice change of subject." I paused. "Maybe I wasn't about to make a comment about how pretty you are. Maybe I was going to say you look too smart to be punching numbers all day."

She smiled, but it didn't reach her eyes. My heart pounded, but I couldn't tell whether it was the hangover and nausea or the attraction I felt. She was smart, funny, kind, and, yes, pretty.

"You've lived on the outer reaches of existence and seen the edges of humanity, and it's changed you," I said. "I can see it in your eyes. Same as mine."

The room fell silent as she studied me for a moment.

"You're a strange one," she said at last.

"That I am," I conceded. "And so are you."

We fell into silence again. I heard indistinct sounds coming from somewhere else in the building, and a car passed outside. Did she like me? Did I deserve to be liked? Was she just serving out her time for the notes I'd laid down? Money was the great corrupter. It skewed everything. Made intentions warped and unclear, like reflections in a carnival hall of mirrors.

"So, you think you're pretty?" I asked, and she feigned outrage.

"I'm not that dumb. Of course I know I'm pretty. Hazard of the job."

"I thought we weren't allowed to talk about your job?"

She tilted her head, as if studying me afresh. "You're almost as funny as you were last night."

"I don't remember being funny at all."

"But you were. Until you lost steam. Then you put your head on my lap, and I stroked your hair until you fell asleep."

For some reason the revelation cheered me. Even if I couldn't remember it, I'd had the kindness I'd craved.

"I figured you were paying for some human contact. I think that's the other reason a lot of men come here. It's not just about the animal. They're lonely."

"As long as I wasn't a total asshole," I said.

"Far from it." Her smile was full of mischief.

"What did I say?" I asked.

My ringing phone saved her from having to respond.

"Excuse me," I said.

"So polite," she replied as I answered the call.

"That guy you were talking about last night," Jim said without any greeting. "Walter Glaze." My gut tightened at the name. What the hell had I been saying? "There's some kind of thing for him. I'm outside the cathouse."

"What? Now?" I asked.

"Yeah, now. Dry your dick and get dressed," he commanded before hanging up.

"Something wrong?" Felicity asked.

"I have to go," I replied, forcing my aching body to rise.

I ignored my dizziness and the cold sweat nausea that sent bile into my mouth.

"You okay?" she asked.

I nodded. "I'm sorry."

"That's a shame," she said. "I don't have to leave for fifteen. I was enjoying our conversation."

"Sorry to be a drag," I said, staggering to the door.

"I don't do this for everyone," she said, "but let me give you my number." She took my phone from my hand before I could reply, and I watched her type her name and number into my contacts. "Call me when you want another deep and meaningful conversation."

"Okay," I replied without really thinking.

I spilled out of the house and oozed into Jim's Continental, which was parked opposite.

"Man, you stink," he said, switching the AC to max.

"Morning," I replied.

"There's nothing good about it," he snapped, and I almost pointed out I hadn't used the word *good* but thought better of it. "You think I wouldn't remember you telling me my car had been used in a homicide?"

Shit.

Oh shit.

He knew.

"We're gonna find out who this guy really was and what they know about who killed him."

"But the cops—"

"Fuck the cops," Jim said, all teeth and burning eyes. "I don't give a shit about the cops. If this guy was connected, I don't want his gangland buddies coming for me."

"I don't think he was connected," I said, remembering all the incriminating websites that had been deleted. What had I told Jim? What warped view of reality had he remembered?

"I don't give a shit what you think," he snarled. "I want to know who knows what about who killed him. And if anyone knows too much, I'm going to fucking end you."

Friends sometimes say they're going to kill each other. *I'm gonna kill you*, friendly punch, smile, and more jokes. This wasn't that. This was a real threat.

I felt sicker than I had at any point that morning. I wished I was back in the cathouse with my head in Felicity's lap, her fingers running through my hair, soothing me to a better place.

I didn't want to be in this car with the devil, but I was, and he growled at me before putting the giant hellcraft into gear and taking me away.

CHAPTER 65

Jim's foul mood didn't improve as we headed west. Hungover, coming down from the speed and cocaine and whatever else we'd blasted, tired and annoyed at being implicated in a homicide—his weathered face, mean at the best of times, was twisted like an old tree disfigured by a storm.

"Can we go to my place?" I asked. I really needed fresh clothes.

He silenced me with a look.

"What the fuck were you thinking?" he asked after a while. "Man's gotta do what's necessary to put food on the table, but you used my fucking car, Peyton. Fuck!"

I was getting a good read of his moral compass now. He wasn't concerned about murder, just the fact I'd implicated him.

"I'm sorry," I said, but I wasn't talking to Jim. I was apologizing to the ghosts of the innocent dead who lived within me.

They didn't reply, but I could feel them there, judging me.

"Fucking sorry," Jim said. He crinkled his nose. "You're a sorry, stinking fuck, that's what you are."

"Where are we going?" I asked.

"Just shut the fuck up," he said.

Most people would be afraid of someone who'd put three bodies in the ground, but Jim Steadman wasn't most people, and I wondered if he had his own skeletons buried somewhere. Why had he served time?

We rolled through LA, along the broad streets and boulevards, past the shiny skyscrapers, full of people with bright lives, toward the ocean that once inspired hope, but now made me think only of my own horizon. If it hadn't been for Skye, I'd have walked beyond the coastal breakers and never looked back. But my life was hers. It wasn't mine to give or take anymore.

Eventually we turned off Santa Monica Boulevard, a few blocks from the Pacific, which shimmered between the low-rise condos.

We navigated a run of twists and turns and came to Charters, a private school laid out on a lot that occupied two blocks. Charters is famed as a school for the children of the rich and talented. Movie producers, actors, and financiers use the place to imbue privilege and entitlement, so the next generation learn to believe the opportunities gained through their parents' money and connections were earned by merit.

The school was busy for a Saturday morning, and when we pulled into the packed parking lot, I realized why. A huge banner hung from the side of the main building, and on it was a photo of Walter Glaze alongside the words *Walter Glaze Memorial Fundraiser.*

"We shouldn't be here," I said as an attendant in an orange vest waved Jim into a space.

"Why?" Jim asked as he swung his huge car into the spot. "I found out about it on Facebook. It's a public event and there's a ton of people here. We'll blend in, find out who knows what. For charity, of course."

He didn't wait for a reply and got out. I had the feeling I should stay in the car, but I don't think he would have taken that as any less than betrayal, so I followed reluctantly.

"I don't know what I said last night," I tried. "I was drunk. Wasted. I was probably talking trash. Spitting up garbage."

"Right," Jim responded, but he didn't break his stride. "Don't try to bullshit me now, Peyton. I'm no snitch, but I'm not going down for you or anyone else. I'm going to find out what I need to do to protect myself. And since you put me in this mess, you can help me clean it up."

We were directly under the banner and Walter Glaze's giant photo, in the shade of the main building, and I still felt waves of nausea lapping up my throat. More cars were pulling up, and they were disgorging somber family members, friends, and community-minded folk who were all heading for a gate not thirty feet from us.

I followed Jim like a condemned prisoner being led to the chair. He had his own gravity, and no matter how much my mind scream danger, my feet couldn't resist his pull. Was I weak? Probably. But part of me also wanted to see whether I had put us at risk. I wanted to find out what the family knew.

We reached the edge of the main building, and through a chain-link fence I saw an outpouring of love. Food and activity stands lined the playing field, and dozens of families, hundreds of people, were taking part in a celebration of a man's life. Pulling a trigger on another life was the only way I'd experience something like this, because no one I knew would inspire such emotion in so many. I certainly wouldn't. I didn't have many friends anymore. The engineering corps didn't have the same spirit of comradeship as frontline combat units, and the few buddies I'd made had turned their backs after my conviction. I didn't have much by way of family. Some second cousins still anchored in Skokie, living the same Lake Michigan life I'd escaped.

"We need to leave," I said to Jim as we neared the gate.

A couple of high school students greeted people with photocopied maps of the stalls.

"There's the family," Jim said, pointing at a cluster of people at the center of the field. A dozen children and adults, all in black.

"Jim," I said, grabbing his arm.

"Get the fuck off me," he responded angrily.

A little too angrily, because kids glanced at us and then pretended not to have heard.

Jim pulled his arm clear. "You do what you want. But remember, traitors are made of wood, and they burn easily."

"No," I said loudly enough for the kids to hear. "You're right. We should pay our respects."

"Stall maps?" one of the kids said as we walked in.

"Thanks," I replied, taking the sheet.

Jim brushed the other kid's arm away and stalked on like an animal on grim business. How did he do it? I wanted people to like me. Even people I didn't like. Jim couldn't care less.

I went after him, feeling sicker with every step, praying he wouldn't land us both in trouble, and wondering why anyone would frame a family man who'd inspired so much love. Why would someone pay one hundred grand to murder a guy who could fuel such an outpouring of devotion and grief?

CHAPTER 66

I'd been manipulated. Scratch that; I'd allowed myself to be manipulated. I'd wanted that money. I'd been desperate for it. I'd lapped up whatever lie made it palatable. And here I was, now responsible for three murders I had not even the slightest justification for. Which made my surroundings press in like crushing jaws of guilt.

Jim wasn't so conflicted. He crossed the grass, which had wilted in the heat, and headed straight for Walter's family. I followed a few feet back.

"Which one's the widow?" Jim asked of an old woman on the edge of the group.

She nodded toward a dark-haired woman who stood at the center of things, her arms on the shoulders of two young boys in black suits. Tiny pallbearers. Small replicas of Walter Glaze, undoubtedly his sons. Next to them was a girl, who was clearly Walter's daughter, and she wore the same black dress as her mother. Both widow and grieving daughter had their hair pulled back in severe buns.

Jim made his way to Mrs. Glaze, and I hovered nearby.

Two men eyeballed Jim and moved closer to the family. They were brothers or cousins, perhaps? Certainly people who wanted to protect Widow Glaze.

"Ma'am, I'd like to present my condolences," Jim said with the pomp of an Alabama gentleman attorney. "You've suffered a terrible and egregious loss."

I was grateful he didn't look at me to hammer home the clear message. I was the cause of all this. I was surrounded by suffering and pain. My bullets had torn holes in this community.

See what you've done, Walter's ghost said. *See my kids, my family, my friends. My wife. Look at her.*

I can't, I said inwardly. *I can't look at her. I'm sorry. I'm so sorry.*

How could unspoken words to a ghost make any of this better?

I wiped my eyes.

I was supposed to be the good guy. The arm of justice. But I was the villain. The bringer of sorrow. If I'd done my homework better, dug into my victims' backgrounds, taken my time, I might not have made such a terrible mistake.

"Did you know my husband?" Mrs. Glaze asked.

"My associate and I were regulars at his nightclub," Jim replied, pointing me out.

Mrs. Glaze eyed me like she might a dead animal lying on top of a steaming pile of garbage. I didn't know how I looked, but I'm sure it wasn't funereal. I was a disgrace, and it was bad enough to have killed the man, but to show up to his memorial like this made me feel just plain rotten.

"He always took good care of us," Jim said.

"Thank you," Mrs. Glaze replied, and I think she imagined that was the end of the conversation.

Jim lingered, though. "Do the police have any leads?"

Mrs. Glaze stiffened, and I wished right then and there the grass would part and a clawed hand would drag me to hell for my eternal punishment.

"Why don't you go play with your friends?" she suggested to her children, and the trio moved away without a word.

"I'd sure like to see the perpetrators get their punishment," Jim added.

Your friend is digging your grave, Walter's ghost said. *Word by word.*

I couldn't disagree.

The cousins or brothers, big men in tight black suits, shuffled closer.

"Who are you again?" Mrs. Glaze asked.

"Name's John Sewell," Jim lied. "Friends call me Johnny."

"I'm not your friend." Her voice could have chilled the core of the sun.

The sound of the fair around us seemed to grow faint, and I willed Jim to walk away. The monsters at his shoulders were bristling.

"I'm sorry," Jim said. "I didn't mean any disrespect."

I breathed easier.

"I just heard your husband got mixed up with some bad people."

Mrs. Glaze went from ice to fire in an instant. Her eyes shone with rage, but that didn't stop Jim.

"Drugs and whatnot. I just wanted to know if there was any truth to all them tales."

The hands were fast, the arms strong, and the brother-cousins pulled Jim back so quickly he almost left an afterimage of himself. Mrs. Glaze teared up and sought comfort in the arms of an older woman standing next to me.

"Get out!" Mrs. Glaze yelled. "Go!"

I didn't need any further encouragement and hurried after the two big men hauling Jim away.

He didn't put up a fight, just eyed me coolly, and allowed the brother-cousins to push him through the gate. Jim nearly hit a family of four coming in, but they swerved, and he stepped clear.

"I'm sorry," I said to everyone, and turned to go after Jim.

I almost had a heart attack right there on that very spot.

Rosa Abalos was leaning on the hood of the Lincoln Continental, and a patrol car was parked inches from the rear fender, blocking us in.

"Mr. Steadman, Mr. Collard, what brings you here?" Rosa asked as we neared. She was as casual as a beachside brunch on an August Sunday.

"Don't you even think of harassing us, Detective," Jim replied instantly. "What are you doing here? Following us?"

What was she doing here?

I looked at Rosa and Jim. Did they know each other? Was this encounter staged for my benefit? To achieve what? Pin me for my crimes? No, Jim wouldn't do this, would he?

What do you really know about him? Gibson's spirit asked.

He's just some drunk you run with, Walter's ghost said.

Frankie Balls is a better fit, I responded inwardly. *Jim is my friend, and this is just an interfering cop.*

"We're doing community outreach, Mr. Steadman," Rosa said. "Making sure there isn't any trouble. Murderers can sometimes turn up at these sorts of events."

Rosa looked at us pointedly.

"We came to find out if the family might have any information on the killer. Since you made it clear you're gonna try to frame us for whatever's happened here, we've got just as much interest in solving the case as you," Jim replied, and I was almost overwhelmed by the scale of his audacity.

Rosa smirked. "So, you're a couple of gumshoes, out here seeking justice. A pair of vigilantes."

"Concerned citizens," Jim said.

"What about you, Mr. Collard? Are you concerned?"

"I feel sorry for his poor family," I replied honestly. "Felt that way ever since you told me about the case. It's just heartbreaking."

"It sure is," she remarked.

"We've paid our respects," Jim said. "Now we'd like to leave."

He and Rosa eyed each other for a few seconds that might have been a century. Was this the moment she took me in?

Finally, she looked toward the cop car and nodded, and the driver rolled on.

"Goodbye, Detective," Jim said, sliding behind the wheel.

"Be seeing you," Rosa replied, stepping away from the Continental.

I got in beside Jim and made every effort not to tremble or cry tears of relief. He must have had stone balls the size of the asteroid that wiped out the dinosaurs and cratered half the planet, because he betrayed nothing as he backed out of the spot and drove us away from the Walter Glaze memorial.

CHAPTER 67

I felt sick and my heart jackhammered unevenly like a trip-hop break-beat all the way back to Rick's. My companion—I'm not going to call him friend, because friends don't seriously threaten to kill each other—said nothing.

My life had taken yet another wrong turn. A bad one. Somewhere out there was someone who'd manipulated me into killing three innocent people, turning me into a murderer. Was it Jim? Some random who'd manipulated me? Frankie Balls? Was Rosa Abalos involved? Or was it someone else entirely?

How could I have been so stupid to trust a total stranger?

We live in a world in which we're taught not to trust. The old man at the end of your road might abduct your child, her teacher or priest might be an abuser, politicians take money from vested interests and lie to the people who elect them, media spins fake news, businesses pollute the four elements, the billboarders hide their money from tax collectors and avoid paying their fair share, doctors push opiates onto unsuspecting patients, and the lessons in dishonesty and manipulation go on and on. And yet in this age of distrust, we are all so naive. We take the word of a stranger on social media as gospel. We trust a guy with a friendly profile picture who claims to have uncovered evidence of a satanic conspiracy at the heart of government, or the friend of a distant cousin who says a Silicon Valley billionaire plans to inject everyone with nanoparticles.

Look at me rationalizing my stupidity. I can't be dumb alone, so I have to implicate everyone. We're all being radicalized, pushed further left or right, taught to distrust authority by strangers we trust to tell the truth about why we shouldn't trust authority, creating a paradox that will ultimately consume every pillar of society, until it collapses on us all. And here I am catastrophizing. My world is ending, so it must be ending for us all.

The truth is I was an idiot. I was played for a fool by someone much smarter than me, and I had no idea who or why. And I needed to find out, because when Rosa Abalos came calling, I wanted my attorney to be able to give her another name. I wanted to be in a position to cut a deal. I wanted a way to avoid prison, and a plea bargain would do it.

So, for all Jim's sass, I had become a concerned citizen. Concerned with my own freedom, and that turned me into an investigator. I needed to know the identity of my patron and why he or she had paid me to kill Walter Glaze, Farah Younis, and Richard Gibson.

What a mess. Who the fuck ends up in this situation? Looking into murders they've perpetrated, like some bizzarro detective. It was an indication of just how far I'd fallen from normal society.

"You tell me if you catch wind of anything," Jim said as we rolled into Rick's parking lot.

Mine was the only car there.

"And I don't think we should see each other for a while. Not with that cop sniffing around you."

I nodded. That was fine by me.

"Later," I said as we stopped.

Jim sneered as I got out, and his tires actually screeched as he raced out of the lot.

I climbed into the Range Rover, stinking of fear sweat and eighty-proof vomit, but I soon got the AC going and felt better as I drove up to the hills.

The wafer-thin relief I felt was devoured entirely when I turned into my driveway and saw Rosa Abalos's car parked outside my cottage. She was sitting on the step by the front door and got to her feet as I came to a halt.

"This is starting to feel like harassment, Detective," I said, trying Jim's line of attack. I didn't have his stone confidence and was worried my words just made me sound like I had something to hide.

"No harassment, Mr. Collard." She held her hands up. "I'm just here to check you're okay. Your friend seemed angry. I wanted to make sure you're not under any duress."

"I appreciate your concern, Detective, but I'm A-okay."

I walked to my front door, key in hand, and she stood to one side.

"You know your buddy has served time for manslaughter?" Rosa said. "Got out fifteen years ago. Lot of people thought it was murder, but Mr. Steadman's lawyer convinced the court it was a bar fight that got out of hand. Had all the evidence about premeditation excluded."

My heart started dancing around again, bouncing in my chest like a drugged-up clubber on a massive rush. Was Jim behind this? Why? Was he settling an old score?

I focused on my key as I unlocked the door. I couldn't look at Rosa. She might see my fear and interpret it as guilt.

"Wasn't like your experience, which seems as though it was a genuine accident," she said. "She was nineteen, wasn't she?"

I froze with the door half-open.

"Freya Persico, the girl you killed in the crash."

I was a statue on the threshold of my home.

"You were a good man before the accident. At least that's my read on things. I checked your military record. Commendations, citations, nothing stellar, but nothing bad either. A family man."

I pinned a dispassionate mask to my face so she wouldn't see how accurate her assessment was. I longed to be that man again, but I was about as far away from him as I'd ever been.

"What made you drink that day?" Rosa asked.

"I don't really remember," I lied. "What's this got to do with these murders?"

Rosa stepped close enough for me to smell her vanilla perfume.

"Prison changes a man. And I don't just mean up here." She touched her forehead, and I wanted to run inside and slam the door, because it was as though she was reading my mind, and I was worried she would see celluloid visions of guilt projected by my treacherous brain. "I mean practical changes. New friends. Associates. People who want jobs done."

"You think I met someone inside?" I scoffed. I could play this part easily because it was the truth. "I hated prison. I made no friends. Or associates. You think I met a killer?"

"I think you might have met someone who wants people killed," she suggested. "I can see what Freya Persico's death did to you. It's written all over your face, and it's obvious in the map of your life. Guilt drove you off the rails, Mr. Collard."

I felt naked, as though she'd stripped me beyond my bones, down to my very soul. She was looking at me like she could see my shriveled heart in my rib cage, my shredded soul fluttering like a torn flag beneath it. She took another step forward and held my gaze.

"Guilt, Mr. Collard. It's like rust. Once it finds a way in, it eats away until there's nothing left. Nothing useful or good anyway. If you had a hand in the murders of Walter Glaze or Farah Younis, the guilt will get you."

"I don't know those people." My voice was so pathetic, even I didn't believe me.

The hot sun, her piercing eyes, the rotten tightness in my chest, my nakedness before her combined to make the world unbearable and close as it swam around me.

"Okay, Mr. Collard," Rosa said, stepping back. "I see we're going to have to take the long road."

"I don't know what you're talking about," I mumbled.

"Yes you do, Mr. Collard." Her eyes frosted over, and she gave me an ice-cold stare. "You know exactly what I'm talking about."

She backed away, eyeballing me until she reached her car.

The pressure eased and the world stopped spinning as she drove off.

I leaned against the doorframe for a moment and caught my breath before stepping inside.

CHAPTER 68

hat's a great model," the sales assistant said as he approached. He was beaming like sunshine on a clear spring day. "Sends everything directly to a hard drive in real time. Or if you buy a subscription, they will record the footage to the cloud."

He was about twenty, with the good days of his life ahead of him. His light brown hair, swept into a parting, flopped around as his head moved. His blue Best Buy uniform hung on his slim frame, and more than anything I wanted to trade places with him and have the promise of an unlived life rather than the wreckage of decades strewn in my wake.

"You looking for home security?" he asked.

His name tag said Kevin. We were the only people in the camera aisle of the Best Buy in West Hollywood, a one-stop shop for all consumer electronics located on La Brea Avenue.

"Yeah," I replied. "I need a couple of cameras linked up to a recorder."

He reached for a box from the top shelf. "These Blink cameras are battery operated, and like I said they can record to a drive or the cloud. Weatherproof and a long battery life. And they're motion activated."

I examined the box, nodding at the list of features. I used to know how to design these sorts of things.

"You could buy a set of three cameras and try to optimize position," Kevin said, "but a set of five is only a hundred bucks more, and surely that's worth the peace of mind?"

I didn't begrudge him his commission. Hopefully he'd do something better with my money than I ever could.

"Five is fine," I replied. After all, for once in a very long time, poverty wasn't my biggest problem.

Kevin's smile brightened. "Let me show you the recorders."

Three hours later, I'd finished drilling the mount for the fifth camera and was fine-tuning its position on the exterior wall of my cottage, aiming it at my gate. The other cameras covered the rest of the property line.

Satisfied with my work, I climbed down the stepladder and started packing away the drill and other tools I'd bought.

My phone rang, and *Anna Cacciola* appeared on-screen.

"Hello," I answered.

"Mr. Collard, it's Anna Cacciola. I know what links those murders. Are you near a TV?"

I was sweating from my work in the afternoon heat, but a cold chill dropped down my spine like an icicle falling from a gutter.

"Uh-huh," I responded, walking through the gate to the cottage.

"Switch on Fox-11," Anna said.

I rushed inside and shut the door behind me, feeling a little sick as I found the remote and switched on the local news station. I was shocked to see photos of Walter Glaze, Farah Younis, and Richard Gibson next to the somber anchor.

"TMZ cites sources within LAPD who say the three killings were linked by ritualistic mutilations. The victims' bodies were horribly disfigured while awaiting autopsies in local morgues. Police say the targeted nature of the mutilations suggests they were also done by the person who murdered the trio. Details have not been released, but some are dubbing these murders the work of the West Coast Ripper."

I flushed with the heat of fear.

Shit. Shit. Shit.

The West Coast Ripper? Shit! I hadn't mutilated those bodies. It wasn't me!

I dropped the phone, ran to the bathroom, and threw up in the toilet. I'd lost count of the number of times I'd hurled in my life, but this was different. I was trying to shed an evil that was part of me, and no matter how much my belly purged, this sickness would never go.

I flushed, staggered to the basin, and washed my face. I looked at myself, hardly recognizing the sunken-eyed, gray deadbeat who'd taken over the body of a once happy and hopeful man. It had been like a possession, a corruption of the soul so gradual, I'd hardly noticed the devil moving in.

Are you sure you didn't cut us up? Farah's spirit asked.

I didn't do that, I responded, but could I be certain? I was a drinker, a drug abuser. I skipped through life, losing hours like a needle on a scratched record. How could I be sure of anything?

It couldn't have been me. Could it? I couldn't have broken into those places to commit horror after murder, could I?

Desperation had turned me to murder. Greed had enabled me to be manipulated. Self-pity had made me careless about my life. Guilt had isolated me. These were my original sins, and now I was implicated in ritualistic murder. Tied to crimes of unimaginable horror that must have been perpetrated by the person who'd hired me.

My patron.

I thought the first thump was my heart, but the second was louder and clearer.

Someone was banging on my front door.

Not banging.

The crash and splinter that came next made the situation clear.

They were smashing their way inside.

CHAPTER 69

My first thought was *Cops!* and I ran into the corridor. Shouts filled my home, and I trembled and shook as I rushed toward the back door, but loud footsteps grew close, and hands grabbed me. I was hurled forward into the door and hit my head against it. Dazed, my vision sparking with flashes of light, I was manhandled roughly and punched in the back.

These weren't police.

I glanced around to see faces I recognized. Horrible, monstrous faces I thought I'd escaped. Frankie Balls, Cutter, Curse, and the rest of their crew. How had they found me?

Cutter had me by the shoulders, and he dragged me back along the corridor into the living room. He swung me around so I was face-to-face with Frankie.

"Peyton fucking Collard." Frankie's breath stank of old cigarettes. "You really think you could hide? Maybe if you'd gone to Mars. But in fucking LA, you're mine."

He slugged me in the gut, and I groaned and crumpled.

"Stay with us," Frankie said, slapping my face. "Nice place. Zebra, get to work."

A large man, with a face that spoke of nothing but anger and hatred, nodded at four others, and they started ransacking my place.

"Please don't," I said.

"Don't what?" Frankie asked. "Collect our money? You owe us, Peyton. We're here for dollar dough, my man."

There was well over $600,000 somewhere in my home, and these jackals were set on finding it.

"You tell me where it is and things will go easier." Frankie sounded as though he was giving mortgage advice to newlyweds, all friendly with a kind heart made of sugary best interests, but he punctuated his words with a knee to my groin.

"I don't have any money," I gasped.

Two punches; a left and a right.

Tears filled my eyes and blood ran from my nose down the back of my throat. I gasped for air and swallowed.

"I don't have anything." I almost choked on the words.

"We know you do," Frankie yelled.

He pulled a pistol from his waistband and forced it into my bloody mouth. The barrel scraped against my teeth, sending a shudder into my bones.

"You still don't remember me, do you?"

I stared into his eyes but drew a blank. Had we been inside together? Served in the army? I had no idea who he was, but he clearly thought I'd wronged him or owed him.

"You took me down with you, Peyton fucking Collard. This is restitution," he said.

I had no idea what he was talking about. Who was he to me? What was this connection he kept talking about? How did he think we knew each other? He was confusing me with someone else?

"Tell me where the money is, or I'll blow your fucking head off," Frankie snarled.

How did he know I had money? Now and before?

His face was twisted, like a king of devils. His demons were working up a storm, tearing my home apart, searching for my fortune.

You're going to die here, Walter's ghost said.

I know, I agreed, and quietly accepted that I had nothing to lose.

This man would probably kill me whether I handed him the money or not.

He pressed the gun farther, until I was almost gagging on the bloody metal.

One bullet.

That was all it would take to leave this world behind.

Whatever hell waited for me had to be better than this, and if there was nothing that would be fine too. Oblivion would be a step up from hell. Toni would find the money, using the instructions I'd mailed to Anna Cacciola on my way back from Best Buy. I'd thought I had to make plans for being busted by the cops. It never occurred to me to worry about Frankie, at least not so soon. How had he found me?

The devil's crooked path takes him into every nook of the world. I'm pretty sure one of my Sunday-school teachers had once said that.

At least Skye would live the life of her dreams and become a doctor if I kept silent.

And the evil that seemed to follow me around would end, and all the bad I'd ever perpetrated would be avenged. Wrongs would be righted, not by law and order, but at the hand of the worst of all villains. I suppose it was a fitting death.

"I know what you're thinking," Frankie said. "Better to eat the bullet. Only you ain't got such a nice end ahead of you, Peyton fucking Collard. If you don't give me the money, I'll put you in a wheelchair and roll you to the corner of Wilmington and Alondra, where you can spend your nights watching your daughter turning tricks for me in a roach motel. I'll work her day and night, Peyton, and when she's birthed a litter of degenerate bastards I'll raise as my own, turning them dark and metal hard, like these men, I'll execute her in front of you."

I burned with hatred and the anger and self-loathing of impotence and struggled against my captors.

"Then and only then I'll give you a bullet to eat," Frankie said, pulling the gun from my mouth.

"There's nothing here," Zebra yelled.

"You have two days. I want fifty grand for starters," Frankie said.

He whipped me with the pistol, and after the second blow, my mind gave up.

CHAPTER 70

When I came to, all of me hurt—my ribs, my stomach, my jaw. Everything.

The house had been trashed. The kitchen cabinets had been opened, doors ripped off, drawers flung around and smashed. The living room was a wild tornado mess. I staggered over to the French doors, looked at the garden, and was relieved to see it hadn't been touched.

The money Frankie Balls wanted, the price of blood for the three dead, was buried beneath the jasmine bush near the back fence. I'd bought a small safe from Home Depot when I got my tools and ladder to install the cameras and had buried my fortune in the earth like the pirates of old. I mean, who would think to look in the ground?

I left the living room and went to my downstairs bathroom. I almost cried out when I saw the mess I was in. I washed away the map of drying blood, but there was nothing to hide the bruises on my face.

I went back to the ransacked living room. The camera monitoring system was still connected to the power outlet, but it had been tossed onto the floor. The motion sensor had been activated and the hard drive was recording. Its alarm was going off. I pressed a button to deactivate the irritating sound, put the device on the couch, and hobbled outside.

Even the sunshine felt rotten, stinging my tenderized skin as I crossed the driveway to my Range Rover. I was horrified to see they'd keyed my beautiful car, marking the paint with white scores of abstract graffiti.

Someone had tried to draw a penis, but it was missing its shaft and just looked like a sick mushroom.

I sighed and regretted it immediately as my ribs joined the chorus of pain. The car was unlocked, and the glove compartment was hanging open. The gun I'd used to kill Richard Gibson was gone. I shuffled along to my mailbox and pulled open the metal door to find a familiar package inside.

Back in the living room, I ripped open the package. It was another message from my murderous and quite obviously deranged patron, the real West Coast Ripper. The money was wrapped in a tight bundle. One hundred hundreds. The paper belt declared $10,000, which meant there would be a million-dollar price on the next head. There was another URL printed on a piece of card.

I opened the browser on my phone. I was too tired and pained to bother with trying to conceal what I was doing anymore, and some part of me wanted to start to build an evidence trail, linking me to my anonymous patron. I wasn't an assassin anymore, or a murderer. I was a detective. I needed to know who was behind this.

I clicked on the audio recording on the website, and the machine voice came on.

"You now know the people you killed weren't villains, so we won't play games anymore," the recording said.

How? I wondered. *How did this grotesque, inhuman voice know that I knew I'd been lied to? Was it the voice of a devil who could see my warped soul?*

"The people you've been killing are not the criminals you were led to believe, but they have to die. The next is Alice Polmar of Sedona. Kill her and you will receive one million dollars. You can establish a trust fund for your daughter. Refuse, and evidence of your role in the other deaths will be sent to the police. You will die in prison and your daughter will lose everything. Scroll down."

I did as instructed and saw three photographs. One of me forcing Walter Glaze into his car, the second of me fleeing Farah Younis's building, and the last showed me shooting Richard Gibson. All three photos were candid, taken by someone who'd been following me.

I laughed a good and hollow chest full of air. Lie with jackals and you get eaten. I was no vigilante. I wasn't even a killer really. I was just a tool. A puppet. My strings had been pulled by the true villain, someone who would have a hold over me for the rest of my life.

I had to find this person and learn the truth about why he'd killed and mutilated these poor folk. I had to free myself from his grasp. I moved onto the floor and crawled to the solid-state hard drive and small LCD screen that were connected to the motion-activated cameras and pressed buttons that took me to the moment the system had activated.

A car pulled up in the mouth of my driveway and a young woman—black hair cut short like a lioness, no, a panther—jumped out. She wore a flowing white dress. An angel in army surplus boots. Heaven and war combined, like some Valkyrie. She ran to my mailbox, deposited the package, and returned to her ancient silver Honda Prius.

As the Valkyrie's chariot pulled away, I saw hope.

I'd recorded the car's license plate.

CHAPTER 71

I woke in a mess, slumped in the chair by my front door, surrounded by the wreckage left by Frankie Balls and his men. Everything came back in a flash, and the inside of my head burned as my memory returned. I had a couple of days before Frankie Balls would come looking for me. The cop was breathing down my neck. My patron was threatening me with exposure to coerce me into another murder. I would need my A game to wriggle away from all the jackals biting at my heels. I needed the man I'd once been, not the wretch I'd become.

I picked up my phone, which lay in the mess of my living room, and searched Google for my next target, Alice Polmar of Sedona, Arizona. There was no gossip this time. No bulletin boards or faked websites to convince me she was a bad person. Just a website for her family-run restaurant, Alice's, and photos of her with her four children and nine grandchildren. Light brown hair, the color of sugared apple pie crust, and a warm smile that said, "Welcome, friend." This was clearly someone who didn't deserve death.

I shook my head and sank a little further into the depression that had gripped me since I realized I'd been played for a fool. This manipulative patron had turned me into an extremist by exploiting my need for money, and now I was trapped. Kill a sweet old lady, or risk a lifetime in prison and the ruin of my daughter's dreams?

What would you have done?

Of course, if I killed Alice Polmar there was a chance I'd face that outcome anyway, but maybe I'd be able to bargain my way out of it if I could find out the identity of the person behind this. Unmask the puppeteer.

I dialed a number. "Anna Cacciola," I said when Anna's assistant answered. "It's Peyton Collard."

"Mr. Collard," Anna said a few moments later. "How can I help?"

"I need to find someone," I replied. "I have a photo and a license plate."

"Why?" she asked.

I was expecting the question, so I offered the best excuse I had.

"Some lady has been harassing my ex-wife, and she asked me to help find out who she is and why she's bothering her."

There was a brief pause.

"Sam Larabee. He's a PI we use from time to time. Ethical, thorough, and discreet. I'll text you his details."

"Thanks," I replied.

"I hope he can help," she said before hanging up.

Sam's info came a little later. I downloaded the footage and stills of the Valkyrie and her car from my camera system to a USB drive, got into my keyed Range Rover, and drove south toward Westmont.

I wanted to confirm a hunch I'd had ever since I'd seen the beautiful Valkyrie on my surveillance footage, and pulled into a mini-mall parking lot. It was the sort of place that attracted businesses operating on the margins of society, drawn by low rent. A pawn shop, laundromat, cheap liquor store, and, behind barred windows, Ryder Bail Bonds.

I parked in front of the office and went to the glass door, which was reinforced with a metal grille. I pressed the bell and, after a short wait, was buzzed in.

I was greeted by a wiry tattooed man with crew-cut gray hair and dark, suspicious eyes. He stood behind a metal mesh that rose from a high counter.

"Yeah?" he asked.

"Syd?" I replied.

"I'm his brother." He turned and yelled at an open doorway. "Syd. Some guy here."

The office had two walls of wanted posters, police notices, and court judgments pinned to corkboards. There were a couple of hard plastic chairs near the window, facing the counter.

Syd Ryder emerged from the doorway and joined his brother behind the mesh. They could have been twins were it not for Syd's long hair, which was bunched in a tail.

"Yeah?"

"Peyton Collard. We spoke a while back," I said.

"Yeah. I remember."

Not much of a conversationalist.

"I wanted to show you a photo of someone. See if she paid my bond."

When I'd called him, after I'd been sprung from jail, Syd had intimated my savior had been an attractive woman. What were the chances of two unfamiliar beauties throwing money at me?

"I can't give out confidential information," he replied.

"I'm not asking you to. I'm trying to find this person to figure out why they sprung me. You don't have to give me a name or anything—"

"I didn't catch a name," he interrupted. "Not one I'd give you anyway."

"Okay," I continued, "all I need is for you to nod if it's her."

He shrugged, and I passed the USB drive through a six-by-eight-inch opening cut just above the countertop.

Syd's brother took the device and plugged it into something on the other side. He opened a laptop screen.

"Which file?" he asked.

"Exterior Valkyrie JPEG," I replied.

He clicked his mouse, and a moment later Syd nodded.

"Thanks," I said. "Appreciate it."

"Just make sure you honor your bond," he replied as his brother handed me back the drive. "Me and Karl don't take kindly to folks we have to hunt."

CHAPTER 72

I don't have Anna's deep pockets. I've checked your credit score and I'm going to need payment up front, Mr. Collard," Sam Larabee said.

I thought Anna Cacciola had given me the wrong address; 4000 Warner Boulevard in Burbank turned out to be the address of Warner Studios, and Larabee had one of the small, old production offices on the lot.

"I gotta ask," I said, trying to change the subject. "How—"

"The office," Larabee cut me off. "I did a service for one of the executives here, and he insisted I take it. Rent free for life."

"Must have been quite a service."

"It was. I don't fuck around, Mr. Collard. Which is why it will be payment up front."

Larabee wasn't quite the grizzled private detective I'd imagined. Apart from the office on the studio lot, which was just surreal, he was a rolled-up sleeves, white shirt, and slacks kind of guy. Skinny and tall with a hard edge and a stern, but somehow charming smile. He reminded me of a young Matthew McConaughey, not just in looks. His tough but fair surface seemed designed to conceal unfathomable depths. He didn't bother trying to impress me with his background; we both knew Anna's recommendation was enough.

So, we sat in his office surrounded by the fakers and dream-makers, and he listened while I spun a yarn of my own, telling him why I needed to find this mystery lady. I think he suspected I was lying, but he was probably the kind of guy who assumed most people were liars.

"Shouldn't be too difficult to find her if you got the license," he told me when I was finished. "My assistant will send you a bill. I'll get started once it's paid."

"Thanks," I said before he showed me out.

His assistant, a preppy mid-twentysomething called Otis, who looked like he might have worked his way up from the studio mail room, took my details and promised to send me the bill within an hour.

My phone rang as I left the building.

"Pey," Toni said when I answered.

I relaxed, then. She never used my pet name if she was mad. She must have forgiven me for showing up at her place drunk with Jim.

"What the fuck have you been doing?" Uh-oh. I'd misjudged it. She was mad as hell.

"Some guys came round here and threatened me and Skye. They said you'd better get them their money."

My heart fell into a black pit of despair. Frankie Balls wanted me to know they would make good on their threat.

"I'm sorry—" I said, but she cut me off before I could get any further.

"Fuck! Peyton, this is our daughter. You can ruin your own life, but don't you dare put her in danger." She started crying. "Don't you dare."

"I'm sorry," I said, stopping by my car. I was shaking. What had I done?

"That's not good enough, Peyton. You need to fix this. Whatever it is, you need to make it go away."

She was right, of course. I had to step up, even if I paid a heavy price.

"I need to see you," I said.

She hesitated.

"Please, Toni," I said. "I have to. It's part of how I make this right."

"Peyton, I don't want to—"

"Toni, you might not love me anymore, but I still love you. You were my first, Toni, and Skye is my only. I need to see you."

She hesitated.

"Okay. I'm at home. I sent Skye to play at Laura's house. They'll bring her home for dinner."

"I'm on my way. Be there in about thirty minutes," I replied before hanging up.

I made it to Toni's in thirty-five minutes. I checked my phone as I walked toward the broken gate in front of her building, and saw the bill from Otis Huxley, Sam Larabee's assistant. I paused, used my online bank to pay, and sent an email to let him know before hurrying through the gate. I crossed the yard and knocked on the back door, and Toni answered almost instantly.

"Oh my God," she said when she saw my bruises. "Did they do this?"

"Yeah."

"Come in." She led me into her tiny apartment. I sat on the couch and she joined me.

"You remember the summer Billy Whipple kicked my ass?" I asked.

She smiled and nodded, but there were tears in her eyes.

We'd been kids together. She knew me better than anyone. She was my love. My friend. So close to me and yet so far. If anyone could sense I was a dead man walking, it was her.

"This is nothing like that," I said. Billy Whipple had been a beach bully, and I stood up to him on the shores of Lake Michigan, only to be buried face-first in the sand. Ass in the air, mouth full of dirt, it had been something of a joke at high school. If someone got beat up, they'd gotten Whippled just like Collard. "These guys are nothing like Billy. They mean business. I don't see a good ending here."

"Oh, Peyton," she replied. I don't know if she had a whole angry speech planned, but she was all sympathy and pity now. "Why did this happen?"

I didn't have time to explain. I knew part of her would be glad to see the back of me. The part that had fallen in love with Jack.

"I've sent my lawyer some information. If anything happens to me, you're to go see Anna Cacciola. She's got a code only you'll understand.

A story really full of references from childhood. It will lead you to the money I've left Skye."

"Peyton," she said, her eyes shimmering. "They can't kill you. They won't kill you. What have you been doing?"

"Bad things," I replied, and her tears fell. "I've been doing bad things. I wish I hadn't, but I was desperate to be a good man, a good father, and someone used my desperation to manipulate me. I'm sorry."

"Me, too," she replied. She exhaled and took my hands. "Just give them the money. We'll be okay. Skye needs a father. Her father."

I was surprised.

"You and I, Peyton. We're still just kids. No one prepared us for this world. No one tells you what it's going to be like. That you have to figure it all out for yourself. That there are no do-overs."

"I can't give them the money," I responded. "My life is a mess. There might be no do-overs, but there are endings. I can't control how the story goes, but I can control how it ends. I'm not a good man, Toni. You want to save me? Skye has a chance with that money. If I can do one good thing, I can be at peace."

"Do you know why she wants to be a doctor?" Toni asked.

I shook my head, barely in control of my emotions.

"She thinks if there had been a doctor there that day, Freya Persico would still be alive," Toni revealed, and I felt the lump in my throat tremble, ready to give way to a flood. "She doesn't want any other families to go through the pain we've suffered."

The revelation was too much for me at that moment, and I started crying as Toni embraced me. She cried too.

"I want to do right by her," I sobbed. "I want to make this better. For her."

"I thought I'd lost the good man I'd married," she said. "But he's still in there. He's still trying."

I heard a key in the front door, and a moment later Skye entered, bemused to find her tearful mother holding her sobbing father.

"Er, hi," she said.

Toni let me go and wiped her eyes. I did the same.

"Hi, honey. How was Laura?" Toni asked.

"Good. Hi, Dad," Skye responded.

"Hi, kiddo," I said. "Are you okay?"

She nodded as she put her bag on the small kitchen table. "You mean those guys? Mom said they were just trying to scare us."

"They were," I assured her. "I'm gonna take care of it. You don't have anything to worry about. I'm going to make everything right."

Skye brightened, and Toni took my hand and held it fondly, and for the briefest time I had everything I needed.

CHAPTER 73

Sitting with my ex-wife and daughter, I had a fleeting taste of the life I'd lost, and for a short time I was able to pretend nothing bad had happened, that we were all together and that they still loved me.

But it didn't last. My phone rang, and a number I didn't recognize appeared on-screen.

"It's Sam Larabee," he said when I answered. "I found the woman who's been troubling your wife. You're not going to do anything stupid?"

"Who needs the heat? I'm sure Anna told you the charges I'm facing. I'm an idiot sometimes, but I'm not violent."

Ha! Farah's ghost said, and for a moment I saw her one-eyed face.

"I just want to talk to her, and if she won't listen to reason, I'll give her details to the cops," I assured him. "I'm sitting here with my wife and daughter—"

"Ex-wife," Toni cut in.

"And I swear in front of them I won't do anything stupid."

Toni looked puzzled, and I raised my hand to indicate everything would be okay.

"Her name is Jessica Yallop. Twenty-seven. Lives in the Hollywood Hills on Beechwood Drive. Otis will send you her details so we have an email trail, Mr. Collard," Larabee told me.

"I understand. You don't have to worry. I appreciate the quick work."

He grunted and hung up.

"What the heck are you into, Peyton?" Toni asked.

"Nothing," I replied. "Well, not nothing, but nothing I can't handle."

Yeah, right, Walter's ghost said. *You're a dead man walking.*

"I've got to go," I said, getting to my feet.

"Whatever you're into, Peyton, you should go to the police." There was so much sadness and resignation in Toni's voice.

"I can't," I replied, and she and Skye didn't bother trying to conceal their disappointment. My words were as good as a written confession of guilt.

Skye followed me to the back door and surprised me by taking my hand. "You okay, Dad?"

"I'll be fine, kiddo. I'll see you around."

She smiled, but it was a lie writ large.

Toni said nothing as she watched me leave, and I walked away from her place with the uneasy feeling that would be the last time I'd see them. I choked up at the prospect I'd miss the rest of Skye's life, but if my sacrifice was what it took to ensure her future, I'd make it without hesitation. Did that make me a good man? I didn't think so. Good men don't get mixed up with murder.

At least Skye would never have to worry about money, and erasing my deadbeat influence from her life might actually be better for her. There are too many similarities between me and my father, and the worst thing I could imagine would be for Skye to end up anything like me. Frankie Balls would have no reason to hurt Skye if I wasn't around. He wouldn't know where the money had gone and wouldn't be able to extort a dead man. My exit was the only way to keep my daughter safe.

I climbed into the Range Rover and checked my phone to find an email from Otis, giving me Jessica Yallop's address on Beechwood Drive. It took me an hour to cross LA south to north, and I spent most of it sitting in nose-to-tail traffic on the Hollywood Freeway, watching the lowering sun drop toward the horizon.

Jessica Yallop lived in a low-rise horseshoe-shaped apartment block with rusty balconies that overlooked a small swimming pool filled with greenish water. I parked on the street outside her building and used my phone to google her. I found the profile of a twenty-seven-year-old actress who'd been in a few short films and one low-budget feature. She had sandy-blond hair, delicate features, and clear skin, and reminded me of a *Pretty Woman*–era Julia Roberts. Her eyes were warm, and there was a longing that I might have imagined because I was desperate for the love and kindness of others.

If she was the mastermind behind the murders, the world was more upside down than I thought. There was nothing about her that suggested she had the funds or the motive to have Walter Glaze, Farah Younis, and Richard Gibson killed, and no obvious connection to the new target, Alice Polmar.

I got out of the car, headed up the path to the 1950s apartment block, and climbed the exterior stairs to the third floor. I walked along the shared balcony, looking for 3F, and when I saw the corroded metal badge with the correct number and letter, I knocked on the door. A moment later, Jessica Yallop opened it.

She was beautiful even without the makeup and lighting of her headshots. Hollywood was full of such beauty, and most of it would be chewed up and spit out by an industry as merciless as it was ambitious.

Jessica tried to slam the door the instant she recognized me, but I stuck my foot out and followed up with my shoulder, barging my way in. She cried out as she stumbled back, and I hurried inside and shut the door behind me.

"Get the fuck out before I call the cops," she yelled. "Help!"

She tried to run past me, but I grabbed her wrist and held it tight.

"Settle down," I said. "I just want to know why you've been paying me to kill people."

She froze. I couldn't have shocked her more if I'd slapped her.

"What did you say?"

She looked at me afresh, her eyes wide with fear.

"Please don't hurt me."

"What? I'm not here to hurt you. I just want to know what's going on."

I let go, and she backed away. I looked around her tiny apartment. Lots of books, manuscripts, movie posters on the walls. She was in a pair of linen shorts and a black vest.

"You don't know, do you?" I said.

She sat on her couch by the window that overlooked the balcony and put her head in her hands. "Oh my God. He promised it wasn't anything illegal."

"Tell me what you know."

She glanced up with fear in her eyes. "A guy contacted me through my website. Said he needed someone to deliver packages. Offered me two thousand bucks a package."

She started crying.

"I knew nothing legal would pay that kind of money, but you know how you con yourself into believing something when you're desperate. Acting is tough, and I needed a way to make my rent."

I scoffed and nodded. I was very familiar with the power of desperation.

"You ever meet the guy?"

She shook her head. "He leaves my money and your packages in an old newspaper dispenser on Proctor Avenue in the City of Industry. Sends me messages on a cell he left there telling me when I need to collect."

She was claiming to be a courier. A cutout to protect my patron's identity. Her story seemed to stack up. She certainly didn't look like she had the resources to pull off a sting of highly paid assassinations.

"How did you know my new address?" I asked.

"He gave it to me."

How the heck did he know? I wondered.

I considered the question and everything else she'd told me in silence.

"Did you really kill people?" she asked after a while.

I didn't answer, and her crying grew more intense.

"I could go to jail," she sobbed.

Typical self-centered twenty-first-century thinking. No thought for the poor victims she'd helped erase or their families. I might have committed the crimes, but at least I felt bad about it. Still, her self-interest in avoiding prison would save me the trouble of having to threaten her. She understood our fates were now linked, and her silence was essential to protect herself.

"Do you have the phone number he uses to text you?" I asked. "And the address of the drop?"

CHAPTER 74

The newsstand was outside an abandoned supermarket. The faded old sign said Tucker's, and it was easy to see why the independent store hadn't been replaced by Ralphs or one of the other big SoCal chains. The building was in a run-down part of the City of Industry, an east LA neighborhood devoted to manufacturing and commerce. Old empty warehouses spread out in every direction, blown clean by the cruel wind of recession. The whole block was ripe for redevelopment, but until then no one would revive the market, which would have once relied on trade from local workers. It was approaching 10:00 p.m., and the streets were deserted.

The newsstand itself was one of the old vend-yourself up-and-over glass-fronted boxes that opened and closed for a quarter. The *LA Times* masthead was just about visible at the top of the box. The mechanism was broken and the money safe long gone. The main cabinet now rose with a gentle pull.

I set up three motion-activated cameras around the newsstand. One was mounted on a streetlamp, another on the cracked wall that stood at the edge of the old supermarket parking lot. The third was placed in the entrance of the warehouse opposite, and I concealed the wireless recorder in a broken mailbox next to it.

Sam Larabee, the private detective I'd hired, returned my call when I was making final checks on the system.

"Mr. Collard, sorry for the late call, I was at dinner and only just got the message from Otis," he said when I answered. "What can I do for you?"

"Can you trace a cell number?" I asked.

"More trouble with your ex-wife?" he suggested.

"Yeah. I went to see Jessica Yallop, and she says she's being paid to harass my ex-wife. Doesn't know who the money's coming from."

A partial truth is always stronger than a total lie.

"Once I have a name, I can go to the police," I said.

He hesitated.

"I just need a name," I pressed.

"Send me the number," he replied. "Same as before: Otis will email our bill. Once it's been paid, I'll get started."

"I appreciate it," I replied before he hung up.

I checked the small screen on the hard drive and cycled through the three cameras to ensure I had a good view of the newsstand and the street and sidewalk around it. Satisfied with my work, I switched off the screen and put the drive on motion-active mode before placing it back into the broken mailbox. It wasn't a floating bridge across a contested river, but it was battlefield engineering of sorts, and it felt good to exercise long-dormant habits. I used a padlock to secure the metal cover, picked up my tools, and returned to the Range Rover, which was parked in the otherwise empty supermarket lot.

The scorings on the side of my car were ugly, but I had bigger things to worry about, so I tried to ignore them as I climbed into my once-beautiful machine and started the engine. As the air-conditioning kicked in and an ice-cold artificial breeze hit me, I reflected on what had brought me here.

Murder, Walter's ghost said.

Greed, Farah's spirit added.

Stupidity, Gibson's specter joined in.

They were all right, and it was this evil that would free me. My patron had followed a pattern. A package naming the target and a down payment, and a second package with the bounty for the hit. In order to draw my mysterious employer to this newsstand, I'd have to kill the next target.

Alice Polmar—sweet grandmother of nine, pillar of the Sedona community, kindly old lady—had to die.

CHAPTER 75

The air-conditioning kept the relentless sun at bay. Heat hit the windshield in pulses and tried to blaze its way into the icy cab of the Range Rover. If you've ever made the drive from Los Angeles to Arizona, you'll be familiar with the burn of the desert. It's a brutal, desolate environment, made habitable by a combination of technology and old west stubbornness. Some say more of the world will be like this in years to come. I hope not, for Skye's sake. I want my child to have a better life in a nicer world than me.

I'd spent the night at home and had tried to pick up the mess. The emergency locksmith I'd called had done a good job on the front door. He'd installed a couple more locks and a security bar designed to make it more difficult for anyone to invade my cottage.

With the place a little tidier and more secure, I'd passed a restless night disturbed by guilty premonitions of what I was about to do to Alice Polmar. I didn't see I had much choice. If I didn't kill her, my patron would expose me, and the only way I could identify him was to draw him out with another death.

So, I woke early and set off for Sedona, and by midmorning was out of the city, driving along the I-10 with Joshua Tree to my north. I couldn't see any of the majesty of the national park from the interstate, just barren hills and arid scrub shimmering in the pizza oven heat.

I stopped at Times 3 Family Restaurant, a diner in Quartzsite, a little over halfway to Phoenix. It was a lime-green 1950s-style pagoda with an aluminum roof a stone's throw from the highway. Outside the dry air crackled with heat, and I felt myself wilt as I crossed the dirt parking lot, but inside was cool and done out like a classic American diner with red leather booths and stools surrounding a horseshoe counter. The walls were lined with family mementos and large colorful paintings of the lush green Arizona mountains I was heading for. I could see them clearly through the big windows.

I took a stool at the counter and ordered a patty melt—a cheese-burger and onions—and a Coke. It reminded me of days out with my dad when I was really young, before I knew he was a lush. We'd have burgers and Cokes in a joint near Lake Michigan. I can't even remember its name, but it was done out like Times 3, and sitting there eating my sandwich, I was transported to happier days. Looking back, I realize my dad was probably so fond of burgers because the grease blunted the worst of his hangovers. But for a short time, sitting at that counter, I pretended I was that kid again, with no idea of the harsh realities that were heading my way.

Writing this, it seems odd I was sitting there romanticizing a drunk who probably set me on the wrong path in life and was a terrible role model. He wasn't all burgers and Cokes. When he was mad and Mom couldn't get me out of the house, he'd beat me. Discipline for some in-fraction, perceived or real. For my own good, he'd slur.

I'd make allowances as a kid, but now I look at Skye and wonder, how could anyone strike a child they love? How could they hit their baby and feel good about it? Like hitting a husband or wife, boyfriend or girl-friend, how can true love yield anything but the truly loving? I wondered if Dad secretly resented me. Maybe I was like Skye is to me, the promise of an unwritten life. I want hers to be the best it can be, but maybe he was jealous of that potential and wanted to warp me the way he'd warped himself?

I sat at the counter and watched a few customers come and go. I wasn't in any rush. I was on my way to kill an old woman to protect myself and guarantee my kid's future. What better reason for murder, right? I'd done it under the illusion I was a vigilante angel of vengeance. I'd even killed by accident. But here I was taking decisive action to protect my money and child. What would you have done? What would you do now if someone like Frankie Balls came knocking at your door? Sitting in your bath, lying in your bed, traveling on the subway, would you be able to do what was necessary to protect yourself or your family? Could you get yourself out of my jam?

I wasn't sure I could. How could I kill an old lady without the propaganda that had riled me up against the others? Alice Polmar didn't deserve to die, so I was left weighing her against me, and I couldn't honestly say I deserved to live. Skye was the only reason the old woman's life was in the balance. Would you kill an innocent to save your kid?

I paid my check and went outside to be assaulted by the afternoon sun again. I drove east, watching heat shimmer over the scrub desert, dancing around the coarse bushes and rocks that had persisted there for eons before human eyes ever saw them.

North of Phoenix, the desert gave way to the pine forests that stretched across the upper reaches of the state. The trees stood proud, like soldiers guarding distant hillsides. America is the land of the road trip, and it is easy to see why. The country is majestic and inspiring, and I felt moved by it. I wanted this feeling to last.

CHAPTER 76

Alice Polmar didn't deserve to die.

Arriving in Sedona shortly before sundown, I drove to her eponymous diner on Schnebly Hill Road, near Oak Creek, and parked in the busy lot out front.

It was a little after six and the place was packed with families. I could see excited kids at almost every table, eating and talking with friends and family. The diner looked like a postcard-perfect snapshot of American history, all whitewashed board, red bricks with bright white mortar, and stars and stripes draped everywhere. The red, white, and blue motif spilled into the interior, and it was obvious this place was run by people who loved their country.

My heart thumped as I got out of the car and walked to the diner, adrenaline sharpening every sense.

The noise was a battlefield assault after such a peaceful drive. The clatter of cutlery and dishes sounding like artillery, the clamor of voices was machine-gun fire, and somewhere beneath it all, a bed of country music.

"Hello, welcome to Alice's," a cheerful lady in a red-and-white-checked dress said as I neared the host's station.

She was early forties and had a genuine warmth that reminded me of my mom. She could always make me feel better.

"We don't have any tables, but I can set you up at the counter."

"That would be great," I replied.

Her enthusiasm encouraged hyperbole. No counter could be great, not today, but I felt obliged to play along.

"Right this way, sir," she said.

She grabbed a menu and led me between rows of booths where America sat feasting. I was green jealous of the good-time happy faces and felt as though I was a different species as I sat on a chrome and red leather stool at the counter.

"It's your lucky day, sir," the greeter said. "Alice is going to take care of you herself."

My pounding heart went into overdrive when I looked along the counter to see Alice Polmar talking to another customer. She glanced at me and smiled, and I felt queasy. The beat of death pulsed in my veins, because that's what I was to my victims.

The deadbeat.

She, on the other hand, looked like Uncle Sam's younger sister and shone with the wholesome qualities of the American dream. She wore the same red-and-white-checked dress as her staff, but she set hers off with a blue neckerchief that was tied at a jaunty angle. Her hair had been styled in a short bob, and her makeup drew out her best features: plump lips, round cheeks, and generous eyes.

My patron was asking me to murder Mother America.

This was no drug dealer, no cartel lawyer, there was no deception or artifice that could conceal what this person was, and right there in that moment she was the embodiment of mothers everywhere and I was being asked to kill her.

"What can I get you?" Her voice was like soft and sweet apple pie filling.

"Coffee, please," I croaked, feeling even queasier.

"And some pecan pie? It's scrumptious."

Scrumptious? *Who even uses that word?*

Good people, Walter's ghost said. *Educated people.*

Take a long look at her, Farah's spirit added. *Does she deserve what you did to us?*

I knew she didn't.

"That sounds good," I said, trying not to betray my inner conflict.

Alice winked, smiled, and got on with fixing my order.

The pie was the sweetest I'd ever tasted, but guilt turned it to sewage in my mouth. I watched Alice flit around the counter like a butterfly, tending to everyone with equal care. Yes, it was good business, but what she was doing went beyond dollars and cents. She really cared. Even about the man who'd been sent to kill her. She checked on me a couple of times, and of course I lied and said the pie tasted amazing. It would have to someone else.

After a while, I left and sat in my car and watched the place until finally, a little after nine, when the sun had gone and stars dotted the sky, she emerged, got into an old Jeep Cherokee, and drove out of the lot.

I started the Range Rover and followed.

I'm not proud of what I did next, but I couldn't see any other way out.

Her taillights led me through town, and we turned off the highway onto Red Rock Loop Road, a narrow winder up into the high hills. We climbed a steep rise toward the heavens, and the road curled round a sugar mound–shaped mountain. When we took the second bend and could no longer be seen from the highway or town, I accelerated along the otherwise deserted road and pulled alongside her.

I'll always recall the puzzled look she gave me, which turned to horror as I swerved. I didn't even have to make contact. Her reflexes did the job for me, and she drove herself off the road.

CHAPTER 77

Were you hoping for redemption?

Were you under the impression that beneath all the murder and selfishness, I was a good man?

Three hours into my drive back to LA, as I sped through the darkness of the desert, the only lights were the stars high above me and the beams of the occasional passing vehicle. I had the radio on, and a little after midnight, the KFYI News and Talk station gave me the breaking-news bulletin I'd been waiting for ever since leaving Sedona. The host announced in a sober voice that prominent Sedona local Alice Polmar had died in the burnt-out wreckage of her Jeep Cherokee, which had been found at the bottom of a cliff, just off Red Rock Loop Road, some three hundred feet below the spot where it had crashed through the barrier. The large SUV had smashed on the rocks below, and the ensuing fire had been so hot her remains had not yet been recovered.

They went live to the scene, where the officer in charge made an appeal for witnesses and told the KFYI host their working theory was that an animal had startled Alice on her way home.

In a way they were right.

I was an animal. A deadbeat. A rare breed that didn't really have any business on earth.

The journey back to the City of Angels was difficult because I knew I'd face trouble ahead. I counted lights on the highway and watched the grayscale clouds drift across the stars, trying to prolong what I suspected would be my last moments. The world is a truly beautiful place if you look at it in the right frame of mind.

I finally reached my cottage in the hills shortly after 4:00 a.m., turned into my driveway, and immediately regretted coming straight home.

Blazing lights blinded me, and I instinctively stepped on the brakes.

The car stopped inches from another, and my heart thundered. I put the Range Rover into reverse, but my path was blocked by two more sets of bright lights pulling up behind me.

Please don't be Frankie, I prayed inwardly. *I'm not ready to die just yet.*

"Mr. Collard, please switch off your engine and exit the vehicle with your hands up," Rosa Abalos said, stepping between my car and the one in front.

My heart shifted down a gear. This wasn't death. This was incarceration.

I did as the detective asked, and the world suddenly seemed very still when I killed the Range Rover's huge engine. I stepped into the warm night with my hands raised.

"What's this about?" I asked, inching toward the back of my car. I couldn't afford to be caught. Not now.

"You know what this is about, Mr. Collard," Rosa said, stepping forward to bring herself out of silhouette. She looked irritated.

I sensed movement behind me and glanced around to see three uniformed cops exit two LAPD cars.

I couldn't be taken. I had to learn the identity of my employer, or I'd have nothing to bargain with.

I took a couple of steps toward the back of the Range Rover.

"I just need to get something," I said, reaching for the rear door handle.

"Keep your hands where I can see them," one of the cops behind me yelled, and I looked over my shoulder to see he'd pulled his gun.

Death was back on the table.

I began to tremble, but as scared as I was, I had to gamble.

For Skye.

I moved quickly, pulled the handle, and opened the back door.

There, lying unconscious on the back seat of the Range Rover, was Mrs. Alice Polmar of Sedona, Arizona.

You were probably a little disappointed when you thought I'd killed her. A part of you knows I'm a murderer, but another is intrigued by me, otherwise you wouldn't have stuck with my tale this far. You want redemption. You want to know there is hope, that our mistakes can be put behind us. You want to know even the worst of us is capable of change.

And so do I.

If there's hope for me, there might be hope for us all.

How could I ever have been redeemed if I'd murdered Mother America? Besides, I realized as I drove through Sedona, contemplating the contours and folds of time, that I didn't have to kill her, I just had to convince my patron she was dead.

The sight of Alice Polmar lying on my back seat had the desired effect. It was a huge distraction.

"Get away from her," the gun-toting cop yelled, and I was happy to oblige.

"Detective, there's a woman in here," another shouted to Rosa, who hurried over.

I moved to my mailbox, while the three cops ran forward to help the old woman. I pulled open the metal door and saw a package that was too small to contain $1 million. It looked like one of the instruction messages.

"Hey!" Rosa Abalos yelled, recovering from the distraction of Alice Polmar's discovery.

I grabbed the package, ignored more shouted commands, put my foot into the mailbox, reached for the top of the wall, and hauled myself over to freedom.

CHAPTER 78

I landed in the scrub by the side of the road. Footsteps crunched across my drive, but I was already running, and pushed through the bushes to the south of my property. My only hope of haggling my way out of a murder rap was to identify my patron, and these cops were intent on robbing me of the liberty to do that, so I flew through thick foliage.

Branches tried to stop me, but I was desperate, and I took the nicking, scratching, and scoring pain, increasing my pace when I heard sirens nearby. The cherry glow of the police cruisers lit up the night.

These cops thought I was a murderer and mutilator and that they'd discovered me with my next victim in my car. As far as they were concerned, I was a monster, and this was a Most Wanted manhunt. I didn't expect gentle care if they took me into custody. The thought spurred me a little faster, but in the main I knew my life was over if I didn't find the person who'd instigated the murders. I'd pulled the trigger, but I'd been manipulated by someone who wanted these people dead for unknown reasons. The mutilations suggest some kind of revenge or punishment.

I ran through the bushes and burst into my neighbor's garden. Motion-activated lights illuminated the place immediately, and it seemed as though the glare was burning me as I raced across the lawn toward the fence on the other side. Darkness was my friend. Light would shine me toward prison.

I climbed over the fence and forced my way through more bushes until I reached another lawn. A dog barked and came sprinting toward me. A Doberman, all bright white fangs and black snarls. I ran to my right and flew up and over a chain-link fence while the dog snapped loud barks at me from the other side.

I ran onto a quiet road and slowed to a walk. I needed help, somewhere to lie low, but my roster of friends had run thin. I couldn't trust Jim, and I didn't want to put Toni and Skye in even more danger. A face filled my mind, the only person who'd shown me any real kindness recently. Felicity's work would make her naturally suspicious of cops and the instruments of justice, and she'd seemed kind and understanding.

I took out my phone and dialed the number she'd given me.

"Hello?" Felicity said.

"It's Peyton Collard, we . . ."

"Peyton. I remember."

"Listen, I could really use a place to crash. I've run into some trouble. I know it's late and we hardly know each other, but I can pay."

"Are you calling as a client or a friend?" she asked.

"Friend," I said.

"Then let's be friends and not talk about money. I'm just finishing for the night. I can meet you at my apartment."

She gave me an address near Venice Beach.

"Thanks," I said.

I couldn't believe my luck. I certainly didn't deserve it.

"See you soon," she replied before hanging up.

I smiled. Felicity had made me feel good, and she was helping me in my time of need. Something about her just felt right.

CHAPTER 79

Felicity had a tiny studio apartment in a blue, wood-paneled building on Pacific Avenue in Venice, two blocks from the ocean. It was on the ground floor with a small garden front and back, and she was there when I arrived, greeting me without makeup. She wore a pair of jeans and a black T-shirt and looked even more attractive than I remembered.

"I'm sorry to ask," I said. "You don't even know me."

"I've developed a pretty good spidey sense," she replied. "Hazard of the job. You don't seem dangerous to me."

I didn't think I was, but right now, the families of my victims and LAPD would disagree with both of us.

"I'm harmless," I said.

She smiled as I stepped inside.

Her living room had a hardwood floor, a cream couch, and bold botanical prints that spoke to a love of nature.

"It's been a rough night," I said. "A rough few years in truth."

"Why don't you have a seat and tell me about it?" She gestured at the couch. "Can I get you a drink? Something to calm the nerves?"

"Water," I said firmly, determined to make some changes.

A few minutes later, we were on the couch, me with my hands curled around a cool glass of water, her trying to conceal her fatigue.

I told her everything. I started with the accident and the death of Freya Persico, because that was the event that derailed me. I told her about the time I served, the beatings I took in prison, the hard life I endured inside, the divorce, the mess I made when I was released, falling into drugs and alcoholism. The longer I spoke, the more I struggled to believe the disaster my life had become.

It was off the scale.

Then came the offer and the murders. She listened intently, and her face hardened when I spoke of Walter Glaze, Farah Younis, and Richard Gibson. I didn't lie or downplay what I'd done. I was honest about my willingness to kill for money, a willingness born from desperation and because I had been manipulated into believing my victims were evil.

If Felicity judged me harshly, she didn't show it. If she was afraid, she didn't show that either. She sat silently. There was no hint of tiredness anymore. She was too engrossed, and we'd pushed through the veil of night to the dawn.

I told her about discovering I'd been manipulated and recounted the abduction of Alice Polmar and the events that led me to her place.

When I finally fell silent, she said nothing. She simply looked at me, her face shining in the dawn light, her eyes cold. I braced for a slap. At the very least, I expected to be told to leave.

Instead, after a pause that seemed to last an age, she took my hands.

"It's okay," she said, and her eyes softened.

Kindness.

I wasn't prepared for kindness, and tears of relief came to my eyes.

"I wondered what connected us when we met," she said. "It's the eyes. When you take a life, I think a part of you dies, and you can see the loss in a person's eyes. I didn't register it before, but I see it now. Part of you is gone."

That's exactly how it felt to me, that a piece of me had died with each victim. I was so grateful and relieved to have found someone who understood me, I could hardly speak.

"It's okay, Peyton," she assured me. "It really is."

"But I've done terrible things." I almost choked on the words. "You don't understand what it's like to live with the guilt."

Her eyes started to shimmer. "I do. I told you I don't judge people. You can only truly understand someone if you've shared their pain. I've shared yours."

She hesitated, and the stillness weighed heavily upon me.

"I was in New York. A guy, turns out he was an off-duty cop, started getting rough with me. I was pretty sure . . ."

Her voice broke as the first tears rolled down her cheeks.

"He was going to kill me. We struggled. I shot him with his gun. The cops didn't believe me. He was a family man with four kids. They said I'd tried to rob him. If it hadn't been for two other women coming forward saying he'd tried to strangle them during sex, the cops would never have bothered investigating. They tied him to the murders of three working girls. He'd assaulted many more. He knew most people don't care about us, and he was cunning, good at covering his tracks."

She looked at my hands, and I watched her eyelashes flicker as they shed more tears. She was being kind to me. We weren't the same. She'd killed to save herself. I'd done it because I'd been drunk and thoughtless the first time, desperate and greedy for the last three. But she'd made her point; few people would understand us as well as we might understand each other.

"I felt guilt for a long time, especially when I saw his wife and kids on the news. But then I thought of the girls he'd killed and the ones he'd hurt, and I knew he'd never be able to do that again. And it felt good to have stopped someone else's pain and given the ghosts of those dead girls some justice."

Who will give us justice? Walter's ghost asked. *You need to suffer for what you've done.*

Felicity must have seen pain in my eyes, because she reached out and stroked my face. "It's okay."

I wanted to make her feel better, to protect her from all the wrong in the world. She brought out emotions I'd long forgotten, and I saw what she'd been talking about. There was something in her eyes that went beyond sadness, as though some part of her was dead. Something was missing in both of us, taken by the deaths we'd caused. Maybe we could fill the gap for each other?

I can't undo what I've done, I told Walter's ghost, *but I can be a better person and atone for my mistakes. Remorse. Real change. Redemption, guided by the memories of the people I've wronged.*

I wanted a better life. Not up in the billboards. Something more meaningful. Felicity had rekindled a sense of ambition that was real and practical, something that wasn't rooted in destroying myself or others, or reaching for a fake world that would always be beyond my grasp.

"Life isn't fair, Peyton," she said. "We like to believe it is, but that's just a comforting lie that's designed to stop people tearing each other apart with the unfairness of it all. The lie holds back anarchy, but the rich, those who know the truth, they can get away with murder. This patron put you up to those killings, but whoever they are, they're invisible and untouchable. You did wrong, but I understand why. I don't condone them, but I understand them. What you did makes sense when seen through the lens of your life. And that means you're not a monster, because monsters walk alone."

It was as close to absolution as a deadbeat like me could have hoped for.

"What do you need?" she asked.

Death had brought us closer than life ever could.

I don't know whether it was exhaustion or our profound connection, but I answered honestly.

"You."

"I know," she said, before kissing me.

CHAPTER 80

Our physical contact went only as far as a kiss that day, but we were bound by something beyond our bodies. We'd both finally found someone who understood, and later we realized she was the answer to my question, and I was hers.

Felicity took me to Proctor Avenue in the City of Industry, and we pulled up opposite the newsstand. I jumped out of her Honda CR-V and ran to the warehouse doorway, where I unlocked the mailbox and retrieved the recording drive.

I returned to her car, and we watched the footage together. According to the time stamp, shortly after 1:00 a.m., when I'd been on my way back from Sedona, a car pulled up by the newsstand. It was a Mercedes GL, black or dark gray, hard to see in the night gloom. A man climbed out, his face hidden beneath a hooded top. He moved slowly, as if each step was agony, and deposited a package into the newsstand. It was the package I'd retrieved from my mailbox before fleeing the cops. The one I had in my pocket. The footage showed someone new collecting it. I guessed Jessica Yallop and my patron had parted ways after I'd revealed what she'd been delivering. Judging from his movements, the new guy was young and careful. He rode a motorbike and never removed his helmet, which kept his identity hidden. But I wasn't interested in the errand boy. I wanted to know the truth about my patron, and I scrubbed back through the footage and froze on a still from one of the cameras.

"I can't see his face," Felicity said.

"And there's no license plate. At least not from this angle," I said.

I took the package from my pocket and opened it. There was no money in this one, just a card with a URL.

"What is it?" Felicity asked.

"A message," I replied as I tapped the URL into my phone.

The familiar play triangle appeared, and I clicked it to trigger the mechanical voice.

"Mr. Collard, when I first engaged you, I said your targets were to die with two shots to the head. No other way. However, in allowing Alice Polmar to burn, you have invalidated our agreement."

Even the mask of the machine voice could not hide my patron's anger.

"You will not receive the sum promised for this contract. I will contact you with details of your next assignment soon."

The recording ended.

"Why is he so angry about the bodies? They're being mutilated anyway."

I shook my head slowly. The mutilations had disturbed me because I didn't want anyone to think I was guilty of such barbarism, but they troubled me for another reason. Did he want the bodies untouched simply so he could disfigure them?

"I need to find out who this guy is." I pointed at the hooded figure, now frozen by the newsstand on screen. "You think you could run me over to Burbank? Warner Studios?"

Felicity looked puzzled. "You want to go to Warner Brothers? You thinking of selling your life rights? You might want to see how it ends first."

I scoffed. "There's a guy there who might be able to help me out. He's not a faker or dream-maker. He's real."

CHAPTER 81

I t was the strangest date of my life.

We sat on a concrete bench that was engraved with the word *Burbank*. It stood on the corner of West Olive Avenue and Hollywood Way, opposite Gate 4 of the Warner Brothers studio complex. We watched the early cars arriving and waited for Sam Larabee to show up for work. There was a chill morning breeze, and the sun hadn't grabbed the day by the throat yet. The café directly behind us built into the ground floor of a four-story office block was closed, exterior tables and chairs upturned.

Inspired by the studio opposite, we started talking movies. We both loved *Interstellar*, *Magnolia*, and the most recent version of *Dune*.

I kept looking at this beautiful, engaging woman and wondered why it didn't trouble her to be sitting alongside a murderer. Then I'd remind myself she too had taken a life. She understood the immediacy of circumstance. Our situations hadn't been the same, but at least she understood some of what I had been through. A former president could drive along West Olive, and we'd be expected to stand and cheer a great man who might have sent thousands to their deaths. War, sanctions, harmful economic and health care policies, mass murder and maiming made invisible by distance. Here we were, two people with experience of it up close, no judgment, no fear.

Soon we moved on to music, foods, travel, and everything else that spiced life with fun. We shared some tastes—pizza, a love of New York

City, awe of Ariana Grande's voice—we disagreed on others—tuna (she hates), San Francisco (I hate), and Prince (she hates)—but every mismatch prompted jokes and laughter. Being with Felicity was easy.

Love should be easy.

We spent almost three hours waiting there for Larabee, who didn't show until two minutes after ten. I still remember every word of our conversation. Some strange attraction was at work, connecting us beyond what we were saying, cementing our relationship in a realm beyond reason, which is a fancy way of saying I recall it because it was the moment I started to realize I was falling in love. I found my soulmate in the shadow of murder. Which should give hope to all lost and lonely souls. She wasn't just the second love of my life. She was my redemption.

"That's him," I said as I saw Larabee come east along Olive in a green Land Rover Discovery Sport. He took a left into the studio lot. "I don't want you drawn into this. Wait here."

Felicity nodded, and I grabbed the video recorder, which was on the bench beside me, got to my feet, and hurried across the street.

I caught up to Larabee as he was presenting his credentials to the guard on the gate.

"Mr. Larabee," I said, and he craned out of the window to look at me. "Can I talk to you a minute?"

He was surprised, but there was no hint he knew I was being hunted for abduction and murder.

"Mr. Collard," he said. "I've got appointments."

"This will only take a minute."

He nodded wearily. "Let me park."

The security guard raised the barrier, and Larabee pulled into one of the visitor spots just beyond it. He climbed out of the car, walked back, and we stood to one side of the gate.

"I've got some footage of the guy blackmailing Jessica Yallop into harassing my ex-wife. I recorded it in the City of Industry. There's a car, but I didn't get a plate and his face is hidden."

He looked at the video recorder in my hand. "And you want me to find him?"

"I thought there might be a traffic camera or something nearby you might be able to access."

He nodded and took the recorder. "Maybe. I'll have Otis send you a bill."

"Thanks," I said.

He tipped an imaginary hat and returned to his car. I watched him pull out of the space and drive toward his normal spot deep in the Warner lot. I walked away from the gate and crossed West Olive Avenue. As I reached the bench where Felicity waited, my phone rang. It was Toni, and I hesitated before answering, aware the cops might use her to get to me.

"Hello?" I said tentatively.

"Hello? What the fuck, Peyton! Where are you?"

"What's up?" I asked.

"What's up?" Her anger went up a notch. "What's fucking up? I'll tell you what's up. Your daughter just saw you on TV, Peyton. You're wanted for murder."

CHAPTER 82

Every ache, every pain, every sore spot on my body came alive at once as the pressure of my past crushed me. The world faded to a dull gray that went black at the edges, and everything started spinning. I could feel my heart trying to pound its way out of my chest, and my stomach flipped like an Olympic gymnast. I caught sight of Felicity, who was on her feet now, watching me with concern.

"Where are you?" Toni asked.

"I can't say." I couldn't risk the cops using her to reach me.

"We need to meet, Peyton. You need to look your daughter in the eye and tell her you're innocent." She hesitated. "And if you're not, you need to say goodbye."

Her words were like anesthetic. Skye was my world. Everything I'd ever done was for her, so she would never have to live a bad life. All my pain stopped, and for a moment it felt as though my body had died. The magnitude of what I'd done finally hit me. I had very little and my daughter was the most valuable of what little I had, but I'd risked it all. I'd almost certainly lost it all.

"Turn yourself in and we'll come to see you in custody," Toni suggested.

I couldn't do that. Not again. I couldn't face sitting across the table from Skye in shackles.

"I can't," I replied. "Not yet. I'm so close to finding out the identity of the person who's really responsible. If I come in now, the cops will pin it on me." It wasn't a lie, but it wasn't the whole truth either.

Toni didn't say anything.

"Please let me see her. Let me explain what really happened. I don't want her thinking I'm a monster, Toni," I said. "You either. I don't want you thinking badly of me."

I took her silence as hesitation.

"Where is Skye?" I asked.

"With me," she replied. "I couldn't send her into school. She's too upset. And the other kids . . . What the fuck, Peyton?"

"I'm sorry. I'm so sorry. Remember where we spent her fourth birthday?" I asked.

"Yeah," Toni replied.

"Meet me there in an hour. Please."

There was a long pause.

"Okay," she said at last before hanging up.

"What's happened?" Felicity asked as I lowered my phone.

"The story broke. That was my ex-wife." I took a couple of deep breaths and tried to find my center. The world came back to full color, and I no longer felt as though I might pass out. I scanned the street nervously, looking for any signs passing drivers recognized me.

"I need to deal with something, and I can't ask you to put yourself at any more risk," I said. "I'm going to take a cab."

I didn't think her disappointment was fake.

"I don't mind—" she began, but I cut her off.

"I need to take responsibility for myself. I can't pull more and more people into this mess. Especially not you. If I can figure a way out of this, I'd like to see you again."

"Me, too," she replied. "So I hope you find an exit. And if you need anything, you know where I am."

She took a step forward and kissed me, and for an instant all my pain melted away, and the massive weight smothering me lifted.

"Good luck," she said.

"Thanks."

I jogged west, hunting for a cab.

CHAPTER 83

The ocean has always meant something to me. Toni and I grew up a short distance away from Lake Michigan, and whenever life got too much we could run away to the beach and pretend we were in a tropical paradise. The Pacific had the same effect, only there was less pretense. It is vast, and the golden beaches of Malibu are as close to paradise as a person can hope to get on earth.

Toni and I used to love bringing Skye out to the beach near Malibu Pier, and I walked the rough paths from the Pacific Coast Highway through the bluffs that were covered in long green grass.

My phone rang when I was almost at the beach, and I pulled it from my pocket to see Sam Larabee's name.

"Mr. Larabee," I answered.

"Mr. Collard, I'm calling to terminate our relationship," he replied. He sounded mad. "My advice would be for you to turn yourself in. If anything should happen to the individual I identified for you, may I remind you everything is on record, and I will turn any relevant evidence over to the police."

"I didn't . . . ," I tried, but it was no use.

"This call is being recorded to show I advised you not to draw this investigation out any longer than necessary and to immediately make yourself available to police to assist with their inquiries."

And with that he hung up, and I lost my only chance of identifying my patron.

I could feel myself running out of road, and the familiar nausea returned as I crested a rise and was blinded by the glare of the sun shining off the vast ocean. It gave the illusion of going on forever.

Like hope.

Toni and Skye weren't at the spot yet. I'd chosen it for our meeting because if the cops were meaning to use Toni as bait, I'd see them coming from miles away across the golden sand. But I was looking into the distance when my attention should have been on my immediate surroundings.

The attack was silent and sudden. Frankie Balls and his men rose from behind dunes all around me, and Cutter and Curse moved before I could react. Even as they came at me, I realized with horror they must have Toni and Skye.

"Get down!" Cutter yelled, cracking me on the skull with a club.

I couldn't refuse and fell as the world went black.

CHAPTER 84

The sound of my phone ringing drew me back from oblivion.

I opened my eyes and slowly wrangled my wild senses. The back of my head crackled and burned where I'd been clubbed, and as my watering eyes focused, I saw the floor. Cheap linoleum with black and white checks like a chessboard.

I was lying in a windowless room that was maybe twenty feet by thirty. There were stacks of boxes beside an inner door, and an ancient vending machine next to a fire exit.

"Enjoy your nap?" Frankie said.

He was behind me, and when I turned, he kicked me in the gut.

I curled into a ball and tried to clutch my belly, but my hands had been tied above my head. The world became a pain sour mash, intoxicating me as every nerve in my body lit up.

Eventually it cleared, and I saw three large couches arranged in a horseshoe by the far wall. Toni and Skye sat on the one in the middle, and they were surrounded by Cutter, Curse, and the rest of Frankie's men. There were eight of them in total, all snarls and tattoos.

I burned with anger at the sight of my daughter with these thugs, and I struggled hopelessly against my bonds.

"I told you what would happen," Frankie said. "I fucking told you, but you had to go and see the bad for yourself. Fuck around and find out. Hard lessons for the stupid."

I turned my attention to him. He seemed even more arrogant and evil than ever.

"We ain't playing," he said. "We know you've got well over half a mil stashed somewhere."

My nausea and sickness sharpened. How did they know?

I caught Toni's disbelieving glare. There was no hiding my criminality now. People like me didn't come into six zeros without crossing lines, but how the hell did they know how much money I had?

"I see your question, man," Frankie said. "We've known about you since the beginning. The same guy that's been paying you has been paying us to mop up after you. Take pictures of you on your spree. Break into the morgues, cut out parts from your victims. Told us we should make you look like a monster, put the pressure on. Said we should take your share of the loot too. He told us to take every cent he was paying you. Break you."

It took me a moment to process his confession. He and his men were the ones mutilating the bodies. They'd taken the photographs my patron had sent me to threaten blackmail. They knew I was a killer because our mutual patron had engaged them to make my crimes seem even worse than they were. And the man who'd paid me had encouraged them to take my money. He wanted to ruin me on every level.

"Why?" I asked, my voice hoarse. "Why cut them?"

"Why kill them?" Frankie asked, and Skye sobbed more loudly now.

Toni's fury hit me in waves. I'd lied to her and put them both in danger.

"We were paid, man," Frankie said. "Just like you."

"Dad!" Skye yelled. "You promised me."

"And now we want to get paid again," Frankie said. "I want what you've got, Peyton Collard."

Why would my patron betray me to this scumbag? Why mutilate the victims? Who would do this to me? To the innocents I'd killed?

"Where's the fucking money?" Frankie asked.

I knew I couldn't tell them. He'd confessed in front of me, Toni, and Skye, which meant we could all implicate him if he allowed us to live.

He intended for us all to die in this room.

"You don't remember me, do you?" he remarked, leaning closer to me. "Peyton fucking Collard."

Who was he? Why did he think we were connected?

"Let them go," I said. "Please."

He didn't even bother to glance over his shoulder and kept his eyes locked on mine. "Cutter, shoot his old lady."

Toni and Skye screamed as Cutter drew a gun. He grabbed my teenage sweetheart by the arm and pulled her off the couch toward him. Zebra and Curse held Skye back as she desperately tried to fight for her mother.

Frankie lifted me by my hair and shoved a pistol in my face.

"Watch."

Toni struggled as two of Frankie's men grabbed her and pointed her at Cutter's raised pistol. Her eyes caught mine, and I saw her weeping through my own tears.

"Okay, okay," I conceded before Cutter got too close. "I'll show you where it is."

"You'll tell me," Frankie said. "And when one of my guys has the money, we'll let you go."

The lie stank the place up.

"It's in a safety-deposit box. The code is on my phone," I said.

He leaned over me and untied my hands. As I staggered to my feet, I saw I'd been bound to an old pool table. We must have been in a back room in his pool hall on Raymond Street in Compton.

"Who hired you?" I asked.

"Same guy who paid you," Frankie replied. "Mr. Invisible. Who the fuck knows? Who the fuck cares? We get our instructions the same way you do."

"You don't want to know who has the goods on you?" I said. "The person who can tie you to three mutilations."

He hesitated for a moment before smiling. "Don't rope me into your mind games, Peyton Collard." He turned to his men, who clustered around Toni and Skye menacingly. "Give him his phone."

I thought about all the good I could do with that money and all the bad I'd done to get it. I remembered the hard-luck road that had led me here, all the bitter disappointments I'd experienced along the way. I looked into my daughter's tearful eyes and saw nothing but fear and disappointment. I knew our relationship would never be the same again. I thought about what these men were taking from her. Most of all, I thought about pain.

You know me, maybe better than I know myself. You've shared some of my pain, but I haven't even spoken of the things that happened to me in prison. I never learned how to fight like Jet Li or Tony Jaa, but I was given a crash course in how to take a beating. I was taught how to embrace pain, because when you've truly suffered, you're not afraid of anything, not even death itself.

Frankie had his eyes on his men. To him I was just another deadbeat. A gutter dweller who was there to be exploited.

But I was also another kind of deadbeat. A bringer of death, my black heart pounding out its bleak rhythm. My pain, my suffering, my training as a soldier, but most of all my love for my daughter made me dangerous.

I launched myself at him, my eyes focused on his gun. I grabbed it as he tried to punch me, but the blow to the side of my head was feeble. I twisted the pistol up, pointed the barrel at his head, and pulled down.

A jury could have spent days deliberating over whether he pulled the trigger or I did, but the result was beyond question. As he turned his head to try to avoid the shot, a bullet tore into his chin and burst out through his cheekbone with a spray of blood and bone.

His men were shaken, but I'd pictured this moment ever since I'd gotten to my feet, so I didn't share their surprise. Speed and shock were my only allies. As Frankie emitted a wet, gurgling scream and fell to the ground, clutching his face, I grabbed his gun and turned it on the horseshoe arrangement. I shot the two men closest to me before the others even tried reaching for their weapons. Curse and Zebra went next, and then the last three, who'd managed to get their guns out.

In little more than the blink of an eye, I was left facing Cutter, who had his gun to Toni's head.

"What the fu—"

I cut him off with a bullet drilled through his throat.

Toni ducked as he instinctively pulled the trigger, and the shot went high into the ceiling. He staggered back, clutching at the angry wound, making choking sounds, and I put him out of his misery with a final pair of bullets to the chest.

"Peyton!" Toni yelled, and I turned to see the interior door open.

I shot the last of Frankie's shocked men the moment they entered the room. Three of them drilled in guts and chest, the final guy taking the remainder of the Glock's seventeen-round clip.

The echoes of the last shots faded, leaving the room in silence, and I stood tense for a moment, waiting to see if more danger came our way. The smell of gunpowder was overpowering, and it took a while for me to realize the room wasn't silent. My hearing had been blasted by the gunshots, and within a few seconds, I was hit by a shrill ringing and the sounds of Toni and Skye crying. I looked around the room, shocked at what I'd just done.

Twelve bodies down.

Skye looked at me uncertainly, almost fearful.

"It's me, kiddo," I said softly. I put the gun down and stepped forward, my arms out reassuringly. "I'm still your dad."

She sobbed, wiped her eyes, ran over, and threw her arms around me.

"Dad," she cried.

I held her like I was never going to let her go.

"Fu . . ."

The sound was coarse and horrible, and I realized it was coming from behind me.

I turned to see Frankie Balls clutching his face. He looked paper pale, and a pool of blood grew on the chessboard floor.

"Fucker," Frankie rasped. "You ruined my life. You don't even remember. I served you that day. The day you killed her."

I didn't need to hear the name, but he said it anyway.

"Freya Persico."

He died with the girl's name on his lips.

I stood looking at his disfigured face, my memories racing. I sucked in air. It couldn't be.

That day, there was a bartender who served me after the waiter refused. He had winked and smiled and pushed me another glass when I told him I was driving. He hadn't been an innocent party. He'd known I was getting behind the wheel.

Frankie's face was older, more gnarled, his features twisted by the world, but now I was sure it was the bartender.

Freya Persico.

The connection was no coincidence.

I rifled through Frankie's pockets and took a couple of magazines for the Glock pistol. Seventeen shots in each. I grabbed a set of car keys, too, and his wallet and my phone.

I pushed Toni and Skye toward the fire escape. We stumbled away from the slaughter and spilled through the door into the blazing afternoon sunshine. Frankie's keys opened a black Ford F-350 with opaque windows parked outside the hall. I hustled Toni and Skye into the huge vehicle before jumping behind the wheel and speeding away.

CHAPTER 85

No one said anything.

What was there to say?

Skye had just seen her father execute twelve men and had heard I was implicated in other deaths. She didn't know I'd done it all for her. She couldn't. The guilt might destroy her.

Toni's eyes told me I was as dead as a deadbeat could be. They shone with the hatred of someone who never wanted to see me again, and I didn't blame her. I'd gone beyond unforgivable by placing her and Skye in danger. I wanted to tell her I'd also saved them but had the good sense not to open that can of worms. She was furious.

I was shaking and felt sick as the adrenaline died away.

My patron had been paying Frankie Balls to mutilate my victims, and he or she was obviously connected to Freya Persico. Revenge had to be playing a part in this.

Were Walter Glaze, Farah Younis, and Richard Gibson the true victims in this? Or was I? Were they simply the collateral necessary to punish me?

As I drove from Compton north through Los Angeles, I checked my messages. Anna Cacciola had left me three asking me to come in for a police interview. Jim Steadman had phoned me twice and slurred some curses down the line. There were dozens from reporters who wanted to talk to the West Coast Ripper. I had no idea how they'd even gotten my number.

I couldn't go home, that much was clear. The cops would have the place staked out.

I glanced in the rearview and caught Skye looking at me with nothing but disappointment. I didn't say anything. I couldn't.

"Where are we going?" Toni asked.

"Where's your car?" I responded.

"On the PCH. By the pier," she replied.

"I'll take you there," I told her.

She snorted her derision.

"You've done some fucked-up things," she said a few minutes later as we were crawling along with the westbound rush-hour traffic on the 105. "But this is beyond."

"Toni . . . ," I tried.

"Don't you sit there with literal blood on your hands and try to give me any excuses," she said, her tone as sharp as any knife. "You complete fuckup."

I glanced down at the wheel and saw she was right. Little drops of blood were spattered on my hands.

"This is the worst thing you've ever done, Peyton. By a long shot," Toni said.

I didn't respond. What could I say?

I drove them out to the Pacific Coast Highway, and the sun dropped below the horizon as we headed north, part of an unbroken stream of red lights. It was night by the time we reached Malibu Pier, and, after following her directions, I parked behind Toni's gray Honda Civic.

"Get out of town for a while," I suggested. "Stay away until I call you to let you know it's safe. Does Jack have family nearby?"

"Never call me again," Toni said, taking Skye and hurrying from the car.

I won't ever forget the look in Skye's eyes. I saw my reflection in them, and I was a monster.

Toni fumbled with her keys but eventually got them into the Civic, and I watched them drive away, wondering if I'd ever see my kid again.

CHAPTER 86

I didn't regret the deaths of Frankie Balls and his men, but I was distraught at having been exposed in front of Skye. I headed east for a while before turning north into the mountains. I took Frankie Balls's Ford into the wilderness and parked at the head of a trail off Piuma Road in Monte Nido. I couldn't risk being seen in a dead man's car and had no idea whether the carnage at Ocean Beach Pool had been discovered. If it had, this car would be as hot as the sun. I needed to lie low while I figured out my next move.

The stars watched me ride a rainbow of emotions, red anger, orange regret, yellow confusion, green shame, indigo frustration, and violet sorrow. Most colors brought tears, slamming the steering wheel, and kicking the footwell. When the storm cleared, I found what would pass for peace.

I turned on the radio and tuned it to KNX News and Talk. Unsurprisingly, the chatter was all about the West Coast Ripper and his gruesome crimes. Green shame tinted the world, but I kept listening to the velvet-voiced anchor talking to her guest.

"So, you think these crimes are the work of a psychopath?" she asked.

"We don't tend to use that term in my field. Sociopath, perhaps, but certainly someone with troubling mental health issues," the guest replied.

"You're listening to KNX News and Talk. I'm Laura Booth and I'm joined by Colin Washington, clinical psychiatrist and consultant to the FBI. Thank you for being with us, Colin."

"My pleasure," the shrink replied.

"Are you concerned about the most recent development?" Laura asked.

"The disappearance of the detective?"

"Yes. For those of you who don't know, the detective leading the investigation, Rosa Abalos, was reported missing earlier today," Laura revealed. "Do you think her disappearance is coincidence?"

"I wouldn't like to speculate," Colin replied. "But I have known criminals become fixated with the law enforcement officers pursuing them."

I hadn't thought things could get any worse, but here was a truck bearing down on me, ready to dump a load of misery on my shoulders. I prayed the cop was okay and that her disappearance had nothing to do with me.

Frankie Balls had finally revealed how we were connected, and that left me in little doubt these deaths had something to do with what had happened to Freya Persico.

I took Frankie Balls's wallet from my pocket and pulled out his driver's license to discover his name wasn't Frankie Balls, but Mark Francis Batch.

I tapped his real name into my phone, and seconds later Google presented me with a series of search results. The top hits were all news articles, and I clicked on the one ranked highest, a piece on the ABC7 News website.

Frankie hadn't been lying.

Mark Francis Batch of Venice Beach was today sentenced to eighteen months in prison for theft. Batch had been stealing supplies of liquor from his employer, the Sundown Inn, Malibu, for a period of three years and selling the stolen liquor to a criminal gang in central Los Angeles. The theft came to light following the investigation of the death of Freya Persico, who was killed in a car accident. Police looked into Batch's role in the incident as he was alleged to have served the drunk driver who caused the crash, despite knowing the man would be driving.

There had been a time during my prosecution for Freya's death when

I'd searched the internet obsessively, looking for anything and everything on her, hoping to find some nugget that might help keep me out of prison. But there were no stories of drug use or alcoholism that could help make her partly culpable. This piece about Frankie's role had been written after I'd been tried and sentenced, so I hadn't seen it before.

Freya Persico's name was highlighted in the article, so I clicked the link and was taken to another feature written after my sentencing. It was a profile piece that gave an obituary, described my trial, and interviewed her friends. Two things were noticeable. The first was the lack of comment from Freya's family. The second was a throwaway remark from the doctor who'd tried to resuscitate Freya at the hospital.

"The death of a young person is always a tragedy," said Emily Gray, MD, *of Ronald Reagan UCLA Medical Center. "But hopefully some good will come from the lives Freya saved through her death. Her organs will give hope to people who would otherwise have none."*

My hands shook as I typed the names of my four victims into the search bar along with the words *organ transplant*. I received an immediate hit. Alice Polmar had been profiled by a local newspaper, and the article mentioned she'd recently received a new kidney.

"The donor was a young woman who was tragically killed in an automobile accident in California," Alice Polmar said in the piece. "And I will be forever grateful to her and her family."

CHAPTER 87

I started the F-150 and headed for the city. When I reached the PCH, I phoned Felicity.

"Hello?" she said groggily. Had she been sleeping?

"It's me," I replied.

"You're all over the news."

"I know," I said. "Are you working?"

"No," she replied. "Night off."

"Someone's disappeared the cop," I said. "They think it was me."

"Yeah," Felicity responded. "They had a comment from the chief on the news. He's mad. The whole department is gunning for you."

The chief? Gunning? This was all getting too hot.

"I think I might know what links the murders," I said. "I wanted to tell someone in case—"

"Don't say it," she cut me off. "I'm superstitious."

"Frankie Balls served me drinks the day of the accident. And Freya Persico was an organ donor. At least one of my targets received an organ from her."

"You think this has something to do with Freya's death?"

"The barman who blamed me for ruining his life with the accident, at least one of the victims receiving an organ from her, and me the cause of it all. These can't be coincidences. I think it's all linked to Freya Persico's death. I'm going to see Joseph Persico to find out if he knows anything. I should have been to see him years ago. I should have made good. I should have apologized for what I'd done. I can't undo the past, but I can do the right thing now, and maybe he can help me."

My stomach flushed with acid at the thought of Joseph Persico. I'd avoided a face-to-face encounter with good reason. I hated myself for what I'd done to that man.

"What if it's him?" Felicity asked.

"What?"

"His daughter's death might have driven him crazy," she suggested. "He might be out for revenge."

I shook my head. "It doesn't make any sense. People don't kill organ recipients. They're normally happy part of their loved one lives on. If it was revenge, he would have come for me without killing innocents."

Felicity was silent.

"But if he is behind all this, at least I'll have answers. I need to know the truth."

"Please be careful," she said.

"I will be," I replied.

"You want to know what you told me the night we met?" she asked.

I had a feeling it was something stupid and hesitated.

"Sure," I replied at last.

She paused.

"You said I was beautiful," she revealed. "That a man would have to be crazy or stupid not to love me. That you'd be a lucky fool to see out your days with me."

"It's true," I replied without a beat.

She chuckled. "Just promise me one thing. If you get out of this jam, you'll call me."

"I promise."

CHAPTER 88

B el Air Road was a confusing snake that curled up through the folds of the Santa Monica Mountains, splitting into spurs and horseshoes that would have had other names anywhere else, but here in the high royal courts of LA, everyone wants the prestigious address, so the one street split and looped like so many varicose veins.

I'd been up here many times and knew exactly where to find Joseph Persico's home, Rockview House, at the end of a spur near the summit. The street was lined with the homes of the people who paid the dream-makers and fakers, the moneymen who owned the billboards on which the bright smile and golden lives were lived. These were the true rulers of our world, rich in money and power.

It was almost 1:00 a.m. when I reached the huge estate, which lay behind a high, ivy-covered stone wall. A forest of mature trees rose behind the perimeter. I drove up to the gate and pressed the buzzer. No answer. I tried again and again and again, and after five minutes I gave up. Was he out? Asleep? I couldn't wait on the street, not in a neighborhood like this, which had regular LAPD patrols. Inside, there was cover and there might even be answers.

There were security cameras every fifty yards, but I found a blind spot a long way from the main gate. I parked the pickup truck by the wall, stood on the roof, and used the thick ivy to haul myself up and over the top.

I jumped into bushes on the other side and pushed my way through to a clearing between the high cedar trees. I saw lights in the distance, coming from the house perhaps, and instinctively wrapped my fingers around the stock of Frankie's pistol, which was tucked into my waistband beneath my top.

I ran between the trees, aiming for the lights, keeping an eye out for dogs, the Boston Dynamics robots, cameras, and guards. But there was nothing, just woodland stirring in the cool night breeze. The trees gave way to a huge lawn that had been so well tended it would have made an Augusta groundskeeper envy green.

I'd looked down on this place from the high mountain that loomed above it like a shadow, but it was only close up that I got to appreciate the beauty and excellence this high-tech billionaire's money had bought him.

The lights came from a large modern mansion that was made of brushed concrete and glass. It was a two-story structure with wings that spread into the darkness. The east wing, which was nearest to me, featured a thirty-foot-long floor-to-ceiling window. Beyond it was an artfully decorated minimalist living room that was illuminated by a single floor lamp.

I could see pictures on a sideboard and headed for the room.

I made it fewer than twelve paces from the trees before I caught a flicker of movement in the corner of my eye. As I turned, I saw something stalk out of the shadows. At first, I thought it was a giant dog, but its movements were too regular. I heard a noise behind me and saw a second creature. It drew closer, and with a sinking feeling, I recognized them as the Boston Dynamics Spot robots I'd spied from a distance. I hadn't noticed when I'd seen them from the mountainside, but they had some sort of device fixed to their long black backs.

"It's a Taser."

I turned to see the silhouette of a man standing by the front door of the house. I could see the clear outline of a pistol in his right hand.

A third robot covered the ground between us.

"I'm sorry for busting in on you like this, sir," I said, my hands raised. "I don't mean you any harm. There's no needs for guns and such."

"There is, Mr. Collard. There very much is," Joseph Persico replied. "Come in. It's time we had a chat."

CHAPTER 89

As I drew closer to Persico, I saw he was bald, old, frail, and sickly, a far cry from the publicity photos I'd found on the internet, which showed him as a tanned, healthy man in his early fifties.

"Was it you?" I asked, eyeing the pistol.

"Of course," he replied. "Inside."

He gave a lazy wave of the gun, and I suddenly felt sick, realizing I'd misjudged my visit, that the man I'd turned to for counsel on the top of the mountain was my foe.

Golden light fell through the doorway, and I walked slowly toward it. The old man drew close and pressed his pistol into my back as he reached for the gun tucked into my waistband.

The three robots followed us, their feet clacking on the flagstone floor.

Persico's home was a shrine to his daughter Freya. There were photos of her everywhere, and he featured in many of them. She watched me as a baby, a young child, and then as a teenager, her eyes judging me.

You can't escape your past, Freya Persico's ghost said, and I almost fell to my knees under the weight of guilt. She'd been locked up so tight, somewhere deep between my black heart and rotten soul, but now she was free.

"You know who I am now, don't you," the frail gunman said.

I nodded, trembling. "I'm sorry. I'm so sorry."

"I'm not interested in your apologies," he said calmly.

"I didn't mean—"

He cut me off with a blow, swinging the pistol into my face. The world flashed white, and my nerves shot fireworks everywhere. He wasn't strong, but the weight of the gun made the beating count.

"I wasn't there for her when she died," he said with tears in his eyes. "My little girl died without me. Because of you."

He hit me again, and it took more than a moment for me to come to my senses.

"I was in the hospital. Waiting for her to save me."

His words made no sense.

"Downstairs."

He gestured at a doorway to our left, and I opened it to find a wooden staircase that led to a cellar.

As my eyes settled and the world came into sharp focus, I realized he looked even more sickly in the glow of the overhead spotlights. His skin was yellow, with harsh shadows cast by his gaunt features. Was he jaundiced? His eyes were black platters, made so by disease or drugs. I was pretty sure he was planning to kill me.

"Down," he said.

I complied and walked the steps to what I was sure would be my doom.

Persico followed, and the robots stalked down after us, their limbs click-clacking on the stairs.

"You took her from me. You did that. You took my baby away."

"I'm sorry," I responded, but my words weren't enough. They would never be enough.

The cellar was a large twenty-by-forty-foot space decked with solid-wood floorboards that had been polished to a high shine. There were two desks and a table covered by computers, papers, and folders. An open safe stood against the back wall. Next to it was a glass-fronted refrigerator.

Inside the chilled cabinet, I saw human organs: a heart, brain, kidneys, and lungs, which must have been the trophies Frankie Balls had taken from my victims.

It was hard not to be freaked out by the gruesome display, but my attention was drawn to another troubling sight. Rosa Abalos had been gagged and bound to a chair. Her eyes were on me, but she looked drowsy, as though she'd been drugged.

"I never got to say goodbye to my little girl, Mr. Collard," Persico said. "When you killed her, I was in a medically induced coma, awaiting lifesaving treatment."

"If I could take it back, I would," I said.

He ignored my remark. "Do you know who was going to save me?" Persico asked. "My daughter. She was a genetic match for Lazarus cells, T-cell clones that had been grafted from my depleted immune repertoire. I have cancer you see. The aggressive kind, as you can tell. My doctors had placed the Lazarus cells in Freya to grow and multiply within her organs. If she'd lived, it would have been a matter of days until she'd provided the cells needed to save my life."

I looked at the organs in the fridge with a new horror.

"Reagan Medical Center recovered her from the crash. When she passed, they saw only that she was a registered organ donor. Only my doctors, Freya, and I knew about the special cargo she carried, so her organs were listed for transplant. By the time I was revived from my coma and given the novel peptide treatment that has maintained my tenuous grip on life all these years, her organs had gone to others. You didn't just rob me of my little girl. You took my life from me. You took my hope. You turned me into this."

"That's why—" *You used me.*

"There was no legitimate way to recover them, and I had to see if any of them still contain the Lazarus cells I so desperately need to kill the cancer within me. So, in the late hours, I dreamed up a plan that seemed less and less crazy as my body faded. You should have faced the chair for what you did to my girl. You have no idea how much I love her. You got three years in prison. People serve longer for wire fraud." He snorted derisively. "My plan would enable me to recover the Lazarus cells and see you and Mark Batch get the punishments you really deserve."

I struggled to take it in.

"Did you recognize Batch when you first saw him? I doubt it. We're all so different now. You took something good from the world, and the bad that followed warped us all. I kept an eye on you in prison through various guards and inmates who were easy to turn informant. Some even took money to give you an education in the harsh realities of life, and I enjoyed hearing the tales of how they'd beaten you. But your pain still wasn't enough. It will never be enough. I watched your life fall apart, your wife and child leave you, and when you got released, I saw you drink and drink and drink. And finally, you'd made such a mess you were ready for my offer. Desperation turns men to all kinds of evil. I know. It's taken me almost four years to convince myself to go through with this. Four years to tell myself I had to kill the innocent. To weigh their lives against mine. Four years to become desperate enough to do what's necessary. I'm dying, you see. And when a person is facing their end, their morals become malleable. And you grew desperate too. So desperate and easy to manipulate. I made those lies. I created those websites. I told you what you wanted to hear so you could maintain the illusion you were a good man, but you were doing the foulest work. You and Batch, killing and carving up the innocent."

Rosa's eyes were still on me, but they were heavy and vacant. She was definitely drugged.

"He's dead, you know?" I said.

Persico hesitated. "It doesn't matter. I have what I need. There's a desperate, near-bankrupt clinical immunologist with a terrible gambling habit who will harvest the Lazarus cells from these organs, and my life will go on."

"And her?" I nodded at Rosa.

"Unfortunately, Detective Abalos stumbled in here following a lead she didn't understand. She found out about the organ donations that linked the victims, and, like you, she came to talk to me about them.

I had to take measures to protect myself from exposure. She is another innocent who will have to suffer for what you've done. You will kill her before I shoot you. I will tell the world you became obsessed with my daughter, that you tracked down the recipients of her organs and slaughtered them in brutal fashion. Then you came here intent on murder. Hero cop Rosa Abalos arrived almost too late, but she managed to save me at great cost to herself. Her intervention enabled me to grab a gun and shoot you dead."

He waved his pistol menacingly.

"I never meant to hurt you, Mr. Persico, and there isn't a day that goes by that I don't think about what I did, but please don't do this. Let Detective Abalos go. She doesn't deserve this. And neither does my kid. I have a daughter too."

"I know all about Skye, and I want to assure you she'll suffer," he replied. "I want you to know that the sins of the father will be visited on her. After you're gone and I'm reborn, I will make it my business to ensure she fails at everything she ever does. I will thwart her every ambition, crush her every dream. I won't kill her, but I will put her in hell. Just like you did me. Her suffering will be a mirror image of mine. I want you to know that any hope your daughter has of a good life will die with you. It's the least I can do for the man who took away the light of my life. My Freya."

CHAPTER 90

I've had a long time to think about what he said and what he'd done, and he was right; desperation makes people vulnerable. The person without a job, roused into hatred of minorities. The person without money or opportunity, tempted to escape into drugs or, in my case, crime. Earlier in my story, I asked whether you'd kill to make a better life for you or your family, but the truth is we'd all kill if we were sufficiently desperate. We all have a price.

If I'd told Persico's story from his perspective, would you be rooting for him? The wronged, vengeful father rather than the manipulated, murderous deadbeat? Maybe you are rooting for him, a man traumatized by grief, who'd hatched a plan of vengeance. Loss had made him desperate in his own way, and he'd become vulnerable to the extremes of action that so entice those without hope. I'd started him on this path when I drove into his daughter's car.

I'd made him a killer, just as he'd made me one.

If I'd been alone in the world, I would have accepted whatever judgment he had for me. I would have taken torture and death as a just punishment for the suffering I'd caused, but I wasn't alone. I had Skye, and she needed me. She was counting on me to keep her safe, to provide for her, and there was no way I could let this twisted man succeed in his terrible plan to ruin her and make her suffer.

I glanced over my shoulder and saw Persico a couple of feet away, gun pointed at my back. The three robots were a short distance behind him.

"Get on your knees," he said.

"You don't have to do this," I responded.

I knew he wouldn't be fast or strong, he couldn't be, not in his condition, but he had a gun, which always altered the natural balance.

"Down!" he said, and I heard him take a step forward.

I crouched as the pistol whipped through the air where my head had been a split second before, and he toppled into me as the force of the attempted blow threw him off-balance. I punched him, and he lashed out instinctively as he fell back. He caught me on the temple with the gun, and my world swam.

The robots clattered around us, trying to get a line on me, and I staggered forward, my head spinning, aware I was finished if Persico could get his gun up. I swung for him, but my aim was off, and it was my turn to swipe air. He hit me with the pistol again, and this time he knocked me down. Darkness tore at the edges of my vision, and I was on the verge of passing out. One more blow and I'd be done.

But there was no further blow. Persico composed himself and stepped toward me, and I saw the muzzle of his gun rise toward my head as if in slow motion.

I thought of Skye and my love for her. I thought of all the things she'd lose if I died here. Desperation swept over me and gave me the strength to fight for my life.

As Persico brought the pistol level with my head, I leaped at him, covering the short distance between us before he had the chance to react. The robots reared onto their hind legs, clearly programmed to protect their principal, but Persico shielded me from any attack.

I grabbed the pistol as he fired instinctively, and the three robots, reacting to the danger, shot their Tasers but missed me and hit Persico in the back. He grimaced and looked at me in horror as three high-voltage devices discharged a surge of electricity into his body.

His cry was despairing and final, and he fell to the floor, surrounded by his expensive machines. They dropped to their fours and lowered what passed for their heads.

They didn't react as he convulsed at my feet, and when he finally stopped shaking, I stepped forward and checked his pulse. His glassy eyes stared up at me as lifeless as his body.

Persico. Joseph Persico, the man whose daughter I'd killed in a car crash. The man who'd wreaked havoc in so many lives. The man who'd made a murderer of me was dead.

CHAPTER 91

I freed Rosa Abalos and removed her gag. She was heavily sedated and couldn't stand, so I laid her on the floor, where she passed out. If I stayed with her, or took her in, I'd be implicated in what had happened here, so I left her with Persico's body and, after checking the open safe and stuffing the contents into a large bag, I pressed the panic button nearest the front door and fled the estate with the alarm blaring into the night.

I left Frankie Balls's pickup by the estate wall and fled the scene on foot. The cops passed me as I made my way down Bel Air Road, and I caught a cab on Sunset. After a quick pit stop, I asked the driver to take me home, where I was immediately arrested by the officers keeping watch on my property.

They took me to Hollywood Station, a modern redbrick precinct on Wilcox Avenue, and I spent the night in a cell.

I didn't sleep.

I couldn't.

I thought about Joseph Persico and his daughter, about the foolish choice that ruined my life and the lives of so many others. I thought about the poor people I'd killed, the innocents who hadn't deserved to die, and the guilty, Frankie Balls and his men, who had earned their violent endings. Most of all I thought about Skye and what kind of future she'd have if I didn't get the money I'd taken from Persico for the killings. Because at the end of it all, money, this artificial construct, this counterfeit proxy for life, is the great divider.

I never wanted my daughter to be a victim. I wanted her to have the money and power she needed to have a good life. I didn't design this game, but I understood the rules now, and I wanted my daughter to have all the pieces she needed to be a winner. I didn't want her to be a deadbeat like her dad.

Soon after the first fingers of dawn reached my cell, a cop opened the door and took me to an interview room where I found Anna Cacciola waiting with a groggy Rosa Abalos and another detective, a man in his early forties.

"Have a seat, Mr. Collard," he said. He had hard eyes, a gaunt, almost sharp face, and a shaven head. "I'm Detective Aaron Wilkins, and I'm here to assist Detective Abalos while she recovers—"

"I'm fine," Rosa cut in.

"If you're not in a fit state to conduct this interview," Anna suggested, "you should recuse yourself."

Rosa was too tired or hungover to bother trying to conceal her irritation. She looked drained but had gone to the effort of putting on a black trouser suit. Her colleague was in a dark gray two-piece.

"I'm fine," Rosa repeated.

I took the seat next to Anna, and the cop who'd brought me in shut the door.

"Can you tell me what the hell is going on?" Rosa asked.

Did she remember what had happened at Persico's house?

"My client doesn't have to say a thing," Anna cut in before I could answer.

"Well, we've got a dead man up at a Bel Air estate who abducted me, apparently shot dead by his own security robots. We found body parts taken from the victims of three murders, all organs donated by his daughter."

"Maybe he resented the donations?" Anna suggested.

"Maybe," Rosa conceded. "Only your client was responsible for his daughter's death, so that raises questions."

"I don't think so," Anna countered. "And even if it did, my client doesn't have any answers."

"We've got a slaughterhouse out at Ocean Beach Pool. A pistol found at Joseph Persico's house appears to have been used to execute twelve men, associates of a gangster who went by the name Frankie Balls."

"Doesn't sound like much of a puzzle to me," Anna remarked.

"How so?" Rosa asked.

"Seems a pretty clear-cut criminal conspiracy," my attorney replied.

"And your client doesn't know anything about it?" Rosa said.

"Did you find anything linking Frankie Balls to Joseph Persico?" Anna asked.

Rosa exchanged an uncomfortable glance with Aaron.

"You both know it's better to clear the air now rather than embarrass yourselves in front of a judge," Anna suggested.

Rosa sighed. "A cell phone with photos of the victims was found in Frankie's pool hall."

I played it cool. I'd used Frankie's thumb to unlock his phone and had deleted any photos of me, leaving behind only their surveillance images of the victims.

"We examined the location history of one of the phones and discovered it had visited all three morgues at the times the victims' organs were taken, and also found packages with handwriting that matched samples from Mr. Persico's property," Rosa continued. "As well as significant sums of money and Walter Glaze's watch and wallet."

I could have punched the air in celebration of Frankie's arrogance or stupidity. He'd kept the things he'd taken from my house on Edgebrook, belongings that linked him to the first murder.

"What about Alice Polmar being found in your client's car?" Rosa asked.

"Mr. Collard has explained he heard Frankie Balls discussing Mrs. Polmar in Rick's Bar and went to warn her she was in danger. She was startled when she saw my client and drove her car off the road."

That part was true. Alice had run her car onto the dirt and crashed into a tree. The collision had knocked her unconscious, so I'd put her into the back of the Range Rover, pushed her car down the cliffside, and watched it explode in a fireball before heading back to LA.

"My client rescued her, and, not knowing how best to keep her safe from an imminent threat, panicked and put her in his car, where she was eventually found by you and your fellow officers. Unharmed and not in any danger, correct? Is Alice Polmar going to press charges?"

Rosa shook her head slowly.

"Of course not, because she accepts my client's explanation and knows he treated her well and tried to protect her. In fact, you and your colleagues put her in greater danger because you failed to give my client the chance to explain himself and he fled, fearing for his life. Mrs. Polmar might have been shot by one of your officers who drew on Mr. Collard, a long-serving veteran who has not had good experiences with law enforcement."

Rosa took a deep breath. "We found deposits into Mr. Collard's bank account. Small sums over several days, totaling somewhere in the region of seventy-five thousand dollars. Can he explain where this money came from?"

Anna glanced at me before turning to Rosa with a look of steel. "He found it." She paused. "It was left to him by his aunt. He won it gambling on basketball. I don't know, and as far as I'm aware, Mr. Collard's finances aren't under investigation. I'm sure he will be declaring the income to the IRS for tax purposes."

I nodded.

"What I do know," Anna went on, "is that Mr. Collard used the money to pay rent on a house for himself and his daughter, and to settle my retainer. Perfectly legal purposes. If you have chain of evidence on the cash deposits and can identify the notes and their provenance, let's talk, but otherwise, I'm pretty sure the presumption of innocence applies."

Anna leaned forward and eyed Rosa, and I could have sworn the temperature in the room dropped a couple of degrees.

"I'm going to sum up what we're looking at here, just in case there's any doubt. You have evidence of a criminal conspiracy between Frankie Balls and his associates and Joseph Persico. Evidence Frankie Balls was involved in the murders of these poor people, organs extracted from their bodies on Persico's property, and the exchange of money between the two parties. You have had nothing but cooperation from Mr. Collard, and he clearly saved one of the potential victims from a very real threat."

Rosa's facade crumbled, and she finally looked embarrassed.

"So, I really have to ask," Anna went on, "what is my client doing here?"

CHAPTER 92

There were a few questions that niggled the cops, like what had happened to the security camera footage at Rockview House the night of Persico's death. The disk had been wiped, and they assumed Persico had switched the system off to avoid having any record of Rosa's abduction, when in truth I'd erased all the drives before I left the building.

They also couldn't figure out why the open safe was empty. I'd found over $1 million inside. I guess it was the money Persico had planned to pay me for Alice Polmar. I'd stuffed the cash into the large bag and had gotten the cabdriver to stop off at the City of Industry on my way home. I'd hidden the bag in the lockable mailbox opposite the newsstand Persico had been using as his dead drop.

After the cops released me, and I'd thanked Anna Cacciola for her amazing work, I went back the next day to collect the cash, and, with my house now free of police surveillance, I dug up the money buried in my backyard. Later that day, after I'd showered, I stepped into my bedroom and admired stacks of hundred-dollar bills spread across the place. By my reckoning, I had just over two million bucks. Enough for a different life. A better one. Not just for Skye, but for me.

Felicity and I are together now. She set up a private practice after qualifying as an accountant and has a small office in Malibu. We live in a cottage in Topanga, and I spend my days making use of my engineering skills to help around the community, building and fixing things.

Felicity's expertise as an accountant came in handy, and she advised me on how to launder the money. It's deposited in an offshore Cayman Islands bank account and is earning a nice return, which keeps me in iced teas. I don't much like them, but I'm sober now.

With my innocence proven to the satisfaction of the cops, Toni's hard-line no-contact stance softened. She had questions and suspicions, but I managed to convince her I'd been the victim of mistaken identity. Frankie Balls had really been after someone else. Skye is doing well at school, and Felicity and I have her every second weekend and during vacations. Jack and Toni are married now, and I feel pretty okay about that. I'm glad to see my old sweetheart happy, because I'm grateful to have found love and happiness with someone else. And I love Felicity more than I can say. She's redeemed me, and she's also helped me with this book. Any fine writing is hers. The less fine is mine.

Anna got me off the criminal damage charges over the incident with the sheriff's car, and she made me promise never to do anything stupid again. I don't know if she suspected I was guilty of the murders of Walter Glaze, Farah Younis, and Richard Gibson, but I was happy to oblige and swore I'd live a wholesome life.

I'm not troubled by the ghosts of my victims anymore. At least not frequently. Sometimes when I'm hovering on the brink of sleep, in the space between life and death, they come to me, but they don't say anything. They just watch me silently, and I imagine they're just waiting for the day I join them. I hope they're kind to me when that happens. I like to think our worries and fears stay with our bodies and wherever we go next, only the purest elements of our soul make the journey. Like when we come into this world, we leave beautiful and innocent.

So, I guess I'm redeemed.

I'm a better man.

My life in recent years was one of trauma, but now I'm healing. I feel guilt and sorrow for the people I hurt, but my life improved in every possible way, so I can't really say I would have done anything differently. Does that make me bad? What would you do if you could change your life for the better? Transform it beyond recognition? Would you be willing to hurt someone else?

Before you answer, think about the car you drive and the contribution it makes to climate change, the cheap clothes that exploit the underprivileged workers who make them, the taxes you pay that fund war, the many small, invisible, and often distant cruelties we unwittingly perpetrate every single day. Is the immediacy and visibility of my crimes what makes them reprehensible? Or are we all on a sliding scale of guilt?

Does living implicate us in death?

Breathe easy.

Relax.

I might just be trying to make myself feel better by implicating everyone in some grand exchange of life for death. You probably haven't done anything wrong. Least not on the same scale as me.

True redemption can't come without recognition of guilt, and I know what I did was wrong.

I promised a version of the truth in this work of fiction, and you've had it. Take from it what you will.

If the cops ever come knocking on my new perfect life, I will of course deny everything and disown this book as the product of an overactive imagination. It's simply the product of my creative mind, knitting together a different version of the facts of an investigation everyone is already very familiar with, so don't waste your time, Detective Abalos.

The case is closed.

ACKNOWLEDGMENTS

I'd like to thank my wife, Amy, and our children, Maya, Elliot, and Thomas, for their support and constant inspiration.

Many thanks to Loan Le and Elizabeth Hitti, whose editorial notes were priceless, and the rest of the team at Simon & Schuster, who do such a great job editing, designing, promoting, and selling my books.

I'd also like to thank my agents Nicola Barr and Jenny Bent for their guidance and insight.

I don't know what to make of Peyton Collard. Is he an evil man? He does good at times, but he's definitely not a good man. Maybe he's an everyman, pushed by circumstance into doing very bad things. Desperation can do that, so it's in society's interest to minimize desperation—at least in my opinion.

Where does our responsibility end and another's begin? The law has a narrow definition of causation and responsibility, which isn't really suited to challenges such as the pandemic or climate change. When we consider these issues, do we need to steer by a different compass? We have more power to affect each other than ever, and in this world of greater connection, increased proximity, we need truth and trust, but both are in decline.

As wealth is concentrated into fewer hands and more and more people have less and less, what duty does the collective have to ensure no individual suffers? Every society has a different answer, and this book doesn't pretend to offer one, but we need to keep the question at the fore-

ACKNOWLEDGMENTS

front of our minds, particularly in times of hardship. What do those in the billboards owe someone like Skye?

These questions were the birth of *Deadbeat*, and Peyton Collard is intended to embody this complexity. He killed his victims, but is he guilty of instigating their deaths? How should we feel about Peyton? About his life at the end of the book? Some people will hate how he's living, while others will love it. I believe those feelings say more about us than they do about Peyton. I think when all is said and done, the best I can say about Peyton is he's a mirror we can hold up to ourselves. What we see in him is a reflection.

I love him and loathe him, so it's hard for me to express anything other than conflicted feelings. The clearest sentiment I have about him is that he's interesting. I hope you agree and that you enjoyed his tale.

I'd like to thank the many authors, booksellers, librarians, and reviewers who continue to support my work. Most of all, I'd like to thank you, the reader. Without you, I'd have no reason to write, so you make the magic happen.

If you enjoyed *Deadbeat*, please review and share the book.

Until next time . . .

ABOUT THE AUTHOR

Adam Hamdy is a bestselling author and screenwriter. He lives elsewhere with his wife, Amy, and their three children, Maya, Elliot, and Thomas.

Follow Adam on X @adamhamdy and Instagram @adamhamdyauthor
www.adamhamdy.com